D1732773

BOOKS BY TRACI ANDRIGHETTI

Franki Amato Mysteries:

Limoncello Yellow

Prosecco Pink

Rosolio Red
(holiday short story)

Amaretto Amber

Danger Cove Hair Salon Mysteries:

Deadly Dye and a Soy Chai

AMARETTO AMBER

a Franki Amato mystery

Traci Andrighetti

To the memory of my Uncle Joe Fraser for teaching me to appreciate Jaspers and Jasperettes.

ACKNOWLEDGEMENTS

Every time I write a book, I look at the finished manuscript and wonder where it came from. The only thing I can say for sure is that *Amaretto Amber* and the books I wrote before it would not have happened if it weren't for Gemma Halliday. I never thought that I was a writer until she convinced me otherwise, and for that I'm forever grateful.

In terms of the plot, I would like to thank Daniel Joseph Gomez for patiently answering a slew of questions related to the entertainment industry, and to K'Tee Bee, a fan and great friend, for suggesting that I have Franki's meddling nonna visit the French Quarter. That idea formed the basis for this entire story, and I shudder to think of what the book would've been without it.

Speaking of fans, I'd also like to say how much I appreciate the support of the Sardis Library Book Club Ladies and the NBPLRomance Readers. Thank you for all that you've done for me—your emails, book clubs, Facebook posts, pictures, and tweets—and for authors and readers everywhere. I have always loved libraries and the people who run them!

As for the technical stuff, I owe a huge debt of gratitude to Detective Ruben Vasquez and pathology expert Dr. Judy Melinek for their professional expertise. I would also like to thank Dana Brown for helping me with the dental references in *Amaretto Amber* and Dr. Michael Lessner, my absolute favorite dentist of all time (go see him—without fear!).

If you couldn't tell from my books, I'm fascinated by foreign language and by names. So, when Suzie Gaspard Quebedeaux joined my street team, The *Giallo* Squad, I told her that I was going to use her awesome Cajun last name in a book. Suzie, I finally did it, so thank you! I also borrowed the entire name of one of my favorite ex-Italian students, Carlos Del Rio, because it just belongs in a book. And Cherie Havard, don't get mad at me for how I used your first name—it was such a perfect fit that I had no choice!

Last but not least, a big *grazie mille* goes to my family for their love, support, and patient proofreading.

Amaretto Cranberry Kiss

Franki loves amaretto, especially when it's mixed with vodka. She's particularly fond of a good kiss, too, but she prefers that it come from Bradley—or Hershey's.

1 cup cranberry cocktail juice
½ cup vodka
¼ cup amaretto
1 ½ tablespoons orange juice

Mix all the ingredients in a cocktail shaker with ice, and strain into a martini glass. Add an orange slice for garnish.

Italian Sunset

This sunny cocktail reminds Franki of her college-study trip to Italy—and of a certain Carlo she met there. Every time she drinks it, she dreams of going back to Rome one day. Maybe a mystery will take her there?

2 ounces amaretto
3 ounces pulp-free orange juice
3 ounces club soda
dash of grenadine

In a highball glass with crushed ice, add the amaretto. Layer the remaining ingredients in the order listed above. Finish with the dash of grenadine. Don't stir, or the sunset will disappear.

CHAPTER ONE

―――――

"It could be the angel of death," I whispered to my Cairn terrier, Napoleon, as I peered from the peephole at the black feather-winged figure on my front porch. "I mean, today *is* my thirtieth birthday."

The dark form shifted, and a bony wrist and hand came into view. The palm was extended upward, and the skin was shriveled and ghostly white.

As my eyes traveled the length of the long, curled fingers, the hand lowered slightly, and I saw a sickening sight.

A Mae West-style cigarette holder.

I sighed and rested my head against the door. "No such luck, buddy," I breathed. "It's Glenda."

"Open up, Miss Franki," Glenda O'Brien, my sixty-something landlady, called in her sultry, Southern voice. "The birthday fairy is here, and she's got a surprise for you."

At only nine-thirty a.m. on the Saturday I'd turned thirty I was in no mood for surprises. And judging from the way Napoleon was rubbing his eye with his paw, he wasn't up for any of Glenda's shenanigans either.

"Like it or not, sugar, you're no spring chicken anymore," she bellowed for the whole neighborhood to hear. "So let Miss Glenda in. She'll make it all better."

I was quite sure that she wouldn't, but I opened the door anyway. Along with the cigarette holder and the set of black wings, Glenda was clad in a studded black leather micro triangle top, a tiny tutu, and thigh-high boots. I couldn't decide whether she looked like a winged Hell's Angel or a geriatric Victoria's Secret model whose wings had been clipped. "Um, is that supposed to be your fairy costume?"

"I just made that crap up so you'd open the damn door,"

she said as she shoved a Bloody Mary into my hand.

I eyed the drink suspiciously. "What's this for?"

She batted her inch-long crimson eyelashes. "Aren't you hung over?"

"No, but I might as well be."

She put her hand on her tutued hip. "The night before I turned thirty, I drowned my sorrows in champagne, and I soaked in it too. A bubbly bath does wonders for a lady's soul and her skin, you know."

On my private investigator's salary, I couldn't afford a glass of champagne, much less a bathtub full. But Glenda was an ex-stripper who'd invested her money in real estate and antiques, including the fourplex we lived in and the not-so-chic seventies brothel pieces in my furnished apartment, so she could afford to bathe in booze. In fact, she had a six-foot-tall champagne glass in her living room for precisely that purpose. "Actually, I wouldn't know."

"Well, don't you fret about that, sugar," she said, waving a bony finger. "Because this year your birthday's gonna be full of fun surprises."

An alarm siren sounded in my head as she took a drag off her cigarette. "What exactly do you mean by 'full of fun surprises'?"

"I can't tell you that, now can I?" she exclaimed, exhaling smoke into my face as she spoke.

I sucked down half the spicy Bloody Mary to calm my nerves. Despite her age, Glenda was as wild as a sorority girl at a Mardi Gras-themed mixer, so one of her surprises could pack a real punch (and not of the delicious rum variety).

She tucked the cigarette holder behind her ear and stepped toward me. "Hold still, sugar."

I eyeballed the lit cigarette, which was dangerously close to my long, brown hair. "What for?"

"You'll see." She pulled a crisp dollar bill from the waistband of her tutu and removed a pin from the teensy triangle of leather tasked with covering her nipple and areola.

I, in turn, uttered a silent prayer to the wardrobe fairy that there would be no malfunction.

"Now stick out your chest."

"No way." I shielded my breasts from both the pin and the ash that was now dangling from the cigarette. We lived in New Orleans, so for all I knew she was about to perform some kind of stripper voodoo ritual to ward off the evil spirits of sagging and wrinkling. "Not until you tell me what you're going to do."

"Oh, quit your bellyachin'," she scolded as she shoved her hand down the V-neckline of my beige sweater and pinned the dollar above my left boob.

"What's that for?" I asked, feeling flustered and felt up. After all, she was the stripper, not me.

Glenda removed the cigarette holder from behind her ear. "It's a local tradition, Miss Franki. Someone pins a dollar to your shirt on your birthday, and then all day long people add money. Sometimes, fives, tens, even twenties."

I drained the other half of my drink as I pondered this possibility. Free money would definitely qualify as a "fun surprise."

My cell phone began to ring.

"You go on and get that, Miss Franki. I'm late for practice."

"Practice for what?" It was none of my business, but I had to know what kind of organized activity would require such a ghastly getup.

Her eyes lit up like a stripper stage. "In honor of St. Patrick's Day and St. Joseph's Day, my old manager at Madame Moiselle's has invited some of us more seasoned dancers to do a show called 'The Saints, Sinners, and Sluts Revue.'"

Madame Moiselle's was the Bourbon Street strip club where Glenda, dancing as "Lorraine Lamour," had made quite a name for herself in the sixties and seventies. She'd also been courted by a slew of prominent suitors, including a wealthy sheikh who asked her to join his harem after he'd watched her "1001 A-labia-n Nights" routine. Ever since she'd retired she'd been helping out at the club, teaching the new girls the tricks of the trade, but I knew that her real passion lay in performing.

"What are you supposed to be, like, a sinner-saint?" I asked, nodding toward her black wings.

Her face fell. "No, sugar," she replied. "I'm a slut. Isn't it obvious?"

"Of course," I reassured. "I don't know what I was thinking."

"No worries," she said with a flip of her long, platinum hair. The corners of her mouth formed a lewd grin. "You have a stimulating day, now."

Her wings flapped as she turned and strutted toward a waiting taxi.

I closed the door and wondered what she'd meant by "stimulating" as I searched for my now silent phone. I found it on the end table beneath a half-eaten bag of Hampton's Cajun Creole Hot Nuts. When I looked at the display, I breathed a sigh of relief—that is, until the phone started ringing again. I gave a sigh of resignation and stretched out on the chaise lounge before pressing answer. "Hi, Mom."

"Happy birthday, Francesca," she said, her usually shrill voice descending with every syllable until it was so low and lugubrious that it sounded like it wanted to jump off a ledge.

"Thanks," I replied, already trying to figure out a way to get her off the phone. These calls from home were typically a downer, but judging from the way this one had started, we were destined to sink to new depths of despair. "Is Dad there?"

"He's at the deli, dear," she said in a dejected tone. "The city shut off the water this morning with no warning, so he had to run some jugs of water over for the kitchen staff."

My parents, Brenda and Joe Amato, had owned Amato's Deli in Houston's Rice Village since before I was born. And if you were thinking that the water issue was the reason for my mother's depression, you were dead wrong. From the moment I graduated from the University of Texas when I was twenty-two, she'd been upset that I wasn't married. The thing was that both of my parents were first generation Italian-Americans, and they believed in the "old country" values. But they didn't hold a candle to my dad's eighty-three-year-old Sicilian mother, Carmela Montalbano. She declared me a *zitella*, which is Italian for old maid, at the advanced age of sixteen—almost half my life ago.

I suddenly realized that my mother had fallen silent, no doubt wallowing in maternal misery. So I said, "That's a bummer

about the water, Mom, but I'm sure they'll turn it back on soon."
Then I made the fatal mistake of asking, "Everything else okay?"

The silence continued, which was the signal that she was
about to segue into the really bad news. "Well, I might as well
tell you, Francesca." She gave a somber sigh. "Your nonna's in
mourning."

Aaaand let the guilt games begin, I thought as I rested
the back of my arm on my forehead. "Mom, she's been in heavy
mourning since nonnu died twenty-one years ago."

"Yes, but she's gone into deeper mourning now that
you've turned thirty. She's started wearing a black veil around the
house, and she's taken a vow of silence."

A vow of silence? That was both worrisome and
wonderful—worrisome because my nonna lived to meddle,
which she couldn't do if she wasn't able to talk, and wonderful
because, well, she couldn't meddle or talk. "So, what's she doing,
then?"

"Sitting on the couch, holding her rosary, and staring at
the portrait of the Virgin Mary," she replied as maudlin as a
martyr. "Your father's just sick about it too. It hurts him terribly
to see his mother in this state."

"Mom," I began, annoyed that she'd played the sad dad
card, "why don't you remind nonna that I have a terrific
boyfriend who I've been dating for over a year?" I asked,
referring to my banker beau, Bradley Hartmann.

"You know your nonna, dear."

Yes, I did. For her, the mere act of dating was equivalent
to living in sin. Single young women were to be betrothed at a
suitable age (by early twentieth-century Sicilian standards) and
strictly chaperoned until the wedding, which was supposed to
take place the minute the marriage banns went into effect. "Well,
she can't expect me to have a two-week engagement like she did.
That's just prehistoric."

"It's a little hasty, I agree. But you've been with Bradley
for a year now, Francesca." She paused. "For your sake, I hope
he proposes at dinner tonight."

I bolted upright, causing Napoleon's ears to do the same.
"What do you mean 'for your sake'? It's not like being unmarried
is an affliction. And besides, you can't put that kind of pressure

on me—or on Bradley, for that matter."

"Now don't confuse me with Mother Nature," she said, lapsing into lecture mode. "She's the one putting the pressure on you. After all, your biological clock has been ticking for some time now."

I clenched my teeth, and a sharp pain shot through one of my upper molars. "Ow! Dang it."

"What's the matter, dear?"

I put my hand to my face. "My tooth hurts."

"You have to take better care of yourself, Francesca," she chastised. "You're not a young girl anymore."

"Mom, that's been made painfully clear to me today," I snapped. "Listen, I need to get going. I'm working overtime this weekend."

"Well, try to have a nice day, dear," she said as though it would be next to impossible.

"Right," I said, biting the inside of my cheek to stop myself from saying something I'd only halfway regret. I also managed to spit out a "love you" because I did love my mother, but not especially in that moment.

I hung up the phone and pressed my molar with my thumb. There was something wrong, all right. I wanted to believe that it was my sweet tooth telling me that I should never have given up sweets for Lent, because I could seriously go for a jar of Nutella right now.

Instead, I grabbed the bag of Hot Nuts and tossed a couple into my mouth. No sooner had I bit down than the pain jolted into my sinus cavity. This was no sweet tooth—this was a sign. On top of being husbandless and childless, I was destined to be toothless too.

* * *

"I'm back, Franki," my boss and best friend Veronica Maggio called as she pushed open the door to her PI firm, Private Chicks, Inc., with a package under her arm.

I'd come to the office an hour earlier to escape the bad birthday juju at my apartment. Soon after I'd arrived and told Veronica about Glenda, my mom, and the saga of my nonna's vow of silence, she'd announced that she needed to run a few errands. So I had high hopes that she was going to right the wrongs of this morning's wayward well-wishers. "What have you got there?"

She saw me stretched out on one of the two opposing couches in the middle of the waiting room and stopped short. "Why are you lying down? Aren't you feeling well?"

I started to tell her that my tooth had begun hurting, but then I noticed that the package was a box from the Alois J Binder bakery on Frenchman Street, and I got a better idea. "I think I have low blood sugar," I rasped, going for a sick waif but sounding more like a steady smoker. "I haven't had any sweets since Mardi Gras, and that was over a month ago."

She smirked and placed the box on the reception desk beside the door. "Nice try, but I got you a plain croissant."

"Gah, Veronica," I said, pulling myself onto my elbows. "Sometimes you can be so cruel. Even my parents used to give me a birthday Lent reprieve when I was a teenager, and you know what strict Catholics they are."

"Yes, but you're not a teen anymore," she said as she looked inside the bakery box.

I scowled and lay back down. I should have known that Veronica would rain on my bedraggled birthday parade. When we first met in college, I thought that she was a bubbly blonde party girl, but I soon learned that she was all business and no pleasure. Case in point—she finished college and law school in about the same amount of time it took me to earn a bachelor's degree, and she did it with honors. "You know, you're the third person today to imply that I'm old, and it's only ten thirty."

Her smirk softened as she brought me the box. "I'm sorry you're having such a bad birthday. I don't know why you didn't take the day off."

"I could use the overtime pay, for one thing," I said, glancing pointedly at the lone dollar that hung from my shirt before taking the creamless croissant. "And I had to get out of that apartment. The baroque brothel décor was starting to remind me of an old funeral parlor, and with that creepy cemetery across the street, I felt like I was sitting around waiting to go to my grave."

Veronica rolled her eyes. "Oh, come on," she said, taking a seat on the opposite couch. "Turning thirty's not that bad. I did it six months ago, and I lived to tell about it."

"I know." I picked at the plain pastry. "Honestly, it's not the age that bothers me as much as the familial fallout from it."

"Well, look at the bright side," she said, pulling a vanilla cream napoleon from the box. "Now that your nonna has taken a vow of silence, you're going to get a much-needed break."

I shot her a skeptical look. With that delicious pastry in hand, she could afford to be optimistic.

The door swung open, and David Savoie, our part-time research assistant, entered, carrying two grocery bags. A junior at Tulane University, David could really put away the grub, but you'd never know it from his lanky frame.

"What've you got there, your lunch?" Veronica joked.

He flipped his brown bangs to one side. "Nah, Rouses Market donated this stuff for the food drive. It's mostly potato chips, pretzels, and pralines."

After swearing off sweets, I was so sick of savory snacks that I could just spit—except that I didn't have any saliva left because of all the salt. But my interest perked up at the mention of pralines. "What food drive?"

David placed the bag on his desk in the far left corner behind the couches. "My fraternity is collecting food for the poor for St. Joseph's Day."

I looked at Veronica to see whether she was as confused as I was. "Why is your computer science frat participating in a Catholic festival?"

"St. Joseph's Day isn't just a religious tradition in New Orleans, Franki," Veronica explained. "It's like St. Patrick's Day—the whole city celebrates it."

This was news to me. As far as I was aware, only Italian-American Catholics observed the day. "Okay, but why bring the food here?"

David sat on the back of the couch. "Veronica's letting me keep the donations in the conference room because my frat brothers keep eating them all."

"That's terrible," I said, resolving to slip across the hall to that conference room. I had no intention of stealing food from the poor, mind you. I just wanted to check those pralines—you know, to make sure they hadn't gone bad.

Veronica swallowed a bite of her pastry. "It's predictable behavior from a house full of hungry young men. That reminds me, David," she began, turning to hand him the open box, "I got you a little surprise from the bakery."

"A shoe sole! Dude, thanks," he exclaimed before shoving the sole-shaped pastry into his mouth. Then he retrieved the grocery bag, grabbed the conference room key from the reception desk drawer, and headed across the hall.

"Speaking of surprises, tell me what Glenda has planned for me," I ordered, giving Veronica my sincerest spill-it stare.

She licked cream from her finger in a ploy to avoid my gaze.

But I wasn't fooled. I was positive that she knew the score because she lived in Glenda's fourplex too. In fact, Veronica was the one who'd convinced me to rent the ground-floor apartment across from hers, sight (and cemetery) unseen. And despite the world of differences between her and Glenda, they were as tight as Gwyneth and Madonna—before their unfortunate split. "I'm serious. Out with it."

She pursed her lips and took a deep breath. "You know I'm no spoiler—"

"Just say it," I commanded through clenched teeth.

"Glenda hired you a male stripper," she gushed.

I dropped the croissant. "Why in the hell would she do that?"

She shrugged. "She thought you needed a little cheering up. And in Glenda's world, that can only mean one thing."

Yeah, nude, hard-bodied men slathered in oil. Of course, there was a time and a place for that sort of thing, but not on the day that I had plans with Bradley. "Please tell me that the stripper isn't going to show up during my date. I'm finally getting to go to the Sazerac Bar, and I don't want to get escorted out."

Veronica shook her head. "I'm sure he'll come before then. Glenda would want you to enjoy him all on your own."

"What'd she get me?" I asked—just so I could be prepared, of course. "A carpenter? A fireman?"

She averted her eyes. "A cop."

"What?" Before joining Private Chicks, I'd worked as a rookie police officer in Austin, Texas, and I hadn't stood a fighting chance at that job. "How does she not know that I'd rather have any profession than a cop? Even a Wall Street executive."

"I told her that," Veronica replied, smoothing her blue Versace skirt. "But she said that you needed the authoritative type to bring you out of your funk."

I chewed my thumbnail. "Well, I hope this guy shows up soon. Because from the way things are going, that date is going to be the only bright spot of my day." *In addition to the Bloody Mary and the dollar.*

"Maybe this will help make your day a little brighter," she said, pulling an envelope from her purse. "It's a half day at the spa. I went by there on my way to the bakery, and they agreed to work you in at noon."

"You're the best, Veronica," I exclaimed as I jumped up from my sofa sickbed and wrapped my arms around her—bending my 5' 10" frame at the waist. "That's almost better than a pastry."

She laughed and shook her head. "Only you would prefer a pastry to pampering. Now, I have plans tonight, but I want to hear all the details in the morning—about the spa and the dinner."

"You got it." For the first time today, I was starting to think that I might have something good to recount.

* * *

"What kind of moron would leave their car running in the middle of the street?" I exclaimed to myself. I'd been standing outside Private Chicks for ten minutes, waiting for the owner of the neon orange Nissan Cube that was blocking my 1965 Mustang convertible. Because the firm was located on Decatur Street in the French Quarter, traffic was always an issue. And it didn't help that an Italian restaurant occupied the first two floors of the three-story brick building we were located in. I liked their pizza and pasta but not their patrons, who were prone to parking their cars in the street while picking up to-go orders.

I looked at the time on my phone as I paced the sidewalk. It was twenty till noon. If I didn't leave soon, I could kiss my spa appointment *arrivederci*.

A thirty-something guy holding a green beer and wearing a matching T-shirt that read, "The leprechauns made me do it," approached from the other side of the street. "Hey, uh, is this the parade route?"

"Parade?" I repeated.

"Yeah." He wiped his nose with his wrist. "The parades for St. Patrick's Day and St. Joseph's Day start today at one o'clock."

I blinked. "They do?"

He took a swig of his beer. "They're always the Saturday before so everyone can get in on the action."

"You don't say," I said, narrowing my eyes at the Nissan. If a bunch of floats came down Decatur, I'd miss my massage for sure.

"Sorry to have bothered you," he said.

"No problem," I replied as I zeroed in on the real bother.

Without further ado, I marched to the driver's side of the Nissan and yanked open the door. As I settled into the seat and released the parking brake, I noticed an open box marked "Erzulie's Authentic Voodoo." Curious, not to mention a little concerned, I peered inside and saw around twenty see-through fabric bags containing incense sticks, candles, packets of white crystals, and little vials of liquid. The bags were marked "3-day ritual spell kits," and they were for everything from gaining wealth to garnering protection.

"What a wack job," I whispered as I pressed the gas pedal and pulled the car forward.

"That's my car," a gruff female voice cried.

I looked in the rearview mirror and saw the Nissan's middle-aged owner. How did I know it was her? My first clue was the teased, tangerine hair that was strikingly reminiscent of Endora from *Bewitched*.

"Help! Police!" She waved her purple-caftaned arms. "Stop that thief!"

I pulled up the parking brake and got out of the car just in time to see a thirty-something cop rounding the corner—and buttoning his shirt?

"Officer," she huffed, grasping his forearm, "this young woman was trying to steal my car."

His ice blue eyes looked through me as he fastened his top button. "Is this true, ma'am?"

I hesitated for a moment, not because I was guilty as accused but because a) I was annoyed by that "ma'am," and b) there was something weird about this cop. No officer I knew got dressed on duty, and he seemed uneasy in the uniform, maybe because it didn't fit him. His biceps were straining against the sleeves, and his pecs looked like they were going to pop out of his shirt.

Then it hit me. This was no street cop—this was the stripper cop.

Instantly annoyed, I shifted my weight to one leg and turned to the witchy woman. "Look, I'm late for an appointment, and your car was blocking mine. So I moved it, okay?"

The counterfeit cop cleared his throat. "Actually, it's not okay."

I gave a surly sigh. "I know, I know. I've been a very bad girl, and I need to be punished. But that's not gonna happen, because I'm going to the spa."

I opened the door of my Mustang and flopped into the seat.

"Ma'am," he began in a terse tone, "I need you to exit the vehicle."

I arched a brow. "Or what? You'll cuff me and teach me a lesson?"

He reached into his back pocket and flipped open his wallet.

My stomach tried to take off running as I stared at the New Orleans PD badge, which was as real as the regulation baton on his hip.

"You're under arrest for unauthorized use of a motor vehicle."

As he proceeded to read me my rights, my brain began to process the situation. To celebrate my thirtieth birthday, I wasn't going to the spa or to the Sazerac. I was going to the slammer.

CHAPTER TWO

———

"I'm taking you to the office so you can pick up your *own* car," Veronica quipped as we exited New Orleans's notorious Central Lockup at eight a.m. the next morning.

I clenched my jaw. She was clearly referring to my "unauthorized use" of the neon Nissan, but after spending the last twenty hours in a cold, cramped cell, I was in no mood for her sarcasm. "If you're thinking about a career in stand-up, forget it. You've got no comic timing."

She gave me a haughty look. "I wasn't trying to be funny, Franki."

We climbed into her white Audi in silence and fastened our seat belts.

"And I still don't understand how you, of all people, could've mistaken a real police officer for a stripper," she continued.

"I had a lot on my mind, okay?" I said as I rummaged through my bag for my sunglasses to shield my eyes from the harsh glare of the sunlight and the harsh reality of Central Lockup. "Besides, someone—and I'm not naming names—told me to be on the watch for a stripper cop."

She started the engine. "You're blaming me for this mess?"

I slid the sunglasses onto my nose. "There's plenty of blame to go around, starting with Glenda."

"She was just trying to do something nice for you," Veronica said as she peeled out of the parking lot. "There's no way she could've known that it would backfire like this."

I crossed my arms. "Maybe not, but she knew that I went to jail."

"What?" she exclaimed, hitting the gas so hard that both of our heads snapped backwards. "How?"

"After I called you and got your voice mail," I began, lowering my eyelids into a cold stare, "the officer agreed to let me try someone else. So, I called Glenda. When I told her where I was, she goes, 'I paid the young man extra for *hard time*, sugar. Enjoy the strip search,' and hung up the phone."

Veronica started to laugh but quickly turned the sound into a fake cough. "Well, look on the bright side. The woman whose car you moved dropped the charges. If I were you, I'd pay her a visit and thank her."

"I'm pretty sure 'that woman,' as you call her, is a witch—in both senses of the word. And because of her, I stood up my boyfriend and spent my birthday in the clink where a six-foot-five woman with a severe skin-peeling condition used my stomach for a pillow."

She put her hand over her mouth. "Oh my God, really?"

I nodded, as serious as a death sentence. "And to top it all off, this old prostitute ripped the dollar Glenda gave me right off my shirt."

Her eyes widened. "What did you do?"

"Nothing. She was a spitter." I searched my bag for my phone. "Now, I'd better call Bradley."

"Don't worry, Franki," Veronica said as she hooked a hard left onto South Rampart Street. "I explained everything to him after I got your message this morning."

I spun around in my seat so fast that my purse flew to the floor, and it wasn't because of that left turn. "You told him I was in jail?"

"He called me, frantic," she said, waving her hands in the air when she should have been steering. "What was I supposed to tell him?"

Now I was the frantic one. "Uh, not the truth!"

Veronica groaned and collapsed onto the steering wheel. "Here we go."

I glanced around the car. "Where? Off the road?"

She glared at me and straightened in her seat. "On a wild ride through your trust issues."

It was a well-known fact that I was kind of cagey where

men were concerned. The problem was that I'd kissed more than my share of philandering frogs before meeting my persevering prince. But Veronica was wrong if she thought that I didn't believe in my boyfriend. "I already told you—I trust Bradley. I just haven't always felt the same about some of the people around him, like his snobby ex-wife and scheming ex-secretary."

"Uh-huh," she said, monotone. "If you trust him so much, then why didn't you want him to know that you spent the night in jail?"

I snorted in disbelief. "That has nothing to do with trust and everything to do with image. Bradley is a bank president. He needs a suitable woman by his side, e.g., one in a black cocktail dress, not an orange jumpsuit."

Veronica twisted her mouth to the side. "Are you saying that if you don't present the right image, you're afraid that he'll break up with you?"

"Not at all." I pulled off my sunglasses so that she could see my piercing look. "I'm saying that I need to be suitable, which I can't be if I'm behind bars. So, there's no way I'm thanking 'that woman' when she's the reason I got locked up in the first place."

"You're the reason you got locked up," she said, taking another sharp turn. "As an ex-cop, you knew that driving her car without her permission was a felony, so you need to thank her for saving you from a much lengthier stay in jail."

"All right, sure. I knew it was wrong," I admitted as I checked my seatbelt to make sure that it was securely fastened. "But in my defense, she started this whole fiasco by illegally parking her car."

"And if you'd simply reported her as opposed to moving the car, then she would've been the one in trouble with the law."

Of course, I realized that there was a grain of truth in what Veronica was saying—okay, a kernel. But the way I saw it, the woman should have apologized for blocking my Mustang instead of pressing charges and condemning me to spending the night with a skin-slougher.

I stared out the passenger window at a stretch of strip clubs on Bourbon Street. A platinum blonde in a gold lamé minidress and purple platform heels was pulling a small suitcase on wheels from the side door of Madame Moiselle's. I knew from Glenda that the club closed at four a.m., so the investigator in me wondered why a stripper would be leaving work so late.

Then a thought occurred to me. Veronica always worked late and was meticulous about checking her email and voice mail before going to bed. And yet, she didn't get my message until this morning. "Where were you last night, anyway?"

"I had a date with Dirk," she said in a quiet voice.

Veronica was famously private when it came to her personal life, so all I knew about her new boyfriend was that he was a gemologist, which made him a perfect match for my bedazzled bestie, and that his parents, Mr. and Mrs. Bogart, had made the surprising decision to name him "Dirk" after the late actor, Dirk Bogarde, rather than the obvious "Humphrey." "Wow, this is like your fifth date. Is it serious?"

The corners of her mouth tilted upward. "He's a keeper, like Bradley."

"Speaking of keeping Bradley, I'd better make that call." I retrieved my bag from the floor and resumed the search for my phone to no avail. I thought for a moment and remembered that the last time I'd used it was to check the time before moving the Nissan. "Oh, man."

She looked at me from the corners of her eyes. "What's the matter?"

I put my head in my hands. "I left my phone on the seat of that wacko witch's car."

"Looks like you're going to have to apologize to her now," she intoned as she pulled to a stop in front of 1200 Decatur Street.

I gave her my best stabby stare before exiting the Audi.

"And if I were you," she continued, "I would avoid calling her both wacko and witch. An officer at the lockup told me that her first name is Theodora, but that's all I know."

So, "Endora" hadn't been far off the mark. "She's either a customer or an employee of Erzulie's down on Royal Street, but since it's Sunday, they probably don't open for a few hours."

"Then you have plenty of time to shower off the jail germs," Veronica said as cheerful as a cheerleader. "You smell like a urinal."

I slammed the car door.

As I climbed into my Mustang, I wondered what in the hell I was going to say to the witch and what in heaven I was going to tell Bradley.

* * *

When I stepped inside Erzulie's at eleven fifteen, over-caffeinated and under-rested, I thought that I'd entered the Age of Aquarius. Unlike the other voodoo and witchcraft shops in the French Quarter, which were fittingly dark and creepy, the shotgun-style store was a psychedelic mind trip of color. The walls were orange with purple trim, and pink paper lanterns dangled from the ceiling. Various tables and shelves were draped with turquoise and fuchsia glitter organza, and blue beaded curtains obscured a room in the back. Even the products on the shelves were colorful—yellow gris-gris bags, green spell candles, red voodoo dolls. The place looked like an LSD flashback to the 1960s, and thanks to the patchouli incense, it smelled like one too.

As I looked around the room for a sales clerk, my eyes were drawn to a portrait of a woman hanging above a purple mantel serving as an altar. She had a short, orange and green Afro, which matched her striped, strapless dress, and her right hand was placed in the middle of her chest. A lavender snake was coiled around her left arm, and a large, red heart was suspended from her right earlobe.

"That's Erzulie Freda, the Haitian Vodou goddess of love, sensuality, passion, pleasure, and prosperity," a regal female voice said.

I turned to see an attractive thirtyish brunette in a teal silk Mandarin dress. "Sounds like someone I need to meet." But then I remembered learning about a vindictive voodoo goddess with a similar name during my first murder case. "She's not any relation to Erzulie D'en Tort, is she?"

She smiled. "Erzulie D'en Tort is the Petro manifestation of Erzulie Freda. The Petro gods came from the New World and the West and are more aggressive than their benevolent Haitian counterparts." She gestured toward the altar. "If you like, you can get acquainted with Lady Erzulie by making her an offering. She prefers gifts of jewelry, perfume, flowers, cakes, and liqueurs."

"What a coincidence," I said in a joking tone. "So do I."

A corner of her mouth turned up. "Is there anything I can help you with?"

"I'm looking for someone named Theodora," I replied, approaching the cash register.

With a nod, the woman walked to the back of the room and slipped through the beaded curtain.

While I waited, I wandered around the store. Erzulie's didn't sell any of the typical voodoo and witchcraft wares, like severed gator heads and chicken feet. Instead, the merchandise consisted of more upscale items, such as goat milk spiritual soaps and jewel-encrusted skulls.

There were so many bright, sparkly items that I couldn't resist the urge to touch something. So I picked up a black-stained glass pentagram. Curious to see whether light would shine through the dark glass, I opened the door and held the pentagram up to the sun.

"You're not thinking about taking off with that too, are you?" a familiar voice asked.

I turned to face Theodora. She was wearing a yellow caftan with a necklace and earring set of green cat's eyes complete with slit pupil. Between her attire and her orange hair, purple eye shadow, and pink lipstick, she really blended in with the shop. "Don't worry," I said, returning the stained glass window to the display. "Pentagrams aren't my thing."

"I actually like them, and I'm not even a Wiccan." She leaned forward and shielded her mouth with her hand. "Nothing against the Wiccans," she whispered, "but I don't believe in organized religion."

"Ah ha," I said, taking a step backwards. "So, listen. I'm Franki and—"

"Theodora," she interrupted, grabbing my hand and giving it a shake. "How'd you find me? Are you clairvoyant?"

"Uh, no," I replied, suppressing a sigh. "I saw the box of spells from Erzulie's on your front seat and figured that you must be an employee."

"Oh, I don't work here. I'm a freelancer." She pulled a business card from a pocket in her caftan and pressed it into my palm.

I reluctantly read the card and saw that she was a "witchcraft consultant." Of course, I opted to ignore that little tidbit and focus on her lack of a last name. "Just Theodora, huh? Like Cher and Madonna?"

"No, they have surnames," she replied, toying with her necklace. "When I was born we didn't have last names."

I assumed a standoffish stance. I was a magnet for all the nutcases in New Orleans, and the last time I'd exchanged business cards with one of them, I'd ended up with a psycho psychic as my sidekick during a multiple homicide investigation at a plantation. "That's super interesting, but—"

"Aren't you going to ask how old I am?" she interrupted, blinking.

"U-um," I began, momentarily distracted by the discovery that her eyes were glowing green like her pendant, "my mother taught me never to ask a witch, er, *a woman*, her age."

"Well, I don't mind telling you that I had a milestone birthday last week." She raised her chin, striking a pose. "I turned three hundred."

And to think that I'd felt bad about turning thirty. "Wow," I exclaimed, searching for something sane to say. "You don't look a day over fifty-five."

She touched her teased hair. "That's what I hear."

I stared at the floor while I tried to wipe the stupor from my face. "So, aaanyway, I dropped by because—"

"I know." She held up a hand. "We got off on the wrong foot yesterday—your foot on my gas pedal, to be precise—and you want to make amends."

I scratched the back of my head. "Uh, about that—"

"No need to apologize," she said, giving my forearm a squeeze.

"Honestly, I wasn't—"

"Shht!" She flapped her caftaned arms like yellow wings.

I was starting to get annoyed. This witch wouldn't let me

get a word in edgewise.

"The truth is, yesterday I was having a down day. I have SAD. You know, Seasonal Affective Disorder? And with spring around the corner, I'm prone to severe highs and lows."

Awesome. Of all the witches I could've run into, I had to go and meet the one with serious mood swings. "Hey, no need to explain," I said, trying to keep her spirits on the upswing. "I just came to get—"

"Help with the curse?"

I cocked my head to one side. "No, my phone."

"Well, why didn't you say so?" she asked, pulling my cell from her pocket.

I swallowed bile as I took the phone and shoved it into my bag. This witch was not only a wacko, she was also just plain willful. I knew that I should have left right then and there, but my curiosity got the best of me. "What did you mean by that curse comment?"

"It's obvious that someone has put a hex on you."

Even if you knew nothing about my life, the events of the past twenty-four hours were compelling enough evidence to support her argument, no matter how deranged it may have sounded. "It is?" I asked against my better judgment. "How do you know?"

She looked me up and down like I was the lunatic. "I'm something of an expert in these matters."

I shook my head, trying to knock some sense into it. "No offense or anything, but I don't believe in curses or witchcraft."

"If a witch had sent me to jail," she began in a droll tone, "I'd reconsider that position."

I shot her a steely stare. "I think we both know that had nothing to do with a curse. And besides, it's not like I have any witch enemies. The people I know are more the *malocchio*, or evil eye, types."

Her purple eyelids lowered. "You can put a curse on yourself, you know. If you wish someone harm, gossip about them, or call them names, those are curses that can boomerang back on you."

I'm not going to lie—I felt a stab of panic upon hearing this news. But then I got hold of myself. "If that's the case then

I'm cursed for life, and no witch in the world will be able to undo it."

She crossed her arms, and her pupils turned to slits like the ones on her jewelry. "Try me."

I pulled my bag in front of my chest in a defensive posture. Were my eyes playing tricks on me? Or were hers? "Let me think on it," I gushed, making for the exit. "Now that I have my phone back, I need to make a long-overdue call to my boyfriend."

"Then know this," she said, pointing a yellow-lacquered fingernail at my forehead like a wand. "You'll never be able to have a healthy relationship until that curse is lifted."

I started to tell her that if she knew my family then she'd realize that I could never have a healthy relationship anyway— curse or no. But I didn't want to provoke her. Her mood had taken a turn for the worse, and I wasn't sure what this witch was capable of. "I'll take my chances," I said as I pushed open the door. "Thanks for returning my phone, though."

I hurried from the shop and turned down St. Ann where I'd parked my car, thinking about Theodora's eyes. That pupil thing had to be some kind of magic trick. I mean, what kind of sucker did that witch take me for? And as for the curse, the only thing to blame for my current wretched state was good old-fashioned bad luck—and my family and friends.

I pulled out my cell to call Bradley. The screen was black, so I pressed the power button. Nothing. The battery was dead.

Again, regular old bad luck. Right?

I shoved my phone back into my bag and proceeded down the street. Then an eerie sensation came over me. It wasn't an I've-been-cursed feeling, because I knew that was nonsense. It was more of an I'm-being-followed feeling. I glanced over my shoulder, but all I saw were a few tourists. Still, something didn't seem right. So, when I reached my car, I wasted no time getting inside.

And I told myself that the culprit was probably just the usual dark cloud hanging over me.

CHAPTER THREE

───────

"*Mannaggia a me*," I muttered as I plugged my cell phone into the car charger and contemplated how to explain my stint in the slammer to Bradley. Then a stunning realization hit me—I'd just said "damn me" in Italian, which qualified as cursing myself. I resolved to stop doing that stat.

The phone display lit up, and I scrolled through the list of missed calls. As I'd expected, most of them were from Bradley, and several were from my mother who was undoubtedly dying to find out whether I was engaged. But there were also a couple from Bradley's secretary, Ruth Walker.

It wasn't unusual for Ruth to call since our relationship pre-dated her position with Bradley. We met while I was investigating the murder of her previous employer, Ivanna Jones, and it was instant, well, appreciation. She had an abrupt, judgmental demeanor, but she had an eye for detail and a mind like a Rolodex, which made her an ideal assistant. She was also approaching sixty and quite plain, which made her an ideal assistant for Bradley.

Because I'd helped Ruth to get a job at Ponchartrain Bank, she'd taken it upon herself to keep me informed of certain goings on, and I didn't object. It wasn't spying—it was more like safekeeping. And if you knew even half the stunts Bradley's last secretary, Pauline Violette, had pulled, you wouldn't blame me one bit.

My instincts told me to skip my messages and call Ruth ASAP. I slowed to a stop at the intersection of Dauphine and St. Peter and tapped her number. As a steady stream of tourists passed, I put the phone to my ear and spotted a salon called Vaxing for Vomen. Someone had obviously scratched off the first half of both *w*'s from the glass door. But still. The sign made the services sound more than a little harsh, especially for something like a bikini wax.

The phone rang once, and then someone picked up.

"I heard you went to the cooler," Ruth boomed without bothering to say hello.

"The cooler?" I repeated, imagining myself pulling a beer from an ice chest. Make that a bottle of Prosecco.

"You know, the dungeon? The hole?"

Now I knew what she meant. Unfortunately. "Why don't you just say 'jail'?"

She snorted. "I pretty much did."

I started to say something snarky but bit my tongue, because now I was more worried about whether word of my arrest was out at the bank. "Who told you I went to jail?"

"Who do you think?" she barked. "After you no-showed at The Sazerac, Bradley panicked and asked me to help him call the hospitals."

"Really?" Despite my guilt for making him worry, my heart swelled at the news of his concern. "That's so sweet."

"Well, Lord knows it's not like you to miss a drink."

That heart swell I mentioned? Shriveled right up.

"Anyhoo," she continued, "he called me this morning and said you were in the pokey. Of course, I told him last night that we should've been calling the jails," she added in a lo-and-behold-I-was-right tone.

I floored the gas and sped around some tourists. Not only was I sorry that I'd phoned Ruth, I was also regretting ever recommending her for the job. "Is this what you were calling on a weekend to tell me?"

"Hell no. My weekends are too precious," she said as though mine weren't. "But there's some ugly business going on at the bank that we need to chat about away from the prying eyes and inquiring minds."

I heard the sound of ice clinking in a glass, and I wondered whether she was drinking. Ruth never touched alcohol—that is, unless you counted digestives (she didn't). "What's the ugly business?"

"You."

"Me?" I glared at the phone. She'd better hope that she'd been hitting the bottle. "I don't even work there."

"No, but your bank president beau does. And that new manager they transferred here from headquarters—Jeff Payne?" She gave a humorless chuckle. "Mark my words, he came to The Big Easy looking for more than a managerial position."

I gasped. "You mean, he's after Bradley's job?"

"Darn tootin'." She crunched a piece of ice.

"That weasel!" I exclaimed. "But what does this have to do with me? It's not like I have a say in the hiring."

"You could play a role in the firing, though."

"How about you dispense with the riddles, Ruth?" I flipped on my turn signal and mentally flipped her the bird. "Then maybe I can take part in this conversation."

She made a slurping sound followed by a sonorous swallow. "Do you even know what a bank president does?"

"Yeah, he…presides." Okay, so I didn't know the specifics of what Bradley did for a living, but in my defense, we didn't see each other very often because of our work schedules. And when we did get together, we had better things to do than discuss his job duties.

"There's a little more to it than that," she said as sarcastic as a classroom teacher at a home-schooling seminar. "The president is responsible for the financial well being of the bank and for its credibility with the community, staff, and board of directors."

"And Ponchartrain Bank couldn't have a more honest, upstanding president than Bradley Hartmann," I said, pulling up to a red light.

"I agree," she intoned. "It's his girlfriend that everyone is worried about."

My heart sank. "Why? What have I done?"

"Oh, I don't know…investigating the internal affairs of the bank, assaulting a bank employee, breaking and entering into the bank's security room, stealing bank information."

By this point, my heart had sunk so low that it was sitting on my stomach. "But, I did all those things to protect Bradley," I protested. "And the bank."

"The problem is that no one from the bank asked you

to," she said, and I could practically hear the frown lines around her mouth permeating her pronunciation. "To make matters worse, Bradley didn't press charges that time he and the cop found you in the security room after hours. So now his credibility is in question."

A car horn sounded behind me, startling me from my shock. I took a quick left and asked, "How do you know all of this?"

She drained the rest of her drink with a loud straw-sucking sound. "I might have read a file on Jeff's desktop."

"Does Bradley know?" I whispered.

"He doesn't know that Jeff has a file about him on his desktop, but he's gotten the idea that you're a professional problem."

My heart stopped.

"Oh, blast and damnation," Ruth bellowed out of nowhere. "It's a quarter after twelve. I've got to get my popcorn popped and my Pimm's poured before the Judge Judy marathon starts. Meanwhile, you lay low, missy. Because if you get in trouble again, you could cost Bradley and me both our jobs. And if that happens," she began, lowering her voice like a guillotine, "Central Lockup's going to seem like a sanctuary."

The line went dead.

I dropped the phone and gripped the steering wheel. My worst fear was coming true, but it was even worse than I'd thought. Someone was trying to prove that I was unsuitable for Bradley, so much so that he could lose his job over me (as for Ruth, she could fend for herself).

Explaining my jaunt to jail suddenly got a whole lot harder.

As I pondered my predicament, I merged onto I-10 West. A green Nissan Cube cut me off, and Theodora's pupils popped into my mind.

And I started to wonder whether a person could actually be cursed.

* * *

Napoleon pawed at the pillow covering my face.

"All right, I'll call him," I huffed. "Can't a girl take an afternoon nap in peace?" I felt around for my phone on the nightstand.

Of course, I knew my dog had no conception of the fact that I was stalling on calling my boyfriend. But Napoleon could sense when something was bothering me, and recently he'd taken to hounding me, so to speak, until I started acting normally again. Like a total Cairn terror.

After knocking the lamp and the alarm clock off my nightstand, I was able to find my phone. I pulled off the pillow and tapped Bradley's number.

The call went straight to voice mail.

I tossed the phone onto my hot pink duvet and stared at the matching canopy. My first thought was that the black, French bordello-style bed Glenda had picked out for my "boudoir" was so ugly that I seriously doubted whether a prostitute could get any action in it. And my next thought was that Bradley was so mad he was probably avoiding me.

The phone rang, and I rushed to answer.

"Before you say anything, Bradley, I want to apologize for—"

"Francesca Lucia Amato," my mother's shrill voice scolded from the other end of the line. "What did you do to Bradley this time?"

I pulled the pillow back over my face. Ever since the age of seven when I'd whacked my older brother Anthony over the head with his light saber for cutting my Totally Hair Barbie's long brunette locks, my mother had treated me like a delinquent. I'll admit that I could be combative, but it wasn't like I was a criminal—yesterday notwithstanding. "I didn't do anything to him, Mom." And that was the truth, but what I was about to say certainly wasn't. "Everything's fine."

She slammed the receiver onto what I knew to be the kitchen counter. "He didn't propose!"

"*È una zitella gattara a vita,*" Nonna wailed in the background, as if on cue.

According to my nonna's proclamation, I'd apparently earned two new distinctions since turning thirty: the first was that I was now a zitella *for life*, and the second was that I was also officially a zitella *gattara*, or old maid cat lady, even though I was allergic to feline dander and had only ever owned dogs. "Um, what happened to Nonna's vow of silence?"

"She's been forgetting about that vow quite often today," my mother grumbled.

"Give-a me a break-a, woman," Nonna cried. "I'm old!"

"Like just now," my mother added through what sounded like clenched teeth.

"Dad's not around, is he?" I asked, trying to hide the hopeful desperation in my tone. "He hasn't wished me happy birthday yet." Not that it would do any good, but at least it would get my mom off the phone.

The receiver hit the counter. "Joe! Get on the other line! It's Francesca!"

A blissful silence ensued as we waited for my father to pick up.

Then I heard my nonna praying loudly for a Savior—not Jesus, mind you, but a husband for me.

"Maybe Dad didn't hear you?" I pressed, anxious to get back to my own private hell.

My mother sighed. "It must be that wax buildup in his ears. I bought him a kit to clean that out, but does he listen to me?" She slammed down the receiver. "Joe! Could you stop playing blackjack on that computer and come wish your damn daughter a happy belated birthday?"

There was another blessed moment of serenity while my mom once again waited and while I tried to figure out how I felt about my dad's wax-encrusted ears and that "damn daughter" comment.

"What is that man *doing*?" my mother exclaimed. "Give me a minute, Francesca. I'm going to have to go find him." The phone hit the counter and then crashed to the floor. "Joseph! *Giuseppe*!" she added, as though my dad might not have recognized the Anglicized version of his name.

Nonna stopped praying. "*Madonna mia*!" she cried. "*San Giuseppe*!"

I wasn't sure what was happening, but either my nonna had just had some sort of revelation, or she was invoking the assistance of the Virgin Mary and the patron saint of Italy and the Catholic Church on my behalf.

Someone picked up the receiver. "Franki," Nonna began, her voice not unlike the Godfather's when he made someone an offer they couldn't refuse, "we have-a some hope."

"We *do*?" This was truly news to me.

"I just-a remembered," she rasped. "*La tavola di San Giuseppe.*"

"What about Saint Joseph's table?" I asked, mildly intrigued. It seemed like everyone was talking about that festival lately.

"You know, the *limoni.*"

"I don't know anything about any lemons, Nonna." Except for the fact that life was giving them to me by the bushel these days.

"It's a tradition, Franki. A *zitella* take-a the lemon from-a San Giuseppe's table, and by the next-a year she have-a the husband. But no one can-a see, or it's-a no gonna work."

"Wait. You mean, *steal* a lemon from the altar? To land a husband?"

"Of course," she replied, as though everyone knew that was how hard-up Catholic gals got their grooms.

"Whatever happened to 'thou shalt not steal'?" I asked, scratching my neck uneasily. The good sisters at my Catholic Sunday school had worked hard to instill psychosomatic disorders in us kids at the mere suggestion of committing a sin, so this conversation was making me itchy.

"It's-a like-a we say in *Italia.* All is-a permitted in-a war and-a love."

"All is fair in love and war," I corrected. "We say that in the US too."

"You see? The whole-a world-a can't be wrong."

I didn't bother telling her that Italy and the United States were not the "whole-a world-a" because I honestly didn't think that she'd ever heard of any other countries. Instead, I got down to brass tacks. "So, let me get this straight. You want me to steal a lemon from a Catholic altar devoted to Jesus's father that's intended to feed the poor?"

"You got a problem with-a that?" she asked, now sounding more like De Niro than Brando.

Before I could reply, someone picked up another line.

"I found your father, dear," my mother announced. "He's sitting on the toilet."

To my horror, I heard her handing off the receiver.

"Happy birthday, Franki," my dad said in an animated voice. "Did you have a nice time last night?"

I squirmed at the memory of the skin-slougher and at the image of my father talking to me from the john.

"Bradley didn't pop-a the question," Nonna replied from the kitchen phone.

"Sorry to hear that you didn't get that proposal," my dad said as though referring to a lost job offer. "Better luck next time, eh?"

"She'll have-a the luck," Nonna said. "The luck of the lemon."

"What's she talking about, Franki?" he asked.

"I'll let Nonna explain, Dad. I've gotta run." Then I remembered the toilet and instantly regretted my choice of terms. "Love you and talk to you soon."

I pressed *end* before they could object and held the power button down. I had no intention of talking to anyone else today—not even Bradley. And honestly, if I could've foreseen how these calls were going to go, I would have let that witch keep my stupid phone.

I slid off the bed and headed for the kitchen. Suddenly, I was craving lemon. And as the old saying goes, when life gives you lemons and your nonna tells you to steal one from a Catholic altar to snag a husband, make lemonade—or better, limoncello.

And then drink it.

* * *

My phone was ringing.

I opened an eye, and sunlight scorched my brain. I was lying face up on Glenda's antique bearskin rug in front of the fireplace. The back of my head was resting on the top of the bear's, and his right paw was wrapped around a half-empty bottle of limoncello. Now I understood why I felt like I was coming out of hibernation.

I rolled onto my hands and knees and pulled my cell from the bear's other paw, desperate to stop the noise. The display was dark, so I pressed the power button. Only then did it occur to me that my phone had been turned off.

The ringing switched to knocking, and I realized that the sound I'd been hearing was my doorbell. I made my way to the door holding my phone in one hand and my head in the other.

Still using the one eye, I peered out the peephole and saw slicked back brown hair.

Bradley? I opened the door.

But it wasn't Bradley. The man who stood before me looked like a young Nicholas Cage. And even in my semi-drunk state, I could see that his police uniform was made of cheap fabric similar to the kind used for Halloween costumes.

Glenda!

Stripper Cop Cage cocked a low brow and pointed a finger intentionally close to my breast. "According to a call that came over my police radio, ma'am," he began in an Elvis impersonator-like voice, "you've been evading arrest."

"Actually, I haven't," I said clenching my fists at that "ma'am." "I got out of jail just this morning."

He froze for a moment, and then his shoulders relaxed. "Well, now I'm going to have to do a full body search," he announced with his lip curling like that of The King. He pulled out a plastic baton and gave a lascivious smile. "Up against the wall, and spread 'em."

I ripped the baton from his hands and whacked him over the head, exactly like I'd done to my brother Anthony with that light saber.

"Ow," he said, rubbing his head. "Was that really necessary? I'm just trying to do my job."

My phone began to ring. I looked at the display and pressed answer. "Glenda," I ground out, "if you don't call off your cop, you're gonna have a homicide on your hands."

Stripper Cop Cage's low brow lifted to the top of his forehead.

"That's what I'm calling about, sugar," Glenda said. "I already do."

"Wait," I said, massaging my temple. "How do *you* have

a homicide?"

She exhaled what was probably a puff of smoke. "There's been a murder at Madame Moiselle's, Miss Franki. An ex-house stripper named Amber Brown."

I thought of the blonde I'd seen leaving the club. "Did you know Amber?"

"Not well, but I'm friends with her ex-landlord, Carnie. I called her a few minutes ago, and I think she's going to need your services."

"I'll be right there." I ended the call and checked the time. It was three p.m., which meant that I hadn't burned off the near half bottle of booze I'd drunk two hours before. I grabbed my bag and headed for the door, but Stripper Cop Cage blocked my way and leered at my rack.

"Show's over," I said, referring both to my boobs and his striptease.

"Don't you want me to dance?" He did a sample Saturday Night Fever-style spin and finished with a mimed hair-smoothing move.

"No, I want you to drive," I replied, pushing past him. "And if you even think about copping a feel in the car, stripper copper, the next place you do any spinning will be your grave."

As I tramped toward his tricked-out Trans Am, I had a bad feeling in my gut (related in part to the limoncello). I don't know why, but something was telling me to turn around—to go back inside my apartment and lock the door. But I didn't listen.

Because I was probably cursed, right?

CHAPTER FOUR

———

My stripper chauffer skidded the Trans Am to a stop in front of Madame Moiselle's, and then *he* skidded to a stop and stared slack-jawed through the windshield at some skimpily dressed strippers gathered on the second-floor balcony. "Uh…you need an escort inside?"

"Nah," I said as I climbed from the car. Maybe it was the lingering effects of the limoncello, but just for kicks I bent down and added, "I'm really only here to see a dead body."

His slack jaw became even slacker, and then he peeled out with the passenger door still wide open.

I smirked and approached a blond police officer who looked like he was barely old enough to drink, standing guard at Madame Moiselle's red double-door entrance.

"The club is closed for the day, ma'am," he announced.

I processed that "ma'am" in disbelief. *Did a citywide press release go out about my birthday or something?*

Glenda leaned over the rail, her hair and breasts hanging down. "She's one of us, Officer, baby."

He looked me up and down and then narrowed his ice blue eyes like a poker player reading his opponent.

I matched his half-lidded gaze and gave him a how-dare-you glare. Not that I wanted to be taken for a stripper, but I sure as heck didn't want some cop who was practically a kid acting like I couldn't be one. After all, us thirty-year-olds could strip too.

"Wait on the second floor with the others," he said, stepping aside.

I mentally thanked Glenda for intervening on my behalf because the police were notorious for not wanting PIs puttering around their crime scenes. Before the officer could change his mind, I hurried inside.

And I experienced an immediate assault on my semi-drunk senses. Madame Moiselle's deep red décor and pink neon signage scorched my eyes, and the stench singed my nostrils. As a rookie cop I'd responded to calls at more than a few strip clubs, and they'd always looked and smelled the same—like sleazy cabarets that stunk of baby powder, stale sweat, spilled drinks, dirty money, and something male, possibly testosterone. This time, however, there was also a sweet, acrid odor that I couldn't put my finger on.

After my eyes adjusted to the redness, I scanned the rectangular room for the scene of the crime. To my left, five officers were gathered around a command post that had been set up at one of two small stages, which, except for the poles running through the center, looked oddly like dining room suites for twenty. Behind the stages, along the far-left wall, there were two men in suits, probably plainclothes detectives, who were conversing on a red, quilted, plush velvet couch that I wouldn't have touched with a ten-foot stripper pole.

I looked to my right and saw several crime scene investigators in white coveralls and Latex gloves standing on a much larger stage next to a full bar. I figured that's where I'd find the victim.

As I took a step forward, a hand gripped my shoulder and pulled me back. I turned expecting to see the boy cop, but instead I came face-to-face with the bastard cop who'd kicked me to the cooler, to use Ruth's term. But this time he wasn't wearing an ill-fitting uniform—he was wearing a form-fitting suit. "What are *you* doing here?"

He crossed his arms. "I believe that's my line, Ms. Amato."

Sadly, the cop had a good memory. And as much as it pained me, I needed to get on his good side to have a shot at viewing the crime scene. So, I opted for the cooperative route. "I'm a private investigator, and I'm here on behalf of a prospective client."

He snorted and bowed his head. "A buddy of mine down at the station told me that your attorney friend said you were a

PI." He grinned and shook his head. "He said you were an ex-cop too. But he was just pulling my leg, right?"

Well, I certainly didn't want to answer that question *now*. So, I turned the tables on him. "What's with the suit?" I forced a half-smile. "Don't tell me you just came from church."

The mocking grin disappeared from his face as he flashed his badge. "Detective Wesley Sullivan. Homicide."

"You're a homicide detective?" Okay, the compliant act was off. "Then what were you doing in uniform in the French Quarter yesterday arresting innocent people?"

"The only person I arrested was guilty," he said with a sardonic stare. "And we like to build up our police presence in the Quarter when the Irish and Italians have simultaneous street parties." His gaze bored into my eyes like a drill. "Because the Italians have been known to pick fights with the Irish."

I bristled at his comment. That was no stereotype—that was a veiled accusation. Now the gloves were off. "Spoken like a true Irishman, Detective." I grasped my chin in a pretend pensive pose. "Correct me if I'm wrong, but aren't the Irish the ones who are typically stereotyped as the fighters?"

He feigned a posture of his own, putting his finger on the cleft in his chin. "Oh, that's right. The Italians are the drinkers. And while we're on the subject, is that alcohol I smell on your breath?"

Crap. I guess I should've taken an extra two minutes to brush my teeth before leaving the house. "That's my lemon mint breath spray?"

He pointed toward the door. "Out."

I blinked. "But I need to see the scene of the murder."

His pointed finger moved from the door to my face. "Do you really think I'm going to let a half-drunk PI with a flagrant disrespect for the law around my crime scene?"

The detective had a point. "Would it help if I told you that I was leaning more toward hungover than half-drunk?"

He put his hands on his hips, pulling back his suit coat in the process and revealing a set of handcuffs. "Would it help if I told you that I was leaning toward arresting you for disobeying an officer?"

"Given your track record? You bet." I spun on my heels

and headed for the door. And to add insult to injury, my tooth started to hurt again.

Now *the alcohol decides to wear off.*

I exited the club and saw the officer on guard talking to a couple of scantily clad young women.

"You need to go straight to the second floor and wait with the other dancers," he said, gesturing toward the balcony. "An officer will question you shortly."

Seizing the opportunity, I waited for the dancers to enter Madame Moiselle's. Then I fell into step behind their six-inch heels and followed them to the pink neon "VIP Champagne Rooms" sign in the far-left corner of the club. They powered up the stairs in their platforms while I plodded along in my two-inch-heeled boots. Of course, I could've kept up with them if I exercised for a living like they did. Possibly.

"Is that you, Miss Franki?" Glenda called.

"In the flesh," I quipped, smiling to myself since I was the only fully clothed female in the joint. The smile faded when I caught sight of Glenda at the top of the stairs in an outfit that made me want to turn around and go back down. She was wearing red, cross-shaped pasties, a white ruffle that was failing miserably at passing for a skirt, a tiny red thong, and red fishnet thigh-high stockings with white go-go boots—naughty stripper-style, not Nancy Sinatra-style. All she needed was a nursing cap, and she'd look like a slutty go-go dancer for the Red Cross.

I reached the landing and shifted my gaze from Glenda to the décor. Everything was red—the walls, the ceiling, the woodwork, the couches, even the bar.

"Let's go into a VIP Room so we can talk in private." Glenda opened the nearest door, and I was instantly taken aback.

"Are they all glowing pink like this?" I asked, shielding my eyes from the neon *Veni, vidi, veni* sign.

"Sure are," she said, flopping onto a love seat. "The idea is that you go from the deep red outside to the vibrant pink inside to evoke lips opening into a mouth or labia opening into a vagina. That's why I decorated your living room in red and your bedroom in pink."

Great. Now in addition to thinking of my apartment as a whorehouse and a funeral parlor, I would forever envision it as a giant orifice.

"But forget the design scheme." She patted the seat next to her. "Come sit beside Miss Glenda so we can discuss the murder."

It didn't take an epidemiologist to know that there wasn't a sanitary surface in the place. "I'd rather stand, thanks."

"Suit yourself, sugar," she said with a shrug. "Now, did you notice anything unusual about the crime scene?"

"Oddly enough," I began, putting my hand on my hip, "I didn't get to see it because the detective who arrested me last night—the one I mistook for the stripper cop you sent me?—he just kicked me out of the club."

She crossed her arms above her red-crossed breasts and looked at me like I was some kind of reprobate. "I can't imagine why."

I wanted to clench my jaw, but I had to protect my tooth.

"But never you mind, Miss Franki, because Miss Ronnie will be here any minute, and she'll charm the pants off that ornery detective. Then you'll be at that crime scene faster than you can say 'strip.'"

"Miss Ronnie" was what Glenda called Veronica. And she was right about her being able to charm Detective Sullivan, including the part about his pants. Veronica had a man-melting move that I'd named "the bat and twirl." All she had to do was bat her eyelashes over her cornflower baby blues while twisting a golden lock around her finger, and men's resistance dissolved. No matter how many times I'd tried to master it, I just looked like I had a nervous eye tic and a hair-pulling compulsion.

"Hey, so what time did you get here this morning to practice for your show?" I asked.

Glenda kicked her skinny legs across the back of the love seat. "What makes you think I came here to practice?"

I eyed her go-go nurse getup. "Well, it looks like you're going for some sort of saintly look."

"I told you, sugar. I'm a slut," she said, staring at me like I was one thong shy of a stripper costume. "And I came to the club because my manager, Eugene, called and said that the police wanted to question the employees about Amber."

I pulled a pen and paper from my bag. "Who found her

body?"

"Eugene did when he came in early to let the cleaning crew in."

I made a note to question the manager. "What time was that?"

"Two o'clock," she said, stretching out a leg to pull up her stocking.

I glanced up from my pad. "Early? I thought you once told me that the club opens at noon for lunch."

"It does, but on Sundays we open at five since it's the Sabbath," she replied as though strip clubs routinely based their operations around religious practices.

I rolled my eyes and noticed a camera hanging from the ceiling, and a thought occurred to me. "Has anyone checked the security system video for evidence?"

"You'd have to ask Eugene about that, sugar."

"Glenda?" Veronica called. "Where are you?"

Without thinking, I opened the door and then stared at my hand in horror. "We're in here."

Veronica entered dressed in a red sweater and a pink skirt, and I wondered whether she was aware of the sex-laden symbolism of her outfit.

"Love the color of the room," she said. "It's so fresh and feminine."

If you only knew, I thought as I reached into my bag for hand sanitizer.

Veronica pulled her pink Miss Sicily bag into the crook of her arm. "Glenda, I heard from Carnie a little while ago. She made an appointment to meet with Franki and me tomorrow morning."

"Did she tell you why she wants to contract a PI?" I asked, rubbing the sanitizing gel into my hands. "It seems kind of odd when the police haven't even begun their investigation, much less questioned her about it."

"She was fairly vague on the phone." Veronica turned to Glenda. "I was hoping that you could tell us more."

Glenda fluffed her ruffle. "All I know is that when I called Carnie to tell her about Amber, she asked me if she had a necklace on. When I told her that she was wearing a chain with a flower on it, she said that she was going to need a private investigator."

"That's bizarre," I said, patting some sanitizer on my neck.

"I guess we'll have to wait until tomorrow for an explanation." Veronica began rummaging through her bag. "In the meantime, Franki, Detective Sullivan has granted us fifteen minutes to view the crime scene."

"Yes," I said with a fist pump. "What did it? The old bat and twirl?"

"A polite request," she replied, opening the door with a tissue.

I definitely dislike that detective.

"I'll call you later, Glenda," Veronica said. "I've got a business proposition for you."

"Ooh, Miss Ronnie," she exclaimed, squeezing her breasts together with her biceps and giving them a little shake. "That sent shivers down my spine."

Funny. It sent chills down mine.

On the way downstairs, Veronica handed me a bottle of Binaca. "Before we talk to the detective, spray this on that booze breath of yours."

"Jeez. All I had was a little limoncello."

"Well, I'm surprised at you, Franki," she said, crossing the club at a clip. "That stuff is loaded with sugar, and you gave up sweets for Lent."

I stopped and gave my mouth a couple of squirts and then jogged to catch up with her. "That's right—sweets, not alcohol. You can hardly expect me to give up liquor when I don't have dessert to comfort me."

Veronica shook her head and climbed the steps to the main stage.

I followed close behind her without paying much attention to my surroundings. But when I stopped and processed the scene in front of me, my breath caught in my throat. I'd never seen anything like it—not as a cop, not as a PI, not even as a devoted crime show watcher.

At center stage was a vintage pink claw-foot tub with a high back, like the one in my bathroom. It was filled to the rim with water.

And a human knee protruded from the surface.

I averted my eyes, perhaps defensively, to the three items on the stage beside the tub—a wooden incense holder with a consumed stick of incense, which explained the sweet, acrid odor that I'd been unable to identify, a purple candle that had burned down to the base, and a bottle of amaretto with the seal intact. It was a brand I didn't recognize, Amaretto di Amore.

Mustering up my courage, I walked over to the tub while Veronica remained rooted near the steps.

Amber was below the water, seemingly looking up at me, with her long, brown hair billowing around her head like a cloud. Her arms were across her chest, and the leg that was protruding from the water was leaning to one side, obscuring her pelvic region. It was as though she was hiding her own nudity even in death.

I looked away—this time out of respect.

"How did Amber end up in a bathtub on a strip club stage?" I asked, breaking the somber silence.

"No idea." Veronica moved to stand beside me. "But if she brought the tub into Madame Moiselle's, then she had help. Or it could've been a prop for the dancers. Glenda would know that."

I focused my gaze on the bathwater.

Veronica turned to me, her brow furrowed. "Are you okay?"

"Yeah," I replied, although I wasn't sure that I was. "It's just that the haze on the water looks like some kind of oil."

She sniffed the air above the tub. "It doesn't have a scent."

"Whatever it is, it makes me wonder whether Amber was taking an actual bath onstage."

She crossed her arms and rested her chin on her fist. Her eyes were fixed on the tub. "It could have been a romantic encounter."

"Or it could have been staged, quite literally, to look like one." I glanced again at the bottle. "I mean, why Amaretto di Amore?"

She cocked a well-groomed brow. "I'm not following

you."

"Why not a common brand, like Disaronno?" I asked, gesturing toward the bar where a bottle of the famous almond liqueur was on display.

"Maybe this was her favorite kind?" she suggested in a questioning tone.

I pulled out my pad of paper. "Or maybe the 'amore' in the name is a sign from the killer."

"You mean to signal a love relationship."

"That or something we don't yet understand." I took a few notes and then knelt and smelled the candle. It was unscented, but the woodsy, vanilla odor from the incense holder was still strong. "Wait a second...I just realized that the incense is similar to the kind they always burn in places like Marie Laveau's and Reverend Zombie's."

Her blue eyes grew wide. "Do you think there's a voodoo connection?"

"We can't rule it out, not when incense and a candle are involved." I stood up and noticed that the CSIs were consulting with Detective Sullivan on the left side of the stage.

Veronica's eyes followed my gaze. "We should examine the body before they take it to the morgue."

I nodded and reluctantly looked into the water.

"When I spoke to Detective Sullivan earlier," Veronica began, "he said that it appears to be a pretty straightforward case of homicide by drowning."

I scrutinized the area around Amber's neck. There was some light bruising and scratch marks, either from the assailant or from Amber herself as she tried to break free. "There was clearly a struggle. The killer probably held her under the water."

"Ms. Maggio," Detective Sullivan interrupted.

"Speak of the devil," I remarked, my hackles rising at the sound of his voice.

"Can I talk to you for a minute?" he continued, ignoring my jab.

"Sure," Veronica said, going to join him.

My phone began vibrating in my bag. I pulled it out and looked at the display—Bradley. Without a second thought I tapped *Decline*. As much as I needed to talk to him, this just wasn't the time.

I shoved my phone into my bag and leaned closer to the bath water to study Amber's neck. My attention shifted to the gold chain that Carnie had been so concerned about. It was either really old or it had been treated to make it look antique. In the center of the chain was a gold filigree flower with a leaf and three gold loops beneath it. As I studied the design, I realized that something was missing.

Veronica climbed the steps to the stage, typing something into her phone. "Detective Sullivan asked that we not speak about the incense, candle, or amaretto to anyone. The police plan to keep them out of the news."

I nodded. "They should keep the necklace out of the news too."

She stopped typing and stared at me. "Why's that?"

I pointed at the gold filigree. "Because someone ripped a charm or a pendant from below the flower."

She held her hair behind her head and leaned closer to the water. "You're right. The middle loop is scratched and bent. I'll let the detective know. But are you thinking that this was some kind of robbery gone wrong?"

"There are so many different ways to interpret this scene, I haven't decided what to think," I replied.

But deep down I knew one thing for sure—Amber's murder was tied to something much more sinister than a simple robbery.

CHAPTER FIVE

———

"You're kidding me, right Veronica?" I asked, gripping my Krewe du Brew coffee mug for support. It was only eight forty-five on Monday morning, so I was hoping that this was some sort of poorly timed office prank.

She reclined in the armchair facing my desk and crossed her arms. "I didn't say that I was planning to hire a permanent investigator—just a temporary consultant."

"Don't get me wrong. I'm glad that Private Chicks is finally solvent enough to afford us some help, but..." I looked at my hands as I struggled to find the right words. "Why in the name of all that is rational would you hire *Glenda*?"

"It's just for this case, Franki." She stood up and clasped her hands behind her back, pacing like she used to do in court when she was presenting opening arguments. "Keep in mind that Glenda has worked at Madame Moiselle's off and on for close to fifty years. Not only does she know all the employees, she's also got a grasp of the inner workings of the club and the entire stripping industry. So, she can offer us a unique perspective on Amber's murder."

She most certainly can. "Okay, but can she investigate?"

Veronica stopped pacing and looked me in the eyes. "I don't think I need to remind you that she's had great insight about some of our hardest cases."

That I couldn't deny. Glenda might seem a little out there, but she was actually as sharp as a stiletto (the dagger, not the heel), and she'd bailed Veronica and me out of a serious jam when we were working our first homicide. But there was one thing I couldn't reconcile myself to—her potential PI outfits. Just imagine Charlie's Angels in their sixties and in stripper/birthday suits and you'll understand my concern.

The bell on the lobby door rang.

"I'll bet that's Carnie," Veronica said, retrieving her laptop from my desk.

I picked up my mug and followed her down the hallway to the lobby, and I was immediately transported to the 1940s.

Standing by the reception desk was a brunette with victory rolls so large they were practically the size of the World War II fighter plane exhaust that had inspired the hairstyle. To complete her vintage *Life* magazine look, she'd selected a navy blue dress with white polka dots, a beaded white clutch, and chunky white peep-toe heels.

But a pinup girl she wasn't. For starters, the woman was a forty-something-year-old man, and a big one too, at six foot four and three hundred fifty or so pounds. Not only that, she was built like the Abominable Snowman from *Rudolph, the Red-Nosed Reindeer*, and she was wearing enough cosmetics to make up the entire Broadway cast of *Priscilla, Queen of the Desert*.

"Hi, I'm Veronica Maggio, and this is Franki Amato. Are you Carnie?"

Her overdrawn lips à la Lucille Ball spread into a smile. "Why yes I am," she replied in a forced falsetto. "Carnie Vaul."

I mentally repeated the syllables. "As in 'carnival'?"

She eyed me warily from beneath her Mimi-from-The-Drew-Carey-Show eye shadow. "It's my drag name. I used to be a carnival clown."

That explained the creepy makeup. But what I couldn't understand was why a man dressed as a woman would want to associate with an institution known for its strong men and bearded ladies. "What's your legal name?"

"Ben Dover," she replied, smoothing a roll—on her head, that is.

I pursed my lips and then muttered, "You're not giving me much to work with."

"What did you say?" Carnie barked. Gone was the falsetto, and in its place was a brash voice that had a quack-like quality similar to that of the Aflac duck.

"She said that you'll be a pleasure to work with," Veronica intervened. She gestured to the lobby couches. "Why don't you have a seat, and I'll get you something to drink."

"Nothing for me, thanks," Carnie replied, giving me the stink eye as she sank into the sofa.

I, in turn, cast her a suspicious eye as Veronica and I took our places on the opposing couch. I'd been duped by a homicide client once before, so I had no intention of falling for any of this ex-clown's antics.

"Do you mind if I vape?" Carnie asked as she opened her clutch.

For a second I was worried that "vape" was some sort of variant of "vamp," but then I saw her remove an e-cigarette. "Have at it."

"Let's get started, shall we?" Veronica asked, opening her laptop. "Carnie, tell us how you knew Amber Brown."

"For the past two years she was my tenant and neighbor," she said, exhaling vapor. "She rented the other side of a duplex I own in The Marigny until about a week ago."

The Faubourg Marigny was an artsy, bohemian neighborhood next to the French Quarter. Tourists flocked to its jazz clubs and art galleries, but I went for the food. "Did she leave a forwarding address?"

She shook her head. "Nothing."

Veronica typed a quick note. "Were the two of you ever close?"

Her lips thinned, highlighting the exaggerated lines of her lipstick. "We were friends, but I wouldn't say we were close. I do drag shows at Lucky Pierre's, and when she was still at Madame Moiselle's we used to get home at the same time and have the occasional nightcap together. Then she quit stripping last year, and we didn't see each other as much."

I swallowed a sip of coffee. "What did she do for a living after she left the club?"

Carnie hefted one chubby leg over the other and draped her arm across the back of the couch. "She said she was leaving the sex industry, but I never saw her going to any job. Honestly, I thought she was hooking again because she'd told me that she used to make extra money that way."

Veronica and I exchanged a look. If Amber had worked as a prostitute, it would complicate the hunt for a suspect.

I crossed my ankle over my knee. "Did she ever bring men to the duplex?"

"Not that I was aware of," she replied with a shrug. "As far as I know, she didn't even have a boyfriend. Amber was a loner, and she didn't have any family."

It always made me sad to hear that someone was alone in the world. As crazy as my family was, I couldn't imagine life without them—well, most of the time. "When did you see her last?"

Carnie took a long vape and thought for a moment. "Friday at around two. I ran into her when I was leaving the duplex to run errands. She came by to pick up some mail. She said she was on her way to a dentist appointment, and since she didn't have a car I offered her a ride. But she opted for the bus."

Veronica looked up from her laptop. "Do you happen to know the name of the dentist?"

"We go to the same guy. Mitchell Lessler."

"Franki, when you talk to him about Amber," Veronica began, "you should make an appointment for yourself."

I rubbed my cheek, sorely regretting ever telling Veronica about my tooth. Now that she knew about it, she wouldn't let up until I had it looked at. And I liked dentists about as much as I liked gynecologists, which was to say not at all. "Did she have any enemies?"

Carnie arched a Bozo-the-Clown brow. "There was one—a platinum blonde from Madame Moiselle's. She used to get as drunk as a skunk and pound on Amber's door in the middle of the night, screaming at her for stealing her best client. I never found out her name, but she had a tacky tattoo of a stripper that covered her back." She scratched her five o'clock shadow. "So unladylike."

I thought of the platinum blonde I'd seen leaving the club, but I hadn't noticed a tattoo. "What did Amber do about it?"

"Well, she never opened the door. But the girl kept coming around, as recently as two weeks ago."

I twisted my mouth to one side. "That's weird, considering that Amber had stopped stripping."

"It's one of the reasons that I thought she'd gotten back into prostitution," she said with a knowing look. "Maybe the client wasn't interested in blowing his money on a stripper anymore when he could get straight up sex."

Veronica stopped typing. "Glenda said that you asked whether Amber was wearing a necklace."

She nodded. "That's why I'm here. A month ago I inherited an antique necklace—a gold chain with a flower and an emerald-cut amber pendant—and it's missing. I showed the necklace to Amber when I first got it, and if what Glenda told me was correct, then I think she stole it from my apartment and was wearing it when she was killed."

I leaned forward with my coffee cup between my hands. "We saw the chain, but there was no pendant. That could either mean that she was killed for the necklace or that the killer took it as a memento."

Carnie frowned like a sad clown. "That's what I was afraid of. That amber was priceless, and I made the mistake of telling that to Amber."

"But amber is fairly inexpensive," Veronica said. "What was so special about this piece?"

She hesitated. "It was from the Amber Room, the one that the Prussian King Frederick William I gave to Tsar Peter the Great in 1716."

Veronica gasped, and her eyes lit up like amber in sunlight. "That's the room the Nazis stole from Catherine Palace during World War II."

"Yes, and it has never been found. Experts say that it's worth at least three hundred and eighty-five million dollars."

After I recovered my ability to speak, I asked, "If the room is missing, how did you get a piece?"

"My grandmother was from Russia, and she was a maid in the palace." She twisted a crown-shaped ring around her French-manicured finger. "When the Nazis dismantled the room, small pieces of amber broke off. They picked up every piece they could find, but they overlooked one that had been cut like a gemstone. My grandmother took it and intended to return it after the war, but her family fled the country. And then when the Soviets began work on a replica of the room in 1979, my mother had the amber made into a necklace."

I swallowed the last of my coffee and placed the mug on

the table in front of me. "So, technically, that pendant belongs to the Russians."

Carnie's face flushed, and her bulbous nose turned as red as Ronald McDonald's. "My mother believed that the Soviets were evil like the Nazis, and she didn't trust them to return the amber to the palace," she huffed. "Besides, after the replica of the room was unveiled, it didn't seem as important."

"Just to clarify," Veronica began in a high-pitched, we-can't-afford-to-lose-this-client tone, "are you hiring us to find the pendant or to investigate Amber's death?"

"Both," she replied. "As soon as I report the theft of the necklace, which I intend to do today, I figure I'll become a suspect in her murder."

She figured right. I knew from my time on the force that she would be questioned, especially now that someone had ripped the priceless pendant from Amber's lifeless neck.

"And even though Amber and I weren't close," she continued, pressing a hand to her ample bosom, "I wouldn't feel right if I didn't have you try to find her killer. I inherited some money with the necklace, so I can cover your expenses."

"It's very admirable of you to honor Amber that way," Veronica said, her voice soft. "We'll do our best to see that the killer and the necklace are found."

I was thinking that we should do our best to find that three hundred and eighty-five million dollar room too. "Is there anything else we should know?"

Carnie bowed her head, causing her double and triple chins to bulge. "Amber felt like bad things had been happening to her since she'd quit Madame Moiselle's, and she was getting really paranoid and superstitious about it."

"Can you give us some examples?" I pressed.

"Nothing specific. But I noticed that she'd started carrying around good luck charms, wearing talismans, things like that."

Veronica nodded. "You've given us some great information. We'll start by questioning the employees at Madame Moiselle's, and we'll check with Dr. Lessler to find out whether he saw or heard anything unusual during Amber's appointment. We'll be in touch in a few days."

Carnie rose to her feet. "I've got a show in an hour." She offered her baseball mitt-sized hand, bending daintily at the wrist. "You've been so kind."

I noticed that she didn't extend the same courtesy to me, but no matter. Because as Veronica saw her out, my mind was already fixated on Amber's superstitious side. And I wondered what, if anything, it had to do with the bizarre murder scene at the club.

* * *

I stepped inside Madame Moiselle's at a quarter after eleven and stopped dead in my tracks.

Glenda stood before me dressed like a stripper Sherlock Holmes.

"Howdy, partner," she exclaimed, adjusting her deerstalker cap.

"You're wearing the wrong hat for that greeting," I said, trying to hide my inner panic as I took in the tiny cape cropped well above her magnifying glass-shaped pasties. "Is that tweed?"

"Yeah, and it's itchier than poison ivy on your privates, so I had to make a costume change." To my dismay, she spun around to reveal her bony buttocks protruding from the round holes she'd cut from the seat of her boyshorts. But on the bright side, she'd left the crotch intact.

"Well, I guess that about took care of it," I said, scanning the club to avoid checking out her cheeks. "Is the manager in yet?"

Mercifully, she turned back around. "Eugene? He's at the police station. Our bartender, Carlos, is in charge until he gets back."

I glanced to my right. "I don't see anyone at the bar."

"He's probably upstairs in the office. I'll take you up there."

Instead of leading me to the VIP Champagne Room staircase, Glenda led me past the main stage, and I noticed that the crime scene had been cleared.

Keeping my eyes fixed on the back of her head rather than on her backside, I asked, "Hey, do you know where the bathtub came from?"

"From the prop room," she replied, pointing to a door behind the stage. "It belonged to Lili St. Cyr."

"Who's that?"

Glenda turned and looked at me like I'd snapped her bra strap (if she'd been wearing one). "None other than the creator of bathtub burlesque, sugar."

As soon as she uttered the phrase, I wondered whether Amber had been recreating a sexy bathing routine for a lover who ultimately killed her.

"In the 1940s and '50s," Glenda continued, "Lili was as famous as Gypsy Rose Lee. Then she retired and ran a well-known lingerie business. Her deep plunge bra made Elvira a superstar. And on top of all that, she even got a mention in *The Rocky Horror Picture Show*."

"That's, uh, quite a list of credentials."

"You can say that again," she said, strutting toward a staircase in the corner. "When Lili passed in 1999, Madame Moiselle's started the 'Wash the Girl of Your Choice' service to honor her memory."

I started to say one of the usual clichés like "she would have been so proud," but I got distracted trying to envision how a client would wash a stripper when the club had a strict no-touching-the-merchandise policy.

Glenda pushed open a door marked *Strippers and Staff Only* and shot up the staircase in her gun-heel boots.

I climbed a few steps, and my message tone sounded. Grateful for the excuse to take a break, I pulled my phone from my bag and saw that the text was from Bradley.

"What's going on? Why didn't you return my call last night?"

My stomach did a belly flop. I should've called him back, but the past couple of days had been rough, to put it mildly. And after seeing Amber, I hadn't felt like talking. So, I sent quick reply saying that I would meet him at the bank for lunch and explain everything—except for the part about me tarnishing his professional image, of course.

"Are you comin', Miss Franki?" Glenda called from above.

"Yeah, sorry." I shoved my phone into my bag, and when I finally reached the landing the tantalizing aroma of sausage teased my nostrils. "*What* is that *heavenly* odor?"

"That's Miss Eve cooking lunch for the girls."

"Wait," I said, holding out a hand to steady myself. "There's a kitchen? *And* a cook?"

She put her hand on her hip. "We don't call her a cook, sugar. She's a house mom. All the quality strip clubs have them."

I immediately began rethinking my career choice. Not that I was considering becoming a stripper. My parents and the Catholic Church had worked too hard to repress me for me to throw it all away by doing something as liberated as that. But an office with a house mom would be nice.

"C'mon," she said, gesturing for me to follow. "I'll introduce you to her."

As we walked down the hallway, I took note of the layout. There were two offices, one across from the other. Then came the kitchen on the left and the girls' dressing room on the right.

Glenda took me by the arm and pulled me into a sunny yellow kitchen where a short, plump woman in her mid-fifties was standing over a huge soup pot. "Miss Eve Quebedeaux, this is Miss Franki Amato, my private investigator partner."

"Well, hiii," Eve drawled, sounding remarkably like Blanche Devereaux from *The Golden Girls*. She wiped her hands on an apron adorned with peaches, possibly symbolizing the state of Georgia. "Miss Glenda's told me so much about yewww," she said, grasping my hands. "I'll bet you work up quiiite an appetite doin' all that investigatin'. Can I git you some chicken Andouille gumbo and a slice of Bananas Foster piiie?"

I blinked and looked for the halo above her graying blonde curls. Then I sunk into a chair at the dining table and managed to utter a faint, "Yes."

"Uh-*uh*, Miss Franki," Glenda said, wagging her index finger (and, unintentionally, her boobs). "You can't have that pie. Miss Ronnie told me that you gave up sweets for Lent."

I shot her a seething look. I knew this hiring Glenda thing was going to be a big bust, and I wasn't referring to her breasts.

"We're actually trying to find Carlos," Glenda continued, planting her bare bottom in the chair across from me. "We've got to question him about Amber's murder."

"Oh, that poor girl," Eve lamented as she fixed me a heaping helping of gumbo. She placed the bowl in front of me and poured me a glass of milk. "I didn't get to know her all that well because she only worked here for two months, but I feel just awful about what happened."

"What was she like?" I asked and then inhaled a huge spoonful of the Cajun goodness.

Eve sat down at the head of the table. "She kept to herself, mostly. Some of the other girls thought it was because she was uppity, but I think she just didn't know how to act in a family setting."

I would've had a hard time seeing a strip club as a "family setting," but now that I knew they had kitchens complete with house moms like Eve, I was a believer. "I've heard that Amber was essentially an orphan. Did she ever mention any relatives to you?"

"Never." She rested her chin on her fists. "The only person I ever saw her with was her pimp."

I almost choked on a piece of chicken. "She had a pimp?"

"Uh-hu-h," she replied in three syllables. "He came here right before she quit the club."

So, Carnie might have been right about Amber working as a prostitute after she left Madame Moiselle's. "Do you know what he wanted?"

"He came to pick her up. And while Amber was changin' into her street clothes, I served him a plate of sauce picante, and we got to chattin'. He said his name was King, and I could see that deep down he was a nice man. So I encouraged him to repent his sins and let Jesus into his heart."

I smirked as I took another bite. The chances of a pimp finding God were about as high as Glenda joining the Cloister.

Eve touched my arm. "And would you believe that right after our conversation he became a minister?"

I lowered my spoon, openmouthed. "How do you know that?"

"Because when I'm coming to work I usually see him at the corner of Bourbon and Dumaine, preaching the gospel to passersby."

Eve's angel status just got elevated to saint, but I wasn't so sure about the status of the pimp preacher. I planned to find that out after lunch.

A Hispanic male who looked to be around twenty-five entered the room and removed a bowl from a cabinet. "Are the girls ready to go, Eve?"

"Oh!" She jumped up from the table. "I'd better go see. Be right back, ladies."

"Carlos, this is Franki, my PI partner," Glenda said. "We wanted to ask you some questions about Amber."

He glanced in my direction. "You're talking to the wrong person. I barely knew her."

"Any information might be important," I said in an encouraging tone. "But could I ask what time you left on Saturday night? It would help to know when the doors were locked."

"Eugene would've been the one to lock up." His thick, black brows furrowed as he spooned gumbo into his bowl. "I had to leave at four fifteen when the club closed because Iris and I got arrested."

"Good grief, Carlos," Glenda exclaimed. "How'd you two end up in the hoosegow?"

He removed a spoon from a drawer and sat beside me. "Things got a little rowdy with some customers who didn't want to leave after last call. So we all went to the tank."

By this point, I was seriously starting to wonder if I'd missed the memo about using euphemisms for "jail." "Who's Iris?"

Glenda flipped her hair. "The bouncer, sugar."

This Iris must be a big girl. "When did you get out of jail, Carlos?"

He splashed Tabasco sauce on his gumbo. "At one o'clock yesterday afternoon after Eugene posted our bail."

So, he and Iris had airtight alibis. "Did you notice anything unusual before you got arrested?"

"Nah, it was business as usual," he replied, stirring his

food. "And I haven't seen Amber around here in a few months."

I looked up from my bowl. "I thought she quit a year ago."

He took a bite and then shifted the food to one side of his mouth. "She did, but she came in sometimes for a drink."

On a hunch I asked, "What did she typically order?"

"The same thing she did when she was dancing here," he replied, resting his elbows on the table. "Amaretto, neat."

Glenda's two-inch false eyelashes opened wide. "It wasn't Amaretto di Amore, was it?"

He shook his head. "We don't carry that brand. Even though it's made here in New Orleans, it doesn't sell as well as Disaronno."

As I'd suspected, there was something weird about that bottle of amaretto beside the bathtub, but I still wasn't sure what. "Is that the kind Amber drank?"

"No, she used to tip me to keep a bottle of Lazzaroni Amaretto under the bar for her."

"Any idea why she wanted that particular brand?" I asked as Eve returned to her place at the table.

He smiled as though remembering something funny. "She liked it because it's the only kind made from an infusion of the Amaretti di Saronno cookies."

I memorized the name Lazzaroni, both because it was pertinent to the investigation and because it was as close as I was going to get to cookies during Lent.

"What are the other amarettos made from?" Glenda asked, twirling her cape tie around her finger.

Carlos swallowed and wiped his mouth with a napkin. "Almond essence or apricot pits."

Eve rolled her eyes. "Amber definitely didn't like that kind."

My body tensed because I sensed that she was about to say something important. "Did she talk to you about amaretto?"

"No, but one time an anonymous admirer had a bottle of amaretto delivered to her here at the club. When she opened it, she got really mad and threw it across the kitchen. It took me hours to clean up the mess." She gestured toward the kitchen window. "And the worst part was that it ruined my chiffon curtains."

My pulse started racing. "Do you remember the brand?"

"Yes, because it was such a pretty name. A-muh-rhet-toe dee Uh-more-ay." Eve sighed and squeezed her shoulders together. "Doesn't it just remind you of a romantic trip to Italy?"

Actually, it reminded me of a senseless killing at a strip club.

And of a murderer with a message.

CHAPTER SIX

———

"You must have been starving," Bradley said as he topped off my champagne.

"Mm-hm." I chewed the last piece of a fourteen-ounce prime rib eye steak smothered in pepper-cream bourbon sauce. Of course, I hadn't been all that hungry since I'd eaten Eve's gumbo before coming to the bank. But Bradley had gone to the trouble of having Dickie Brennan's Steakhouse deliver lunch to his office as a belated birthday surprise, so who was I to disappoint him?

Dabbing my mouth with my napkin, I discretely scoured the room for any sign of the restaurant's famous creole cheesecake. "What's for dessert?"

He looked at me from beneath thick, dark lashes, and the corner of his mouth lifted into a sexy half smile.

I met his gaze, and a warmth spread through my body.

"I was going to order the praline chocolate mousse," he began in a husky voice, "but then Veronica called and told me you'd given up sweets for Lent."

That warmth turned as cold as Veronica's gelid heart. *Just who did she think she was, anyway? A Catholic cop?*

"However," he continued, his blue eyes twinkling, "I do have this for you." He pulled a rectangular box from his desk.

I covered my mouth with my hands. "What is it?"

"You'll have to find out," he replied, sliding the box in front of me.

I opened the lid and gasped. Inside was a gorgeous ruby and diamond necklace. The pendant was teardrop shaped, which, given that this was a thirtieth birthday present, seemed particularly appropriate. "It's stunning," I whispered. "Thank you."

"You're stunning," he said in an earnest tone. "Especially in red."

My chest swelled with happiness. Bradley and I had been dating for a little over a year, and even though I'd had reason to doubt him—actually, *two* reasons considering that he'd neglected to tell me he was married when we started dating and that he once broke up with me to hook up with his evil ex-secretary—it was times like these that I remembered why I was so crazy about him (and, obviously, when I found out that there were logical explanations for the above discretions). But as I gazed at him from across the table, I sensed that something was on his mind. "Is everything okay?"

His jaw tensed, and he glanced at his half-eaten steak. "The bank lost a couple of its biggest accounts last week."

"I'm sorry to hear that," I said, concerned. "Do you know why?"

"I don't." He rubbed his eyes. "I thought that I had a solid relationship with both of the clients too."

I hated to see Bradley upset. It always made me feel helpless, which I didn't like. "Have you tried contacting them?"

"They haven't returned my calls," he replied, depositing his napkin beside his plate. "But enough about business." He clasped his hands in front of his mouth. "Let's talk about you."

Just one more reason that he was the best boyfriend on the planet. "Well, I wanted to explain about—"

There was a knock at the door, and Jeff Payne, the over-ambitious bank manager Ruth had warned me about, entered without waiting for an invitation. With his brown brush cut and perpetual sneer, he looked more like a drill sergeant than a banker. "Sorry to interrupt your tête-a-tête."

I could tell from the smug look on his face that he wasn't sorry at all.

"What can I help you with?" Bradley asked in a polite but strained voice.

Jeff tossed a document on the table. "I need you to sign off on this loan contract."

Bradley turned and put the document on his desk. "I'll take a look at it after lunch."

Jeff's eyes narrowed, and he opened his mouth to say something. But then he turned and stalked from the room.

I looked at Bradley to see his reaction.

"You were saying?" he asked, picking up his champagne glass.

Following his cue to let the Jeff issue lie, I said, "I was just going to apologize for not calling you yesterday. Honestly, it was one of the worst days of my life."

He stopped in mid-sip. "What could be worse than going to *jail* on your birthday?"

There was something about the way he said "jail" that made me wish he'd used a euphemism like everyone else. "Oh, I don't know," I replied, irritated. "Seeing a young woman's dead body, having to investigate her death with Glenda..."

He frowned and put his glass on the table. "You're working on another murder case? And with *Glenda*?"

"Yeah, the victim used to strip at Madame Moiselle's." I almost added that I thought she'd been killed by a real freak, but I stopped myself in time. Bradley worried when I worked homicides, and I didn't want him focusing on my safety when he had problems at work to deal with.

"Strip clubs can be dangerous places," he said, his brow knit with worry. "Do you have any idea why she was murdered?"

"I'm not sure," I hedged. "But listen, I need to get back to work. How about dinner at my place tonight?"

He leaned back and ran his fingers through his hair. "I'm flying to New York later today for an impromptu meeting with the board in the morning. What about tomorrow night?"

"Perfect." I forced a smile as I wondered whether the sudden meeting had something to do with the loss of his clients. Or with me.

Bradley's office phone began to ring. He stood up and glanced at the number on the caller ID. "I need to take this. It's one of the board members I'm meeting with."

"That's fine," I said, rising to my feet. "I'll see myself out."

He reached over the desk and picked up the receiver. "Hey, Bob. What's up?"

While Bradley listened to Bob on the other end of the

line, I took one last look at my beautiful necklace before tucking it carefully into my purse. Then I drained my champagne, and Bradley pulled me into his chest with his free arm, and his mouth descended onto mine. It was a slow, probing kiss that made me want to lie down and keep kissing—for starters.

When Bob stopped talking, Bradley released me. "No problem at all," he replied into the receiver. "I'll have the report ready."

After a kiss like that, I needed a drink. So, I grabbed the half-empty bottle of champagne from the table and filled a go-cup. This *was* New Orleans.

Raising my drink as a farewell, I turned and opened the door.

Jeff recoiled in surprise as though he'd been eavesdropping and stepped quickly from the doorway.

But not quickly enough.

I tripped over his foot and went flying into Ruth's chair, spilling my drink on her desk in the process. When I regained my balance, I turned to give him a piece of my mind, but he was gone.

As I mopped up the spilled champagne with some tissues, my tooth began to throb. Although the sudden aching could've been a result of all the chewing I did eating those two lunches, I blamed Jeff for my pain. And now that I'd caught him listening at the door, I was certain that Ruth had been right—he wanted Bradley's job, and he struck me as the type who would do whatever it took to get it. What I needed to know was whether he'd had a hand in costing the bank those accounts to make Bradley look bad.

And I had every intention of finding out.

* * *

When I exited Vieux Carré Wine & Spirits in the French Quarter a half hour later, I wasted no time unscrewing the cap from the bottle of Lazzaroni Amaretto I'd purchased. I hadn't had a dessert in weeks, so I couldn't wait to taste the liquid cookie liquor. Normally, I didn't drink on the job. But as long as I was working a case with Glenda, I had a feeling that I was going to stay semi-sloshed. So I tipped my head back and took a swig, and I understood why Amber liked the stuff. It was amaretto ambrosia.

Reluctantly, I replaced the cap and headed back to Madame Moiselle's. Then I remembered that King, Amber's pimp, preached near the club, and I decided to make a detour. Glenda didn't have to be with me every second of the investigation, especially if she was going to persist in wearing those stripper sleuthing suits. And with any luck I'd find King holding court on his corner, because it was time for the alleged pimp-turned-preacher and I to have a come-to-Jesus talk about Amber.

I hooked a left on Dumaine, and I caught a glimpse of someone darting from view behind me. Certain I was being followed, I stopped and backtracked a few steps, but the only person in my vicinity was a guy in a gator costume.

He must've thought that I was checking him out, because he lowered his snout and leered at me.

The animal. I turned around, and even though I knew that no one in their right mind would tail a person in a gator getup, I quickened my pace. This was Louisiana, after all.

A block from Bourbon, I heard the strains of a church organ, which was as out of place on the infamous party street as a harpsichord. It didn't take long to spot the source. Behind an electric keyboard stood a tall, thin man in a purple velvet suit with green silk lapels and a frilly gold shirt. Apart from his square white sunglasses and thick rope chain with a giant, jeweled crucifix, he either looked like a Mardi Gras pirate or Prince during the Purple Rain tour.

As I approached, he let out a scream worthy of James Brown.

I jumped backwards as his fingers crashed down on the keyboard.

"Temptation! Intoxication! Fornication! Pregnation!" He pointed at his audience of one, i.e., me. "Brothas and sistas, avoid damnation," he implored, sinking to his knees and raising his arms to the heavens. "God is elevation! So seek salvation at The Church of King Nation." He bowed before a fur fedora filled with cash. "Donations kindly accepted."

To use a –*tion* word, the man was a sight and sound sensation. Actually, "*sin*sation" was more appropriate, because I wasn't buying his religious bit for a second. "I take it you're King Nation?"

He sprung to his feet and smiled like a Cheshire cat, revealing gold front teeth engraved with the letters K and N. "At yo' spiritual service."

I held out my card, and he clasped my hand between his, both of which were adorned with three-finger rings that read "Lawd" and "Gawd," respectively.

Giving him a half-lidded look, I said, "My name's Franki Amato, and I'm a private investigator."

King dropped my hand like it was a counterfeit bill.

It was my turn to smile—like the cat that ate the canary. "I need to ask you a few questions about Amber Brown."

"God rest her soul," he said in a perfunctory tone. "I heard about that nasty biniss at Madame Moiselle's."

"Yes, well, speaking of nasty business," I began with a devil-may-care stare, "rumor has it that you were prostituting Amber."

He jutted out his lower lip. "I ain't seen her in over a year. And in case you couldn't tell, I quit the pimpin' profession. I'm a man of Gawd now."

I glanced at his outfit. "Judging from that suit you're wearing, I'd say you were still a pimp."

"Be easy." He gave me a sideways look as he tugged on his lapels. "The clothes don't make the man. What you cain't see is that I went through an inner transformation."

This I had to hear. "How so?"

"Six months ago, the good Lawd came ta me in a vision. I was in an alleyway, jus' waitin' on my friends and smokin' some grass when the street lamp went out. So I had me a drank ta calm my nerves, and the light done came back on. Then it happened agin—I had a smoke and a drank, the lamp went on and off—and that's when I knew that Gawd was showin' me the light."

Not to be a doubter, but I would've sworn on a stack of Bibles that drugs and a faulty light bulb had more to do with that vision than God. "Do you mind if I ask what you were drinking?"

"Crown Royal, the beverage fit for a King," he replied as his eyes shifted to my left hand.

I suddenly realized that I was talking to a pimp-preacher while holding a bag of booze. "Did you or anyone you know ever send Amber a bottle of amaretto?" I asked as I stuffed mine into my purse. "Amaretto di Amore?"

He grabbed a cane from beside the keyboard. It looked suspiciously like a pimp stick, thanks to the bejeweled voodoo god topper. "I don't know nothin' about no amaretto. My girls only drank the best—Hpnotiq."

I resisted the urge to roll my eyes as I pulled out my pad and pen. "Would you mind telling me where you were between the hours of four a.m. and two p.m. yesterday?"

His eyes narrowed to the size of coin slots. "At my church."

"You were there at four a.m.?" I asked, giving him a get-real glare.

He raised his chin. "I got there early ta write my Sabbath sermon."

Somehow I doubted that. "And where is this church, exactly?"

"You're standing in it," he replied, tapping the toe of his gold platform shoe on the sidewalk. "The streets are my pulpit."

I wrote "no church, no alibi" in my notes. "Okay then, do you have any idea who might've killed Amber?"

"It was the devil's doin'," he exclaimed with a flourish of his cane.

"Yeah, I got that part," I said drily. "I was thinking more along the lines of one of her ex-clients. Any chance you could provide me with a list?"

"No need." He crossed his arms on his crucifix. "They was all named John."

I set myself up for that one. "Do you know what Amber did for a living after she left your, uh, employ?"

He pulled a gold toothpick from the pocket of his jacket and slipped it into his mouth. "She tol' me she was tired of workin' fo' the money, so she was goin' clean."

"That doesn't make sense," I protested, resting the pen on

my cheek. "Did she say anything else?"

"Tha's all I know. Now if you don't mind," he began, gesturing toward a lone wino sitting with his back against a nearby trashcan, "I need ta tend to my parishioners."

"Well, thanks for your time," I said, practically choking on the words. As shady as this King character was, I had to keep the lines of communication open.

He bowed and pointed to the fedora. "Donations kindly accepted."

My lips curled. I reached into my wallet for a five and tossed the bill into the hat. "You'll get more when I get more, *capisci*?"

"I dig," he replied and then raised his cane and whacked the wino, who was making a play for the fedora funds.

So much for Christian charity.

As I walked back to the office, I pondered King's comment about Amber "goin' clean." Of course, King was anything but trustworthy, but his story did line up with Carnie's recollection of Amber saying that she had wanted to quit the sex trade. So, if it was true that she hadn't worked for King or anyone else during the past year, then I needed to figure out how she could have come by money honestly without earning it. And the only way I could think of was that someone was giving it to her.

But who? And why?

* * *

"Come and get it, Miss Franki," Glenda yelled as she threw open the dressing room door. "Miss Eve brought us a bucket of her buttermilk fried chicken."

My ears pricked up at the mention of the decadent Southern dish, and I rushed into the dimly lit white room. Long, black countertops and mirrors with vanity lighting lined the walls, and strippers in various stages of undress stood around a table attacking the meat like sharks at a feeding frenzy. As I gazed at the gory scene, the fourteen ounces of cow in my belly started kicking. "Thanks," I said, clutching my gut. "But I just ate. Twice."

"Well, while you were at the bank, I took the liberty of calling the girls who worked with Amber." She handed me a cardboard pantyhose insert with some writing on it. "I couldn't get ahold of one of them, but I started this list for the other two. It's got their contact information, alibis, and measurements."

Although I was impressed with Glenda's initiative, I was confused about that last item. "Why'd you give me their measurements?"

"To help you size them up!" she cried and then slapped her knee as she doubled over with laughter.

I stood there stone-faced until she got out her guffaws. When she finally recovered, I asked, "So, is Eugene back from the police station?"

"Not yet," she replied, wiping a tear from her eye. "But the two girls I called came in early for their shifts to talk to you."

I glanced at the list. Interviewee number one, Bit-O-Honey, was in the hospital on the night of the murder, and interviewee number two, Saddle, was working at a club in Las Vegas. "Do all the dancers use stage names?"

"If they don't, they should." Glenda flipped her hair. "We need to protect our identities, and the bottom line is that we can make more money with a name that appeals to clients. Personally," she began, putting a hand over her heart, "I went for alliteration and romance with 'Lorraine Lamour.' But young girls today go for things like candy, liquor, and exotic locations."

"Then how do you explain 'Saddle?'" As soon as I asked the question, the answer came to me. "Never mind. I got it," I said, raising my hand in a stopping motion. "It refers to riding—but not horses."

Glenda put a hand on her hip. "It refers to the saddles she makes for a ranch supply store. Honestly, Miss Franki, you need to get your mind out of the gutter."

Yeah, because no one has inappropriate thoughts in a strip club. "That reminds me, what was Amber's stage name?"

She grimaced. "According to the girls, she never used one. They said she didn't care if anyone knew who she was."

I wondered whether Amber's openness had anything to do with the fact that she had no family.

Glenda turned to a chubby brunette who was sitting at

the counter and gnawing on a thigh in nothing but a thong. "Bit-O-Honey, come talk to Miss Franki about Amber while I go get Saddle."

She choked down a chunk of chicken. "Yes, ma'am."

As Glenda left the room, I sat in the chair next to Bit-O-Honey and wished that she would put on a robe. "What was Amber like to work with?"

She stared at me, wide-eyed. "Um, she was a super dancer."

I gave her a reassuring smile. "No, I was talking about her personality."

"Oh." She wrinkled her mouth to one side and glanced up and down like a student wracking her brain for the right answer. "Um, she was super creative?"

I pursed my lips. This was going to be harder than I'd thought.

The door swung open, and Glenda returned with a long, lean black-haired beauty wearing a tan suede bikini and chaps complete with a whip. Judging from the cowgirl costume, this was Saddle.

"Was Amber superstitious at all?" I continued.

"She didn't have time for that nonsense," Saddle replied as she sat down and kicked her high-heeled cowboy boots onto the counter, revealing a crescent-shaped tattoo on her calf. "She was fearless."

"That's right," Bit-O-Honey agreed, shaking a chicken leg, among other things, for emphasis. "For her 'crazy as a polecat' routine, she wore a sexy straight jacket while she worked the pole."

"Wow," I said, trying to visualize that scene. "She must've had powerful legs."

"And labia too," Bit-O-Honey added with a round-eyed nod. "Even though she did put Mighty Grip powder on them."

I froze as an unusual image came to mind that I was sure couldn't be right. "Is that like extra-strength baby powder or something?"

Saddle shook her silky locks. "It helps you stick to the pole."

I knew I shouldn't insist, but I couldn't help myself.

"Then why did she put it...down there?"

"She had to collect the clients' dollar bills somehow, sugar," Glenda intoned as she brushed her bottom with bronzer. "After all, her hands *were* strapped to her body."

My jaw fell open, and it took a long time to get it to close. "Uh, speaking of routines, did Amber ever use Lili St. Cyr's bathtub during a performance?"

"No one would dare because that tub is sacred to us strippers," Bit-O-Honey huffed, pressing a hand to her bare breast.

At this point I was willing to forgo the robe and take a pair of pasties. "Did she have any issues with clients?"

"She didn't like The Fly," Saddle drawled, "but it wasn't like they had a falling out or anything."

I paused. "Did you say 'The Fly'?"

"He's one of our VIP Room regulars," Bit-O-Honey gushed. "And he brings in a jelly jar full of flies and pays us to kill 'em with a fly swatter." She swung at an imaginary fly with her chicken leg as a demonstration.

This time my jaw dropped so low that it almost touched my neck. "Whatever happened to paying a stripper to dance?"

"Clients want all kinds of things in the VIP Room," Glenda explained as she checked out her bronzed behind in the mirror. "Dancing isn't usually one of them."

I shifted in my seat. Before this investigation was over, I had a feeling that I was going to learn a lot of things that I'd never wanted to know about the stripping industry. "Okay, so what about the other dancers? Did Amber have any problems or fights with them?"

The girls exchanged a look.

Saddle's lips thinned. "She had a Hatfield-McCoy-type feud with Curaçao."

For some reason I thought of the woman I'd seen exiting the club the morning after my arrest. "She's not a platinum blonde, is she?"

Bit-O-Honey gasped. "How'd you know?"

"Just a lucky guess," I muttered. "But where is Curaçao now? Did she quit or something?"

"She still works here," Saddle replied. Then she glanced

at Bit-O-Honey. "At least, we think she does."

"She's the girl I wasn't able to get ahold of," Glenda said, brushing some bronzer on her cheeks (the ones on her face). "And, from what I hear, no one's seen hide nor hair of her since her Saturday night shift."

I looked from Glenda to the girls. "What about Sunday when the police had all the dancers come in for questioning?"

Bit-O-Honey threw her hands in the air, along with her chicken leg. "She never showed."

My gut lurched, and it wasn't from that kicking cow. "Has anyone reported her missing to the police?"

Glenda placed the bronzer brush on the counter. "Curaçao is known for her benders, Miss Franki. But I'm sure that Eugene told the police all about this today."

I leaned back in my chair. With Amber dead, Curaçao's disappearance could mean only one of two things. Either she didn't want to answer questions about her enemy's murder or she couldn't because she was dead too.

CHAPTER SEVEN

———

"Curaçao hasn't shown up for her shift, sugar," Glenda said, climbing onto the barstool beside me. "And she's still not answering her phone."

I took a sip of chicory coffee from Madame Moiselle's signature "mammary mug" as I digested the worrisome news. "Do we have an address for her?"

"That child is a free spirit," Glenda replied as though she were the epitome of conformity. "The last we heard, she was sleeping on some friend's couch. You'll have to ask Eugene if he knows who or where that is."

If he ever comes back. Eugene had been at the police station the entire day, and I knew why. Because he'd found Amber's body and had keys to the club, he was a prime suspect in the eyes of the law. The question was, did he deserve to be?

"In the meantime," Glenda continued as she hopped from the barstool in platform penny loafers, "the peep show must go on. Is it all right if I cover for Curaçao? Or do you need me to do some more sleuthin'?"

"It's six o'clock. The work day's over," I said, raising the mammary to my mouth.

"You going home?" she asked, tying her white button-down shirt into a knot beneath her bosom.

"Nah." I swiveled on my stool and leaned my back on the bar. "Bradley left town today, and Veronica offered to look after Napoleon, so I think I'll stick around tonight and observe— you know, see if I notice anything out of the ordinary." *For a strip club, that is.*

"Well, slap my ass and call me happy!" she exclaimed as she demonstrated the gesture. "I'm about to practice one of my acts for The Saints, Sinners, and Sluts Revue, so you'll finally get to see me dance."

I did my best to look enthusiastic, but seeing my sixty-something-year-old landlady strip was not on my bucket list—nor was slapping her ass. Besides, judging from her pigtail braids, micro-mini plaid skirt, and knee socks, I feared that she was about to reenact Britney Spears's "Baby One More Time" video. "You're a slut, right?"

"Yes indeedy, Miss Franki." She curtseyed, purposefully displaying boobs adorned with pasties shaped like crosses—the religious kind, not the Red Cross kind. "I'm a Catholic schoolgirl."

As she turned and strutted toward the stairs, I vowed vindication for present and former Catholic schoolgirls everywhere.

"Ride 'em, cowboy!" a female shouted.

Glancing toward the main stage, I saw Saddle galloping and cracking her whip as the song "It Wasn't God Who Made Honky Tonk Angels" began to play. "I don't care what Glenda says," I muttered, "that woman's name has nothing to do with making saddles."

I spun around to the bar to get one of Eve's honey-garlic chicken wings, but instead I came face-to-face with a turkey. From my up-close-and-personal viewpoint, I put him in his early forties. Apart from a noteworthy mole growing from his right eyebrow, his most distinguishing feature was his complete lack of fashion sense, i.e., baby blue bell-bottoms and a purple and white, floral-print shirt unbuttoned to his navel. If he'd been wearing a denim newsboy cap, he would've looked like one of the Wild and Crazy Guys.

"Hello, luscious. Didn't I see you at Hooters?" he asked, his eyes glued to my honkers.

I wasn't surprised by the lame line or the lascivious linger, but I was struck by the way he seemed to swallow his *l*'s. It sounded familiar, but I wasn't sure why. "Sorry to disappoint you," I began, blowing my honey-garlic breath in his face, "but I'm not looking to hook up. I'm here on business."

His eyes glinted like the gold medallion nestled in the fur rug on his chest. "You're in luck, lady, because I'm the manager," he announced, holding out his hand. "Eugene Michael."

Finally. Opting to skip the handshake, I said, "I'm Franki Amato."

"Amato, eh?" He moved his unshaken hand to his chin and rubbed his unshaven beard. "We could use a fiery Italian onstage."

I flashed a smart-aleck smile. "I'm sure you could, but it's not going to be this fiery Italian." I pulled a business card from my bag and placed it on the bar counter in front of him. "I'm investigating Amber Brown's murder."

He pulled a comb from his back pocket and ran it through his slicked-back hair, and I wondered whether he felt as cool and collected as he was trying to make me believe.

"You must be Glenda's friend," he said, returning the greasy comb to his pocket. "What can I do for you?"

"Answer some questions about Amber," I shot back.

He looked down and gave a frustrated sigh. "I met her the day she came into the club and asked me for a job, and I haven't seen her since she quit." He raised his head, and this time he looked me in the eyes. "So, I had nothing to do with her death, all right?"

Eugene was clearly on the defensive. The way I saw it, either he was tired of being questioned, or he was hiding something. "Do you know why she quit after only two months?"

"Strippers like to move around, look for better money, and in this industry it's easy to do," he said as he walked behind the bar. "You show up to a club, and if you've got good moves and the cash to pay the house fee, you can dance."

It didn't seem right that the women had to pay to work, but then there were a lot of things about this business that didn't seem right. "Carlos told me that you closed the club after he and Iris were arrested. What time did you leave?"

"At around five thirty," he replied as he browsed the bottles on the bar. "Then I went home to bed, and I didn't get up until Carlos called at noon and told me that his and Iris's bail had been set." He picked out a bottle of vodka. "And since no one can vouch for me, I'm evidently a suspect."

I remembered the surveillance camera that I'd seen in the

VIP Room. "What about the video from the security system? If you had nothing to do with Amber's death, that could potentially clear you."

"There is no video because we don't run the system after hours," he replied, placing a highball glass on the counter. "Can I offer you a drink?"

"No, thanks." I wondered whether he was telling the truth about the video. If he was, Amber could've known that the cameras wouldn't be running since she'd worked at the club. But had the killer known this too? "Did Amber have problems with any of the clients?"

He laughed revealing discolored teeth, and my tooth gave a pang of repulsion. "The girls have problems with a lot of the clients," he said, pouring himself two fingers of vodka. "If I told you about some of our VIP Room regulars, you'd take me up on that drink offer."

After Bit-O-Honey's story about The Fly, I was inclined to agree with him. "What can you tell me about Amber's feud with Curaçao?"

"They had a few cat fights over one of Curaçao's regulars, a guy named Shakey." He took a swig of his drink and wiped his mouth. "Curaçao claims that he was going to propose to her and that Amber got wind of it and deliberately stole him."

If Curaçao had lost a husband to Amber, then she could've hated her enough to kill her. But until she surfaced, I couldn't rule out the possibility that she'd met with foul play too, maybe even at the hands of this Shakey character. "Do you think it's possible that Curaçao killed Amber?"

He gripped his glass. "As nuts as that chick is? Definitely."

"What about Shakey?" I pressed. "Do you think he could've done it?"

Eugene shot the remainder of his vodka. "I don't know anything about the guy except that he's a Texas oil man who wears a Stetson. But sure. Why not?"

I pulled out my notepad and jotted down the description, although I didn't hold out much hope of finding Shakey given that he sounded like a few hundred thousand other men in Texas. "Do you have any idea where Curaçao is? Some of the girls told me that she hasn't been seen since her shift on Saturday night, and I'm afraid she could be in danger."

"Don't worry," he said, pouring another drink. "Like I told the police, she parties pretty hard—alcohol, drugs, you name it. Sometimes she takes off for days at a time without telling anyone. But she always comes back."

If Curaçao had a substance abuse problem, she could be somewhere getting high or in withdrawal or worse. "Do you happen to know the name of the friend she's staying with?"

He drained his glass. "Maybe."

I blinked, wondering whether he was expecting a bribe for the information. "It's either yes or no."

"No, it's Maybe," he said, placing the glass on the counter. "That's her name. She danced here once or twice a couple of months back."

Now I wished that I'd asked for some of that vodka, because this case was going to give me a nervous breakdown. "You seem to know a lot about Curaçao. Were you ever intimately involved with her? Or with Amber?"

He moved in close and looked me in the eyes. "Honey, I stay as far away from these chicks as I can get."

A shrill whistle pierced the air followed by a strident "Yippee-ki-yay, y'all!"

I almost jumped from my stool. I glared over my shoulder and saw Saddle exiting the stage as Carlos the bartender pushed a fake altar up a ramp. Glenda must have been preparing to make her ungodly entrance, and that was my cue to look the hell away.

"Tell me something," I said, turning back to Eugene. "What do you think Amber was doing in that bathtub?"

He leaned on the counter with his forearms. "Probably getting it on with some loser who killed her for kicks."

I pretended to look at my notes while I recovered from my revulsion. "Did the police mention anything about a necklace?"

"You mean the amber?" he asked, arching the brow with the mole.

Apparently, he'd been questioned about the pendant even though Veronica had advised Detective Sullivan to keep its existence from the public. "Yeah, I'm curious about whether you have any thoughts on why the killer would steal it."

He straightened and hiked up his pants. "My first thought was that one of the girls killed Amber for the pendant."

I narrowed my eyes. "Why would you think that?"

"Because stuff goes missing around here practically every day," he said, opening his arms wide. "If it isn't nailed down or locked up, the girls take it. And they love sparkly things."

"So," I began, crossing my arms, "all strippers are thieves, huh?"

"Not all of them," he replied, raising a finger. "Just some."

For a second, I figured that he was trying to deflect suspicion from himself. But then I remembered that I had seen one of the girls, probably Curaçao, leaving the club with a suitcase containing Lord only knew what. "You mean, like Curaçao?"

"Primarily her," he replied with a pointed look.

"Eugene," Glenda called as she flounced up to the bar in her stripper schoolgirl uniform. "That darn sound system stopped working again." She gave a haughty flip of her braids. "I just can't work in these conditions."

It had to be divine intervention.

"I'll take care of it," he said, taking one last, lustful look at my breasts before exiting the bar.

Eugene was a creep, but I wasn't convinced that he was a killer. Curaçao, however, was a different story. From the sound of things, she had a healthy hatred for Amber and a strong motive to kill her on top of some psychological issues. I needed to talk to her ASAP.

I just hoped that I still could.

* * *

The legs on the stripper-pole clock above the bar read ten p.m. I yawned and looked around Madame Moiselle's. After four straight hours of shaking, slapping, and sliding, I was spent. And I wasn't even doing the dancing. I was considering calling it a night because, as far as I could tell, everything was on the up and up at the club—thanks in part to the silicone.

My phone began to vibrate on the counter, and Ruth's name appeared on the display.

Eager for a break from the boobs and booties, I grabbed my phone and hurried through the hotbed of horny men toward the exit. But outside on Bourbon Street, it was almost as loud as the club. I tapped answer and covered my ear with my hand in an attempt to drown out the blaring jazz music and the din of the revelers. "Hey, Ruth," I shouted. "I'm glad you called."

"Where are you at?" she barked. "A damn rave?"

All right, maybe I wasn't so glad. "Madame Moiselle's."

A moment of silence ensued, followed by a gagging sound.

"Ruth?" I prodded worried that she was choking on an ice cube or something. "Are you okay?"

She inhaled sharply. "I told you to lay low," she rasped, "so first you come to the bank and get sloppy drunk, then you head straight to a titty bar?"

I grimaced as I realized that she hadn't been gagging, but raging. "Relax, will ya?" I huffed. "I'm here investigating a case. And I didn't get 'sloppy drunk.'"

She harrumphed. "Then why does my desk smell like a saloon?"

Annoyed, I collapsed against the exterior wall of the club—until a woman standing next to me pulled up her "I'm getting married, B*tches" T-shirt to flash some guys on the balcony across the street. "That was no well whiskey," I began, bolting away from the bodacious bride, "that was Dom Pérignon champagne, and it inspired a perfume, FYI."

"Yeah, for cheap tarts," she quipped. "Now what in the hell were you thinkin' drinkin' bubbly at my desk?"

I sighed. Compared to a conversation with Ruth, the strip club seemed like a spa. "Look, I spilled it on your desk because I tripped over Jeff when I found him eavesdropping at Bradley's office door."

"Well, well, well." She took a sonorous slurp. "And I found him alone in Bradley's office when I came back from my mammogram. The doc said my girls are doing fine, by the way."

My lips curled. I was up to my eyeballs in "girls" here at the club and on Bourbon Street, so I didn't need Ruth's old gals added to the mammary mix. "What was Jeff doing in Bradley's office?"

"He said he was looking for some loan contract, but we both know that was a load of bull pucky." She let out a boisterous belch. "So, I waited until he went home for the night, and then I broke into *his* office."

Panic gripped my chest. The last thing Bradley or I needed right now was Ruth getting arrested. "You didn't damage the door or anything, did you?"

"I want to keep my job, thank you." She popped the tab of some kind of can. "If you must know, I picked the lock. It's a skill I acquired in the Girl Scouts."

"For what?" I exclaimed. "The breaking-and-entering badge?"

"Let's just say that it was an inner-city troop and leave it at that."

As I processed her reply, something hit me in the head. I reached down to pick up the offending object—a set of Mardi Gras beads with a plastic penis pendant that said *Madame Moiselle's.*

"Sorry, Franki," Bit-O-Honey called from above.

I looked up to see her—and her bare breasts—leaning over the balcony as I rubbed the welt on my head. "Did you find anything interesting in Jeff's office?"

"You bet your patootie, I did," Ruth growled. "A receipt from Casamento's for two soft-shell crab loaves."

Casamento's was an old Italian restaurant on Magazine Street that looked like a giant swimming pool inside because of the original owner's penchant for imported tile. "So what? I just ate pan bread and oyster stew there a week ago."

"I'll tell you *what*." She chomped a piece of ice. "It's dated the day before Martin Slater, one of those two clients Bradley lost, canceled his account. And according to Bradley's client files, that's not only Slater's favorite restaurant, it's his favorite meal too."

My jaw tensed, and I squeezed the plastic penis. It looked bad—for Jeff—but I needed to be certain that he was turning clients against Bradley. "We need hard evidence." I caught a glimpse of my hand and promptly dropped the beads. "Like an email or letter."

"I'm on it," she said. "Now I've gotta scoot. *The Best of Divorce Court* is coming on."

I knew better than to stand between Ruth and her armchair justice, so I hung up without further ado.

As I stood on the street pondering the situation at Ponchartrain Bank, a guy wearing nothing but a mesh shirt rubbernecked my rack. I laid a lethal look on him and entered Madame Moiselle's. It was cleaner inside the club.

* * *

"Club's closed! Everyone out!"

I bolted up on my barstool at the sound of Carlos's voice. The t & a show had gotten so tiresome that I must've dozed off.

Carlos removed some dirty glasses from the bar. "Glenda asked me to tell you that she was going upstairs to change."

"Thanks," I said. Although I couldn't fathom why she had to change when the costumes she wore at the club were the same as her street clothes.

As he began loading the glasses into a dishwasher, I scanned the room and saw the last of the patrons stumbling out the exit. Now that the club was empty, I wanted to search for any evidence that might've been overlooked.

"Hey, Carlos," I began, sliding off my stool, "when Glenda comes down would you let her know that I'm taking a look around the club?"

"Sure thing," he replied as he wiped the counter where my head had been laying.

Hoping I hadn't left behind a pool of drool, I headed for the prop room behind the main stage to check out Lili St. Cyr's claw-foot tub. When I pushed open the door and switched on the light, I gasped. Many of the items were larger than life so that a dancer could fit inside. There was a martini glass, a birdcage, a fishbowl, and a high heel, just to name a few. It looked like a giant was having a garage sale.

After a minute or so of searching, I spotted the bathtub in a corner to my right beside a three-tiered cake. For a moment, I forgot about the tub and gazed with yearning at the colossal confection. It had been so long since I'd had sweets that I seriously considered taking a bite.

Shaking myself from my dessert daydream, I approached the tub. But my foot got caught on the birdcage stand, and I went flying. Using my hands to break my fall, I bumped into a six-foot-long oyster shell, and the top opened to reveal an enormous fake diamond.

"Some stripper doesn't know her gemology," I muttered as I rubbed my aching wrists.

Since I was already on the floor, I crawled around the tub and examined the exterior. The epoxy was smooth except for a few chips on the lip. Next, I leaned into the tub and noticed scratches down to the cast iron right above the overflow faceplate. Upon closer inspection, I realized that the marks were a crude carving of a mermaid followed by several X's, all of which had circles around them except for the last one. I wondered whether the designs were made by Lili St. Cyr or whether they'd been done more recently, possibly even by Amber.

The sound of shoes scraping on pavement startled me from my thoughts. I looked up figuring that I'd find Glenda.

Instead, a bald man stood over me who was so massive that I halfway expected him to shout "Fee-fi-fo-fum!" Only, it wasn't his size that spooked me—it was his eyes. The irises were ice blue, but the whites were as black as coal. And in that moment, they held the same sociopathic stare as Malcolm McDowell's character in *The Clockwork Orange*.

They say that your life flashes before you when you die, but all I could see was Bradley's worried face as he told me that strip clubs were dangerous.

Then everything went as black as the scleras of the giant's demonic eyes.

CHAPTER EIGHT

The pungent odor of hay assailed my nostrils, and something stabbed at the backs of my arms and legs. I tried to think—to remember where I was—but my mind was in a fog. *Am I back in Texas? In a barn?*

I opened my eyes a crack and saw a flesh-colored mass hanging over me. It was coming in and out of focus, but it looked like...*an udder?*

Okay. It was one thing to wake up in a barn, but it was quite another to be underneath a thousand-plus-pound cow.

Convinced that my eyes were playing tricks on me, I squinted at the mass. There were four teats all right, but two of them were covered with...*purple peace-sign pasties?*

"She's coming to," a familiar female voice said.

"Don't let her sit up," another added. "Wait until the whiskey comes."

I snapped my eyes shut. This was no Texas barn, and that was no udder—it was Glenda and Bit-O-Honey leaning over either side of me in the prop room.

While I pretended to be passed out, I had to wonder whether those pasties comprised the outfit that Glenda had changed into and whether Bit-O-Honey went through life topless until she had to put on a costume to perform.

Warm flesh pressed against my leg, and my eyes, understandably, flew open. Glenda had planted her bare bottom beside me on my sickbed, which I now realized was a big bale of hay, and she was coming at me with a feminine hygiene product.

All of the sudden, I longed to be beneath that cow in that barn.

"What shook you, sugar?" she asked, dabbing at my forehead with a thong panty liner.

The giant's face came back to me in a flash. "There was a huge man in here, and the whites of his eyes were black—like a zombie's."

"Oh, that's Iris," Bit-O-Honey bubbled as her boobs bobbed above me. "You know, our bouncer?"

"Wait. Stop," I said, shooting a pointed look in the direction of her breasts. "Iris is a man?"

"It's a nickname," she explained. "Because his eyes are so blue?"

I massaged my forehead—for so many reasons. "And no one thought the black parts were worthy of a reference?"

"Those are corneal tattoos, Miss Franki." Glenda flipped her hair and, unintentionally, a breast. "And Iris is sensitive, so we try not to comment on his appearance."

I closed my eyes instead of rolling them because it took less energy. If you asked me, any man who tattooed his corneas needed to have a thick skin, both literally and figuratively. "So, I take it that this hay is for one of Saddle's acts?"

"No, it's for The Wrangler," Bit-O-Honey replied.

Now my eyes were rolling because I felt a VIP Room story coming on.

"He's another one of our regulars, Miss Franki," Glenda said as she tamped down the edge of a protruding peace sign. "He likes the girls to neigh like horses and stomp around in hay while he tries to lasso them."

I snorted. "That's not degrading, or anything."

"It depends on how you look at it." Glenda leaned back on her hands and kicked her legs like a Rockette before crossing them. "Here at Madame Moiselle's, we subscribe to a feminist view of stripping."

I stared at her and wondered whether my ears were as woozy as my brain. "And what would that be, specifically?"

"We're exploiting our exploiters tit for twat," Bit-O-Honey explained as she took a seat on the lip of a large stoneware pot labeled "Winnie the Pooh."

I suppressed a smirk. These strippers might know their feminist theory, but they needed some serious instruction when it came to common objects and expressions. "You mean, tit for *tat*."

"No, sugar," Glenda said, batting her purple eyelashes. "She means tit for twat."

Bit-O-Honey nodded. "Amber used to say that we shouldn't objectify ourselves," she began, balancing with splayed legs on the honey pot, "and that men should pay us reparations for exploiting us for so long."

I looked at the ceiling and chewed the inside of my lip. Free money seemed to be a recurring theme where Amber was concerned, but the feminist aspect was new. I wondered again whether she'd found someone to fund her.

"Here's that whiskey," a mousy male voice announced.

I turned my head and saw Iris holding one of Madame Moiselle's signature "cock-tail" glasses, and I bolted up on my bale despite his Mike Tysonesque tone. But when my eyes crossed and his merged into a Cyclops eye, I had to lie back down.

"Iris, you gave Miss Franki quite a fright," Glenda scolded as she took the glass from his hand. "You've got to quit sneaking up on people like that."

"Well, I didn't mean to," he whined, twisting the bottom of his faded Marilyn Manson concert T-shirt. "She didn't see me when I came into the room before because she was looking at Amber's pictures."

I bolted up again, but this time only to my elbows. "Do you mean those etchings in the claw-foot tub?"

He opened his eyes wide. "Yes, ma'am."

I cringed at the "ma'am" even more than at the black scleras. "I didn't realize you knew Amber."

"I don't. Uh, I didn't," he stammered, rubbing his shaved head. "Another dancer told me that Amber did those drawings. Maybe."

"Well, did she, or didn't she?" I asked, pulling myself into a sitting position.

"She did." He gave a lizard-like blink. "That is, Maybe."

"Wait." I held out a hand. "You mean, *Maybe* Maybe?"

Glenda looked from me to Iris and then shot my whiskey. "I'm starting to think that we need to take both of you to the damn hospital."

"I'm fine," I said looking with regret at the empty glass.

"He's talking about a dancer named Maybe. And according to Eugene, she's the friend that Curaçao is staying with."

Bit-O-Honey blinked. "Are you talking about Maybe *Baby*?"

I almost said, "Maybe," but I caught myself in time. "I guess."

"Well, I know *her*," Glenda exclaimed. "She lives over in The Marigny by Carnie."

"That's good, because we need to pay her and Curaçao a visit." I started the process of standing up. "But first I need to go home and take a hot bath and get a few hours of sleep."

"I'm with you, sugar," Glenda said, rising to help me. "Right now, I'm too pooped to pole dance, much less private investigate."

As we entered the club, a member of the cleaning crew turned on what the dancers liked to call the "ugly lights," i.e., the overheads that showed all of one's physical imperfections.

Angling a glance at Glenda's pasties, I asked, "Um, do you need to go upstairs and get your shirt?"

"Shirt?" she repeated as though it were a foreign word. "Now that you mention it, Miss Franki, I did forget something. I'll be right back."

Glenda strutted toward the stairs, and I leaned against the stage for support. I was half asleep and still kind of shaken up, which meant that I was in no condition to drive home. Deciding to let Glenda do the honors, I pulled my keys from my bag and promptly dropped them. When I crouched to pick them up, I saw a flash of light reflect off something between the wall of the stage and the pile of the red carpet. After a few minutes of searching, I found the culprit—a tiny glass tube covered in some kind of oil.

Sitting on my knees, I inserted the tip of my car key into the opening of the tube and lifted it to my nose. It had an earthy odor. As I examined it for branding, I noticed silver stilettos with a stripper-on-a pole heel in front of me.

"What'd you find, Miss Franki?"

I looked up to see Glenda in a white, floor-length feather boa. It wasn't a shirt, but it was a start. "Is this container from a product the dancers use?"

She leaned over and sniffed the tube. "That smells like dirt, sugar. We professionals stick to the basic man magnets—baby oil, cocoa butter, or vanilla perfume."

"That's what I was hoping you'd say," I said as I wrapped the tube in a tissue and dropped it into a zippered compartment in my bag. Because I had an idea of what it was. It was a long shot, but if I was right, it was going to add a whole new dimension to this case.

* * *

My Mustang skidded into oncoming traffic, and then Glenda swerved back into our lane.

"I might've taken that turn a tad too fast," she said, taking a deep drag off her cigarette holder.

I pulled a few of her boa feathers from my mouth and began feeling my head for knots. Because surely I'd suffered a brain injury when I fainted at the club, and that's what had prompted me to ask her to drive. "Would you please slow down and get your foot back inside the car? You're supposed to use it, you know, to *brake*?"

Her head retracted into a flock of feathers. "Well, who ever heard of using two feet to drive?"

"Only everyone who went to driving school," I snapped as I checked my seatbelt. "Where'd you get your license, anyway?"

"License?" she scoffed as she pulled the car to a stop in front of our fourplex. "What would I do with one of those?"

That explained the reckless ride. "Oh, I don't know. Abide by the law, use it for ID?"

"This is New Orleans, sugar." She exited the car and threw her boa around her neck. "Abiding by the law is a matter of personal choice, and everyone knows who I am."

She had me on both counts. I shook my head and climbed from the car, and I wondered why Glenda had parked on the street.

Then I glanced at the driveway, and the screechy-scary shower-scene music from *Psycho* pierced my brain like a blade.

"Glenda," I whispered, "please tell me that Veronica's

boyfriend Dirk drives the exact same car as my mother."

She squinted and exhaled a cloud of smoke. "No self-respecting single man drives a station wagon, sugar."

I put my hand to my mouth. "I was afraid you'd say something like that."

We contemplated the maroon Ford Taurus in silence, and then I crossed myself because I didn't know what the hell else to do.

Glenda dropped her cigarette and stubbed it out with her shoe. "Family shouldn't stay under the same roof, Miss Franki. Do you want to sleep in my champagne glass?"

It was a tempting offer. I'd crashed in her glass once before after partying with some pirates, and it was a little cramped but not half bad. "Nah, I'd better go in and face the music," I said, thinking mainly of that *Psycho* soundtrack. "If my mother is here, then something's up."

"Whatever," she said with a shrug. "Just remember, my champagne glass is your champagne glass, sugar."

I watched with envy as she sashayed up the stairs, and then I slowly unlocked the door to my apartment and tiptoed inside. Even though I was thirty years old and had done nothing wrong, I felt like a teenager coming home past curfew—not that I ever did that, of course.

My mother was stretched out supine on the chaise lounge, snoring with her mouth wide open, and Napoleon was watching me warily from the bearskin rug. Clearly, my mother's unexpected visit had set him on edge too.

I turned and closed the door.

Napoleon growled like the traitorous terrier that he was, and my mother jerked awake. "Francesca Lucia Amato!"

A wave of guilt washed over me. There was something about hearing your mother say your full name that instantly elicited a sense of shame.

"Where have you been?" she scolded as she sat up in a nightgown that looked like it had come from the set of *The Golden Girls*. "It's—"

I waited while she slipped on her bifocals and looked at her watch.

"—six o'clock in the morning!"

"I was working," I said, clutching my bag against my chest as though I were hiding cigarettes or booze—not that I ever did that, either.

"All night?" she shrilled. "I thought that you wouldn't have to work the graveyard shift anymore after you quit the police force."

"I still work in crime, Mom," I said as I deposited my bag on the coffee table, "so I have to investigate whenever the need arises."

"Well I don't know how you're going to raise a family working these hours," she said as she adjusted the hairnet that protected her bouffant brown bob.

I almost replied that the only thing that was going to keep me from having a family was my family, but I held my tongue—between my clenched teeth. "How'd you get into the apartment, anyway?"

She slid her feet into dingy white slippers. "Veronica let us in."

My mouth formed a grim line. So, while I was busting my hump for Private Chicks, Veronica was probably busting a gut at the thought of me coming home to find my mom lying in wait like a lioness in my living room. "Why didn't you tell me you were coming?"

"We wanted to surprise you, Francesca," she said as she struggled to lift herself off the chaise lounge.

The *Psycho* screeching sounded again. "*We?*"

She pushed past me on her way to the kitchen. "Your nonna came with me, dear."

Of course, I couldn't see the expression on my own face, but I imagined that it looked a lot like Janet Leigh's did when Norman Bates pulled open the shower curtain dressed like his mother and wielding a knife.

"We had to share your bed since it's the only one in the apartment," she continued as she opened a can of Folgers.

There went the sleep I'd hoped to get.

"But your nonna kept me up half the night going back and forth to the bathroom, so I had to come out here." She pointed a spoon at me. "Then she woke me up at three a.m. and asked me to get her enema bag from the trunk. You know how backed up she gets before a big trip."

Aaaand there went that bath. "Yeah, so, what's the occasion for the visit?"

"It's a belated birthday present," she replied, spooning coffee into the filter.

The gift that keeps on giving.

"Also," she began, filling the carafe with water, "it's been a long time since your nonna returned to her old stomping grounds."

My nonna and nonnu had emigrated from Sicily to New Orleans and raised my father and my four uncles there. So, I'd long known that a visit from my nonna was inevitable, but I'd naively assumed that my parents would've given me a heads-up so that I could prepare—i.e., stock the refrigerator, buy an air mattress, attend a few therapy sessions.

"And the timing couldn't have been more perfect," she added, pouring the water into the coffee maker, "because your nonna can help her old church friends make the bread for the St. Joseph's Day table."

This time, instead of hearing the *Psycho* soundtrack, I felt Norman's knife stabbing into my flesh. Now I knew why my nonna was here—it was to make sure that I stole a lemon from that damn altar. "Mom, I'm not going to steal from a church."

She almost dropped the carafe. "Well, you most certainly are not, young lady."

To the world at large, I was now a "ma'am," but to my mother I would forever be a "young lady." Was there no end to the injustices? "Mom, I'm talking about the lift-a-lemon-snag-a-spouse tradition."

"Oh, that," she said, shoving the carafe into the machine. "It hardly counts as stealing, Francesca. After all, that food is there to be eaten. And besides, at this point, what've you got to lose?"

Only my last shred of dignity and possibly my spot in heaven. No biggie.

She flipped the switch to the coffee maker. "I've got to go get your nonna out of that bathroom so I can do my business." She pasted a smile onto her face. "And when I get back, we can all sip our coffee and have a nice mother-daughter-grandmother chat."

As my mother headed toward my bedroom, I visualized Janet Leigh sliding down the wall of the shower, slowly dying from the multiple stab wounds that Norman had inflicted.

"Carmela, come out of that bathroom," my mother demanded.

"It's-a gonna be a while," Nonna shouted.

A surge of adrenaline shot through my veins. I had to get out of my apartment while I still had some lifeblood left in me—and before my nonna opened that door.

I scribbled a quick note to my mom telling her that I just remembered an early morning meeting I needed to attend and snuck out the door. I started for the stairs to Glenda's, but then I got a better idea—I was going to give Veronica a piece of my mind for not warning me about the familial invasion.

Marching over to her door, I raised my hand to knock as a man dressed in black bolted from the side of my house. I spun around and saw that he was wearing a ski mask and gloves just as he jumped into a dark sedan parked in front of the cemetery across the street.

Because he came from the area of the kitchen window, my first thought was that he was a Peeping Tom who'd been checking out my mom in her granny gown.

But I knew that couldn't be right.

As the peeper peeled out and sped down my street, a more sinister thought occurred to me. I'd had the feeling that someone had been following me off and on for the past couple of days. Could he be the perpetrator? If so, who was he, and what did he want from me?

More importantly, he'd been to my house at least once—was he planning on coming back?

CHAPTER NINE

———

As I stumbled half asleep up the stairs to Private Chicks, I was about to curse the old building for not having an elevator when I remembered that weirdo witch's warning. I wasn't sure whether cursing an inanimate object could "boomerang" back on me, but I couldn't take any chances. Because in light of this latest "present" from the family, I now firmly believed that I was cursed.

I pushed open the door and glanced at the clock: five past noon. Instead of going to my office, I headed for the kitchen to make coffee. I'd gotten maybe three hours of sleep thanks in part to Veronica, who'd called the cops after my encounter with the masked man. But Glenda also bore some of the blame because before the officers could write up the report, she came down wearing a teeny stars-and-stripes-themed teddy in a "show of support for our men in uniform"—that turned into an actual show.

"Well, good afternoon," Veronica said as I entered the narrow kitchen. She was sitting at the two-seater table looking minty fresh in a pale green pencil skirt and crisp white blouse while nibbling on a salad.

"You know I worked late last night," I grumbled, feeling like wilted spinach next to her in my green button down shirt. "And are you seriously going to nag me after everything you've put me through?"

"I was just kidding, Franki." She stabbed her fork into a piece of lettuce. "And like I told you this morning, there was no way I was going to ruin your mother's surprise."

Veronica was wise to stay on my mom's good side, because the woman could swing a mean pasta spoon—and those things had spikes. "Did I miss anything this morning?"

She swallowed a bite of salad. "Carnie's on her way here. She's found something that might be relevant to the case, so I called Madame Moiselle's and asked Glenda to stop by."

"I can't believe Glenda's already at the club," I said, pouring some of Veronica's leftover French press coffee into my Italians Brew It Better mug.

"She had rehearsal for the revue. And by the way," she began, her eyes growing wide, "she told me what happened with Iris last night. You must've been pretty frightened to faint like that."

"I was, but then I went home," I said, shooting her an accusatory look. "Iris has nothing on the women in my family."

She giggled, but then her smile faded. "Speaking of scary people, I'm concerned about the man you saw at the house this morning."

"Don't be," I said as I reached into the fridge and pulled out my Baileys Bourbon Vanilla Pound Cake coffee creamer. "I've got bigger things to worry about."

She pointed her fork at the Baileys. "Like breaking Lent?"

"This is creamer, Veronica, not cake." I poured a half a cup of the dessert-like liquid into my mug. "And I was talking about my mom and nonna. Can you imagine what they'll do when I tell them about the masked man, not to mention their reaction when they get a load of Glenda's getups?"

She popped a crouton into her mouth. "I still can't believe they didn't hear the commotion outside this morning."

"I'm sure they couldn't hear it over the commotion inside the bathroom." I took a sip of my coffee, which suddenly tasted bitter despite the creamer. "I'm also worried about something that's going on at Ponchartrain Bank between Bradley and the manager, Jeff Payne."

Veronica put her fork down. "Whatever it is, I hope you're staying out of it."

"I'm trying," I said, which wasn't really a lie since I was having Ruth look into the issue for me. "But Jeff is practically dragging me into it."

She narrowed her eyes. "How so?"

"Ruth says that he's after Bradley's job," I began, staring into my coffee, "so he's keeping tabs on any trouble I've caused at the bank because he's trying to convince upper management that I'm a liability."

"He sounds like a real jerk," she said as she carried her plate to the sink. "But you can't change the past, Franki. All you can do is make sure that you don't give this guy any new ammunition."

As Veronica washed her dishes, I thought back to my interactions with Jeff. The only thing I could come up with that might look bad was the champagne incident. But I doubted that he could hold that over me since it was a birthday gift from Bradley.

The lobby bell sounded.

"I'll go," Veronica said, drying her hands.

As soon as she'd left the kitchen, I topped off my coffee with more creamer and hurried into the lobby.

Glenda was talking to Veronica by the reception desk while suited up in a New Orleans Saints uniform that made the team's cheerleaders look like real saints. "I can't wait to find out what Carnie has for us." She shimmied like a player who'd just scored. "I hope it's something scandalous."

"That reminds me," I said, trying not to gawk at her fishnet football pants, "why didn't you mention that Carnie was a man?"

She strutted to the couch in her brown pigskin boots and took a seat. "Because I treat my squirrel friends the same way I treat my stripper friends, Miss Franki."

I stared at her over the rim of my coffee cup. "'Squirrel friends?'"

She batted her game-day eyelashes and picked up a copy of *Woman's Day*. "Girlfriends who hide their nuts, sugar."

I was sorry I'd asked but glad I hadn't gone with the Baileys Hazelnut creamer.

"Oh, Franki, I almost forgot," Veronica began as she consulted a calendar on the desk. "I got you an appointment with Amber's dentist, Dr. Lessler. He had a cancelation for eight a.m. tomorrow."

My hand flew to my cheek. "But my tooth isn't hurting

anymore."

Veronica scribbled something on the schedule. "Well, you might as well have him look at it since you have to go to his office anyway."

"Miss Ronnie's right, sugar," Glenda said as she flipped through the magazine. "You don't want to end up like The Tooth Fairy."

I was half tempted to ask what she meant, but I refused to bite.

"The Tooth Fairy?" Veronica looked up from the calendar. "I don't get it."

"He's an elderly gentleman who frequents our VIP Rooms," Glenda explained. "The poor man's got a full set of dentures, so he has a bit of an oral fixation. He pays the girls to brush with Crest and tips handsomely for their used dental floss."

I glowered at Glenda. The VIP Room stories were starting to set my teeth on edge.

The door opened, and Carnie paraded inside in a strapless, floor-length yellow-feathered number with a Marie Antoinette-sized wig and a Miss Universe-style crown. David stood behind her looking bewildered, and I could certainly empathize. It was disconcerting to see Big Bird dressed in drag.

"Uh, ladies," David greeted red-faced. He squeezed past Carnie and dashed to his desk.

"Lordy," Glenda exclaimed, fanning herself with the magazine. "Miss Carnie's serving up fish today."

"Fish?" I said, still thinking squirrels. "Are you having a dinner party or something?"

Veronica cleared her throat. "Franki, 'serving fish' refers to a drag queen who looks very feminine."

"And this ain't no trout, honey," Carnie said as she took a seat beside Glenda and frowned at my shirt.

No, more like a barracuda, I thought as Veronica and I sat on the opposite couch. "So, what have you got for us?"

"Amber's credit card bill." She pulled a sheet of paper from her breast feathers and handed it to Veronica.

I looked over Veronica's shoulder. "Anything interesting?"

"It's mostly groceries and gas," she replied, running her

finger down the list of charges. "But there's also a purchase from etsy.com and one for Waxing Salon on Dauphine Street."

Glenda patted Carnie's beefy bicep. "Where'd you find this, Miss Carnie?"

"The mailman delivered it last night."

"And you opened it?" I asked, surprised.

"Of course I did." She adjusted her crown. "Amber's dead, and the bill did come to my house."

I shrugged. "It's still a federal crime."

"So's murder," she snapped in her man voice and then raised her chin. "And that's what we're here to solve, am I right?"

I declined to comment. This queen was too regal for my blood.

"And after what the police put me through yesterday," Carnie continued, returning to her falsetto, "I felt like I had no choice but to take the law into my own hands." She batted yellow feather and rhinestone eyelashes. "A lady-boy's got to defend her honor."

"Ain't that the truth?" Glenda said with a shake of her head.

This time I really wanted to comment, but Veronica silenced me with a don't-you-dare stare.

Veronica assumed her attorney air. "What happened with the police?"

"They questioned me for eight hours, using strong-arm tactics to try to get me to change my story." She held out a French-manicured finger. "But FYI PO-lice, this bitch don't budge."

I could attest to that.

"I'm glad you stood your ground," Veronica said. "Did you get a sense of where the police are in their investigation?"

"If they're focusing on me, then I'd say they're nowhere." Carnie turned and shot me a half-lidded look. "What about you? Got any updates?"

I decided to keep the glass tube to myself until I knew whether my hunch about its origin was right. "I've talked to Amber's ex-pimp, King, and everyone in the club who knew Amber except for a dancer named Curaçao."

"Curaçao?" Carnie cocked a Bozo brow. "Like the

liqueur?"

"The Caribbean island," Glenda clarified.

Carnie put a hand to her feathered bosom. "How exotic."

Glenda nodded. "Precisely."

"Now that we've established that," I said with an eye roll, "I'm pretty sure that she's the platinum blonde you saw harassing Amber, but we don't have a picture of her to confirm."

"Well, when do you plan to talk to her?" Carnie huffed.

"When she finds her," Glenda replied. "We haven't seen or heard from Curaçao since Amber was murdered, and she didn't show up for work again today." She crossed her legs, flashing a fleur-de-lis thong. "That reminds me, Miss Franki, is it all right if I cover for her this afternoon?"

"Fine with me," I replied a tad too enthusiastically. "I'll head over to Maybe's house now. Hopefully, Curaçao's with her."

Veronica shook her head. "I don't want you going alone, Franki."

"I'll go with her," Carnie announced. "I'd like to have a word with this woman about Amber."

My enthusiasm waned. "Don't you have a show to do?"

"I can get someone to cover for me," Carnie replied. "My freedom's at stake."

"While you two are out," Veronica began, using the credit card bill to block her view of my imploring look, "I'll have David look into Amber's Etsy purchase."

David shot from his chair. "The dancer from Madame Moiselle's?" He ran over to retrieve the bill. "I'm all over that."

I started to tell him that anything Amber had bought from the artsy online market probably wasn't related to stripping, but I decided to let him dream. He was still young, after all.

Carnie turned to Veronica. "Franki and I could stop by that waxing salon afterward. And if we need to do it on the down low, I could pose as a client." She glanced at her lap. "I've been looking for a new esthetician."

I leaned my head on the back of the couch. It was one thing to investigate with Glenda, but going undercover with Carnie was a whole nother ball of wax. "I think it's best if we stick to the direct approach."

"Well, I'll leave you ladies to your business," Glenda said, rising to her feet. "I've got to go change out of this slut costume if I'm gonna cover for Curaçao." She pointed a gold fingernail at me. "Be safe out there, sugar. You don't want to attract the wrong kind of freak."

I mustered a wan smile. "I'll be careful."

As Glenda said her good-byes, my thoughts drifted to the masked man. But I didn't want to think about why he'd come to my house or what he wanted from me. For the time being, I had to focus on finding Curaçao. She'd been MIA for three days and counting, and with every day that passed the likelihood of solving Amber's murder decreased. If I didn't find her at Maybe's house, I wasn't sure where I was going to look—or what was going to happen with this case.

*   *   *

"Yo, Carnie!" I called from the front porch of Maybe's Creole cottage. "Shake a tail feather, will ya?"

"I'm painting," she replied as she powdered her nose. "A queen has to look polished, Miss Thing."

My lips curled. She'd been sitting in my Mustang preening like a peacock for the past fifteen minutes, and yet somehow I was "Miss Thing." "Listen," I began, struggling to keep my cool, "I agreed to let you tag along for Veronica's sake, but if you're going to drag me down then you can leave."

She snapped her compact shut. "You be careful how you use the word 'drag' around me, honey."

I sighed and looked at the porch ceiling. It was going to be a drag of a day.

Carnie exited the car and adjusted the train of her dress. Then she strutted up the sidewalk like the cock of the walk, and I don't mean a rooster.

I turned and knocked on the door. I smirked when I realized that it had been freshly painted haint blue—kind of like Carnie's eyelids—while the white paint on the rest of the house was peeling. According to a Southern superstition, the blue-green color was believed to keep "haints," or evil spirits, from entering a house. I wondered how that had been working out for

Maybe and Curaçao.

The door opened to reveal a tipsy-looking bleached blonde in high-heeled slippers and a sheer pink robe that left nothing to the imagination. She swayed slightly and shielded her eyes from the afternoon sun with a half-empty bottle of wine. "Yeah?"

I cringed at her high-pitched voice. "Are you Maybe, uh, Baby?"

"Who's askin'?" she squeaked.

"I'm Franki Amato, a local private investigator, and this is Carnie…" I hesitated because I'd about had it with the nonsensical names. "…Vaul. We're looking for Curaçao."

"I ain't seen her for a few days." She started to close the door, but Carnie shoved it open with her huge hand.

"We're going to need a few more minutes of your time," Carnie growled.

Maybe looked so shocked that you could have knocked her over with one of Carnie's feathers. I couldn't tell whether she was surprised because Carnie had blocked the door or because she was drunk enough to have initially mistaken her for a woman.

I held up one of my business cards. "I'm investigating the murder of a dancer named Amber Brown, and I have reason to believe that Curaçao is involved and maybe—I mean, *possibly*—even in serious danger. Can we come in?"

She was silent for a moment, then she waved us into the living room with the wine bottle.

I stepped inside onto a sea of dirty clothes that covered every square inch of the floor, and I held my breath just in case I was kicking up any airborne diseases. I figured the fewer times I inhaled the better.

Carnie entered behind me and glanced from the floor to a stained white couch. "If that's your only sofa, then I'll stand."

For once I had to agree with her. "I'll make this quick," I said, mainly because I wanted to limit my breathing. "Did you know Amber Brown?"

Maybe took a swig from her bottle. "Only what I heard from Curaçao, and she hated her."

Carnie's blue-shadowed eyelids lowered. "Was this

because of that client Amber supposedly stole?"

Maybe took another swallow of wine. "The rich oil guy?"

Carnie shrugged. "I don't know. Maybe."

"What?" Maybe asked.

I rolled my eyes. "No, Maybe, she meant 'perhaps.' And yes, Carnie, he's a wealthy oil baron named Shakey. Which reminds me, Maybe, do you know his last name or contact information?"

"What do I look like?" she shrilled. "A dictionary?"

While I struggled to come up with a reply, Carnie pointed to a picture frame on a shelf beside a nesting doll. "That's the woman who was harassing Amber."

I followed Carnie's finger to a picture of a platinum blonde. She was the woman I'd seen leaving the club the morning Veronica bailed me out of jail. I turned to Maybe. "Is this Curaçao?"

She nodded. "The one and only."

"What's her real name?" Carnie asked.

Maybe tried but failed to arch her eyebrow. "That *is* her real name."

I started to take a deep breath and then thought better of it. "She was asking you for her legal name."

Maybe crossed one arm, but the other fell to her side. "Well, how should I know what she goes by in court?"

Once again, it wasn't the reply I was expecting, but it was clear enough.

"And I thought you said this was gonna be quick," she protested.

"Don't get your G-string in a knot," Carnie barked, "because Lord knows you need to put it on. Now, we just need a few more minutes."

Maybe groaned and flopped onto a blue beanbag chair in a position that my mother would have described as "extremely unladylike."

Carnie put her hands on her hips. "Guuurl, I can see your seafood platter. You need to sit up straight and clamp those legs shut tight like a clam shell."

Maybe pulled her see-through robe together as though

that would have solved the problem. "You sound just like my mother."

"That's because I *am* a mother," Carnie said, brushing her curls back with her hand.

My head snapped up at that announcement.

"A *drag* mother," Carnie clarified as she shot me a sideways stare.

"What's *that*?" Maybe asked, her head tipping precariously to one side.

Carnie fluffed her breast feathers. "A mentor to young drag queens."

How I pitied those poor girls.

"Well, I hope you're not as controlling as my mom." Maybe put the wine bottle close to her "seafood platter" and picked at the label. "Or Amber's."

"Amber had a mother?" Carnie and I exclaimed in unison.

"Uh-huh," she replied, her head tipping in the opposite direction. "Curaçao heard her talking on the phone to her mom a couple of times. She said she sounded like a total control freak."

I crouched beside the beanbag. "Did she happen to catch her name or the name of a town where she might live?"

Maybe's eyes seemed to cross as she tried to focus. "She said her name was Mama."

Carnie and I exchanged a look.

"Why did Curaçao think Amber's mother was controlling?" I pressed.

Maybe's head fell backwards onto the beanbag. "She said she could tell by what Amber was saying that her mom was telling her how to get rid of Curaçao."

"Get rid of her?" Carnie echoed, moving to stand in front of Maybe.

"You know, make her go away," she explained. "But Curaçao said she wasn't going anywhere until Amber paid her back for stealing Shakey."

"How could she do that?" I asked. "With money?"

"No, Curaçao didn't want that," she replied, waving her wine. "She wanted Amber's necklace."

My pulse picked up, and I glanced at Carnie. "Did she

get it?"

Maybe chugged the rest of her wine. "Beats me."

Carnie leaned over the beanbag. "What did she tell you about this necklace?"

She dropped the empty bottle onto the clothes-covered floor. Then she plucked a feather from Carnie's dress and wiped her mouth with it. "Just that Amber stole it from some drag queen with serious RBF."

Carnie's eyes narrowed to slits and her cheeks turned blood red. And with her mad Mimi makeup and Dolly Parton 'do, she looked like she'd walked right off the set of the '80s horror flick *Killer Klowns from Outer Space*.

I looked at Maybe, whose face was frozen with fear. "What's RBF?"

"Resting Bitch Face," she whisper-whined.

Well, if the "drag queen" description hadn't been enough to identify Carnie, the "RBF" certainly had.

Before Carnie could flip her wig and Maybe could flood her basement (drag for "wet herself"), I yanked Carnie out of the house and wrestled her into the car.

As I sped from the duplex, I wondered how I was going to find Amber's mother, and where I was going to look for Curaçao next. Because I'd just learned one thing for sure. Curaçao had ripped that necklace from Amber's neck the night of the murder. What I needed to confirm now was whether she'd killed her too.

CHAPTER TEN

"What is this place?" Carnie squawked from the sidewalk. "A Soviet waxing salon?"

I pulled myself from the car and winced. I'd jacked up my back trying to get Carnie into the Mustang at Maybe's house, and it wasn't the only casualty of the scuffle. Carnie's feathers were ruffled—as in the ones on her dress—and a lot of them were broken. I just hoped that none of my vertebrae were. "What are you even talking about?"

"Guuurl, look at the door," she ordered. "Vaxing for Vomen?"

"That's weird," I said as I pulled Amber's credit card bill from my bag. "I drove by here a few days ago."

Carnie plucked her compact from the feather nest between her breasts and checked her crown. "I thought we were looking for Waxing Salon."

"That's the name on the charge," I replied, glancing from the bill to the sign, "but the address is a match. I guess whoever scratched off the other half of those *W*'s also removed the business name."

"Well, let's go in and get this over with." She pulled down her wig and yanked up her dress. "But from the sound of things, I'd best look elsewhere for my waxing needs."

As I pushed open the door, I felt a rush of gratitude for whoever had altered that sign.

"What'd I tell ya?" Carnie breathed as she entered the waiting room behind me. "It looks like Little Moscow in here."

She was right. The interior was a drab gray with chunky antique furniture, and the only decorations were a portrait of Gorbachev on the wall and a hammer and sickle flag in the pencil holder on the desk. Nevertheless, I found the austere, utilitarian atmosphere to be a vast improvement over Maybe's house.

A sixty-something woman with spiky, maroon-tinted hair and the body of a matryoshka doll emerged from behind a black curtain. "You vant vax?"

My eyebrows shot up. So now I knew that the other half of those *W*'s had *not* been scratched off. "Uh, no. I'm Franki Amato," I said, handing her my business card, "and I'm investigating the murder of a young woman named Amber Brown."

She scrutinized my card like a comrade checking papers at a Communist checkpoint and then slipped it into the pocket of her smock. "Nadezhda Dmitriyeva."

The second she said her name it occurred to me that she looked like Boris from the Rocky and Bullwinkle show but sounded like Natasha. "Are you the owner of this salon?"

Nadezhda sneer-smiled revealing a missing eye tooth, making me glad I had that appointment with Dr. Lessler. "I specialize in Brazilian and Sicilian."

She caught me off guard with that revelation. I'd heard of the Brazilian, but based on what I knew about Sicilian-American women, the practice of bikini waxing was as foreign as foot-binding.

"That's good to know and all," Carnie interjected. "But like the woman said, we're here to talk to you about Amber."

Nadezhda's dark eyes bore into mine as she jerked her head in Carnie's direction. "Who is him?"

Carnie gasped and drew a hand to her bosom. "Listen, Babushka. You've got a lot of nerve throwing shade like that with your Sharon Osbourne 'do."

I held my breath as I waited for the outburst, but the hair jab rolled off Nadezhda like vodka off a Cossack's back.

She pursed her lips and clasped her hands behind her. "What means 'trow shade'?"

"To criticize," Carnie replied, smoothing her feathers. "In this case, my lady look."

Nadezhda raised a well-waxed brow and turned to me. "Amber was regular client," she announced. "For one year."

Something about her sudden proclamation made me suspect that she'd been rehearsing her answers. I decided to put her honesty to the test. "When was the last time you saw her?"

She jutted out her lower lip. "Two weeks since today."

The timeframe corresponded to the charge on the credit card bill, but it was no guarantee that she'd tell me the truth about anything else. "Amber started coming to your salon at around the same time she quit a job at Madame Moiselle's Strip Club. She supposedly wanted to quit the sex industry and 'go clean.' Did she ever mention that to you?"

Nadezhda shook her head, but she was avoiding my gaze.

"What about her financial situation?" I pressed. "Do you happen to know where she was working this past year or if someone was giving her money?"

She walked to the reception desk and began unloading supplies from a cardboard box. "Not my business."

My instincts told me that Nadezhda made everything her business, so I tried another angle. "I know that clients often confide in their estheticians. Did Amber ever seem worried about anything? Or did she mention any problems she was having?"

"She had problem with her mama," she replied, pointing a package of waxing sticks at me. "Ze woman is Nazi."

"Talk about the Commie calling the Fascist black," Carnie intoned as she pretended to admire the Gorbachev portrait.

A pain shot through my backside that I was pretty sure had nothing to do with my injury. "Can you elaborate on that, Nadezhda?"

Her dark brow furrowed. "She call too much. Every time Amber come here, zey fight on phone."

I, of all people, knew that it wasn't unusual for mothers and daughters to argue, but I found it telling that Amber's mother had made such a bad impression on at least two people, and especially on a tough woman like Nadezhda. "Do you know anything about her mother? A name or an address?"

"*Nyet*." She pulled a tub of cream wax from the box.

I swallowed my disappointment as I pulled my pad and pen from my bag. "What kinds of things did they fight about?"

She shrugged. "Sometimes money, sometimes her man friend."

"Wait." Carnie held up her hand in a stopping motion. "You mean Amber had a boy toy?"

She put her hand on her hip. "Zat's right, darlink. What else?"

"No need to get nasty, Nadezhda," Carnie replied, fluffing her curls.

I sighed and resolved to beg Veronica to free me from the cohort cross she was making me bear. "What can you tell us about this man?"

"Nusink," she replied, resuming her unpacking.

I wondered whether that was because she didn't know anything or because she didn't want to tell me. "Do you remember anything about Amber's demeanor during her last appointment? Like, was she happy or depressed?"

Nadezhda took a seat behind the desk. "Her mama call," she replied in a low voice. "Zey have big argument about necklace."

"What about the necklace?" Carnie asked, rising to her feet.

"Her mama did not like." She shook her index finger. "She tell her not to wear."

Carnie gasped. "My mother designed that necklace, and it was fierce."

"Your mama design pentagram?" Nadezhda's lips curled. "Not surprise."

Carnie's clown brows rose to her wigline, and my mind flashed to the stained glass pentagram at Erzulie's.

"Nadezhda," I began, trying to keep a neutral tone, "do you think there was any special significance to the pentagram? Or was it a fashion statement?"

She looked me square in the eyes. "You tell me."

The door opened, and an elderly gentleman with hairy ears entered and did a double take when he caught sight of Carnie in all her yellow-feathered splendor.

Carnie held his gaze in a seductive stare and rubbed her hands down her Big Bird belly.

I rolled my eyes and grasped the door handle. "We'll

leave you to your work," I said, hoping that the man was there to get his lobes weed-whacked. "But I'll be in touch."

The minute we got outside Carnie cornered me. "What do you make of that pentagram?"

"I'm not sure," I replied, heading for the car.

But that wasn't entirely true. Because if the pentagram necklace meant what I thought it did, then this case was about to take a dark turn.

*   *   *

"Bradley!" I exclaimed as he leaned over and planted a kiss on my cheek.

"I figured I'd find you here," he said as he slid next to me in the booth at Thibodeaux's Tavern, aka my home away from home thirty steps from my front door.

I snuggled up to him. "I thought you weren't going to be back until later tonight?"

"I caught an earlier flight." He winked at Veronica who was sitting across from me and held out his hand to her boyfriend. "Bradley Hartmann."

Dirk flashed a movie-star smile. "Dirk Bogart," he said with a handshake. "You're with Ponchartrain Bank, right?"

"For the time being," Bradley replied, slipping his arm around my shoulders.

I shifted uncomfortably. I couldn't tell whether that was a casual remark or an indication that something had gone really wrong at the board meeting, but I knew that it wasn't the right time to ask, especially if I was part of his "professional problem."

"I'm not interrupting, am I?" Bradley asked as his eyes searched my face.

"Actually, we both are." I glanced apologetically at Veronica. "I saw Veronica and Dirk through the window as I was pulling into the driveway, so I decided to pop in and say hello."

Veronica looked from my empty plates to Bradley. "That was an hour ago," she observed drily. "I guess you know that Brenda and Carmela arrived last night for an unexpected visit?"

"No, but I thought I recognized that Ford Taurus parked

out front," Bradley replied with a twinkle in his eye.

For reasons I could never understand, he always looked amused when the subject of my family came up, which was pretty incredible given that when he'd met them last Christmas my mom and nonna had tried to "mafia-wife" him into marrying me. At least *he* could laugh about it.

"Anyway," Veronica began, "Dirk's a gemologist, and he was telling us about the Amber Room."

Bradley cocked a brow. "The room the Nazis stole from the Russians?"

"That's the one," Dirk replied with a nod. "Although the Nazis felt that Germany never should've given it to Russia, which is why they packed it up all six tons of it in '41 and moved it to Königsberg Castle."

I stirred my Campari and soda. "If they took the room back, then where did it go?"

Dirk ran his fingers through his reddish-blond hair. "That's the question politicians, researchers, and treasure hunters have been asking since 1945. The Nazis moved the room again when the Allies began bombing Königsberg, and no one has seen it since."

Bradley turned to me. "Why are you so interested in the Amber Room?"

I averted my eyes. Since Veronica and I were under orders from Detective Sullivan not to discuss certain details of the crime scene, I couldn't let on that this was connected to my case. "I don't know." I hedged, feigning an interest in my drink straw. "It's been in the news a lot lately."

Veronica cleared her throat. "Franki, Dirk says that before the Nazis made it to Catherine Palace, the Russian curator of the room tried to take it apart to hide it, but the amber was so brittle that it starting cracking and splintering, so he had it covered with fake walls instead. He catalogued 28 amber shards that had broken off various parts of the room."

I looked up from my straw and met her gaze.

"I'm assuming that more pieces broke off when the Nazis took it apart too," she added with a slight nod.

I knew what Veronica was trying to tell me—that Carnie's grandmother could very well have picked up a piece of the Amber Room.

"Just think," Dirk said with a shake of his head. "We could all retire on what one of those shards is worth today."

"But isn't amber prehistoric tree resin?" Bradley asked. "I mean, how much could that be worth?"

"The history of this amber is what makes it priceless, and I'm not only referring to the mystery," Dirk replied with a knowing look. "It was a masterpiece of eighteenth century artistry that was widely considered to be the Eighth Wonder of the World. And, in fact, experts agree that the replica of the room the Russians unveiled in 2003 doesn't hold a candle to the 1716 version. Today at auction, a tiny piece of the original room could fetch millions."

I almost coughed up my Campari. Maybe had said that Curaçao wanted the necklace as payback for Amber stealing her man, and if Curaçao had even the slightest inkling of what the pendant was worth, it could've given her more incentive to kill Amber.

Phillip, the bartender, approached Bradley. "Yo, can I get you something, bro?"

He tapped his fingers on the table. "I'll take an Abita. Jockamo IPA, if you've got it."

"Coming right up." Phillip flipped his long, dirty-blond bangs to one side and headed for the bar.

Bradley turned his attention back to Dirk. "Isn't there supposed to be a curse on anyone who searches for the Amber Room?"

I stiffened. *Why was everything coming up curses?*

"That's the rumor." Dirk smiled and raised his eyebrows. "And considering the fate of some of the people who've looked for it, it would certainly give me pause."

I scooted closer to Bradley. "Um, what do you mean 'fate'?"

"The German museum director in charge of hiding the amber died under mysterious circumstances along with his wife, and their bodies vanished," Dirk replied, peeling the label off his beer bottle. "Then a Russian general died in a car crash after consulting with a journalist about the alleged location of the room." He paused to take a drink. "But the most famous incident involved a guy named Georg Stein."

Veronica opened her eyes wide. "What happened to him?"

"He was found dead in the middle of a Bavarian forest," Dirk explained. "Naked, with his stomach slit open by a scalpel."

I jumped and bumped my head into Bradley's jaw. "Ow," I said, turning to look at him. "Sorry."

He rubbed his chin and scrutinized my face.

Phillip returned with Bradley's beer, and I was grateful for the distraction. I couldn't help but wonder whether Amber had heard about the curse and whether she blamed it for the bad things that had allegedly been happening in her life. Of course, I also wanted to know whether the curse applied to someone trying to retrieve the stolen pendant, i.e., me.

"Does amber have any special properties?" Veronica asked.

Dirk put his arm around her and pulled her close. "Historically, people believed it could suppress bleeding and cure certain mental disorders, like hysteria and hypochondria."

Veronica glanced at me and then quickly looked away.

"But these days," Dirk continued, picking up his beer bottle, "the only thing I've heard of people using it for is to treat babies' teething pain."

My tongue went to my tooth, and I wondered whether I could suck on a piece of amber rather than going to Dr. Lessler in the morning.

Now Veronica was openly staring at me, and I shot her a what-the-hell stare.

Dirk swallowed some beer. "In Russian folklore, amber was thought to be a powerful deflector of the evil eye."

This caught my interest, especially in light of Amber's superstitious side. "What else can you tell us about amber?"

Dirk thought for a moment. "Most of it comes from the Russian town of Yantarny, which was named after the word for amber, *yantar*. And there are a few popular myths about its origin. The most well known is the one about a Lithuanian queen named Jurate."

I swallowed the last of my Campari. "Never heard of her."

"Well," he said, straightening in his seat, "legend has it that she lived in an amber castle beneath the Baltic Sea. And one day, she went to punish a young fisherman named Kastytis for depleting the sea of fish, but she fell in love with him instead. The god of thunder was furious that an immortal goddess had fallen in love with a mortal man, so he struck her castle, shattering it into millions of pieces."

"What did he do to the fisherman?" Bradley asked in a wry tone.

"There are several endings to the legend," Dirk replied. "But according to the most popular version, the thunder god killed him, and Jurate still mourns him and weeps tears of amber."

Veronica snuggled closer to Dirk. "What a beautiful love story."

"Actually, it's kind of confusing," I said, stabbing at my ice with my straw. "I thought the amber came from Jurate's shattered castle, not her tears. Plus, she's not a real queen."

Dirk shrugged. "They call her a queen, but she's basically a sea goddess."

"A sea goddess?" I sat straight up, knocking Bradley in the chin for a second time. "Ow," I said, looking back at him. "Sorry."

He narrowed his eyes and took a sip of his beer.

I turned to Dirk. "Is Jurate by any chance a mermaid?"

"Yes," he replied, giving Veronica a squeeze. "She's the queen of all mermaids."

A shiver went down my spine as I thought about the mermaid that Amber had carved into the bathtub. It seemed like a long shot that it would be connected to a Lithuanian legend, but I was convinced that her drawing had some sort of significance to the case. On a hunch, I pulled my phone from my bag and googled *Queen Jurate*.

"It's getting late," Veronica announced, exchanging a look with Dirk.

"Right," he said, practically leaping to his feet. "Pleasure to meet you both."

Bradley stood up and shook Dirk's hand, and Veronica slid from the booth and gave Bradley a hug. "Night." She looked at me. "I'll talk to you tomorrow. After your appointment with Dr. Lessler?"

"Can't wait," I muttered, staring at the screen. I wasn't trying to be rude—well, okay, maybe a little after that dentist dig—it's just that I was surprised by the search results. The first link that came up was a Wikipedia entry about the myth of Jurate and Kastytis, and the second was an article in Forbes magazine titled "Mysteries of the Amber Room." It occurred to me that if Amber had done any research on the room at all, she might very well have come across the myth. What I didn't know was what that meant in terms of the crime scene.

Bradley slid back into the booth. "I don't know what you've gotten yourself into, but promise me that you're not thinking of looking for the Amber Room."

"Do I look like a treasure hunter to you?" I asked as I typed the phrase *Goddess Jurate* into my browser search field.

"I wouldn't put it past you," he muttered.

I turned and gave him a kiss on the lips. "You know me so well."

Bradley's eyes widened. "So, you *are* looking for the Amber Room?"

"Definitely not," I said tapping a link. "But if an international shipment of Nutella goes missing, I can't make you any promises."

He laughed and finished the last of his beer while I skimmed the first paragraph of "Jurate—the Baltic Goddess of the Sea." And I only had to read down to the second sentence to find what I was looking for—the mermaid queen was a "deity of healing."

I chewed my thumbnail as I thought about the bizarre assortment of items at the crime scene and the good luck charms and talismans that Carnie had seen Amber wearing.

Bradley nudged me with his shoulder. "Is everything okay, Franki?"

"Now that you're here, everything's great," I said as I wrapped my arms around his waist and rested my head on his chest. And I meant it, too. There was just one problem I had to work out—whether Amber's death was a witchcraft killing or a ritualistic voodoo murder.

CHAPTER ELEVEN

———

"What are you up to today, Francesca?" my mother asked way too brightly from the opposite end of the kitchen table.

I stared at her while I chewed the enormous spoonful of Cheerios I'd just shoveled into my mouth. She'd been sitting there watching me eat my breakfast for a good five minutes before she asked the question, so I figured she could wait for me to swallow. And besides, I knew that if I answered her with my mouth full, she'd chew me out.

I washed down the cereal with a sip of orange juice. "I have an eight o'clock appointment with a dentist about my tooth. And since he's involved in a homicide case I'm investigating—"

"You're going to a homicidal dentist?" she shrilled.

The spoon slipped from my hand and fell into the bowl. "Take it easy, Mom," I exclaimed. "He was the dentist of a stripper who was murdered."

She confiscated my napkin and mopped up a wayward Cheerio from the table. "You really should be more choosy when it comes to doctors, dear."

I fished my spoon from the chocolate milk. "Are you saying that he's a bad dentist because his client was murdered?"

"It's just so morbid," she replied, frowning at my wet fingers. "And you know what your nonna would say."

"Yeah, *porta iella*," I said, using the Italian phrase for *it brings bad luck.* "So, let's not tell her, all right?" The last thing I needed was a warning from my nonna about all the tragedies that were destined to befall me when things were already spectacularly craptastic.

"Fine with me." She sat back in her chair and resumed

watching me eat.

Nonna entered the kitchen in her everyday wear—a basic black mourning dress accessorized with a cross.

"*Buongiorno*," she said, dropping her purse on the table with a thud that rocked some milk from my bowl.

"Morning, Nonna." I eyeballed her bag as I wiped up the spill before my mother could do it for me. My brothers and I had been wondering what she'd been carrying in that thing since we were kids, and I was beginning to think it was an anvil.

Nonna pursed her lips and patted the cushion of one of the Bordeaux-and-gold Dauphine chairs, which was the same height as her. "So, this-a Glenda..."

My body tensed, and I shoved a bite of cereal into my mouth as I waited for the other anvil to drop.

"...she has-a good-a taste."

I inhaled in surprise, and a couple of Cheerios flew down my windpipe, causing me to start coughing up a lung.

My mother sprung into action, slapping me repeatedly on the back. "This wouldn't happen if you'd chew each bite thirty times like I taught you."

Impervious to my pulmonary plight, my nonna continued to survey the apartment. "It look-a like the noble *palazzi* of-a Sicilia in here."

I made a mental note to scratch all Sicilian palaces off my future travel itineraries—that is, if I lived to take another trip.

My mother suddenly stopped slapping. "By the way, when are we going to meet Glenda?"

"She's..." I wheezed. "...working a lot." I coughed.

"That reminds me," she continued, "I noticed that Bradley didn't stop by last night." She shot me a probing look. "Nothing has happened between the two of you, has it?"

"No, I saw him last night." As soon as I'd said the words, I wanted to smack myself upside the head with my nonna's purse.

"Mah!" Nonna jutted out her lower lip.

When my nonna uttered the Italian sound of doubt, I knew the situation was dire. "Bradley had just flown in from New York, Nonna, so I told him to go home and get some rest. He'll come over tonight."

She tapped her finger on my chest. "If he no wanna see your mamma, he's-a no gonna marry you."

I knew that I needed to do something drastic to defend Bradley, otherwise he was going to get a ruthless reception when he stopped by. So I marched into my bedroom and pulled the ruby and diamond necklace from my jewelry box. Then I returned to the kitchen and dangled it in front of my nonna's face. "Would a man who isn't going to marry me give me this?"

"Eh, *sì*," she replied with a combination shoulder shrug and hand flip.

I put my hands on my hips, bracing myself for the speech to come. "How do you figure?"

She crossed her arms and raised her chin like Mussolini standing on his balcony. "Because it's-a not a ring. And as-a the saying go, 'why buy-a the goat when you can have-a the milk for free'?"

"It's a *cow*, Nonna. A *cow*," I stressed as I returned to my seat at the table. It might seem pointless to insist when neither animal painted me in an attractive light, but I didn't want to be compared to a goat because they had beards—like so many women in my family.

"A cow, a goat, an *ippopotamo*." She waved me away. "It-a no make-a the difference."

"It-a make-a the difference to me," I proclaimed, especially now that she'd thrown a hippopotamus into the mix. "Why can't you understand that Bradley and I don't want to rush into something as serious as marriage?"

"Rush-a?" she cried, throwing her arms in the air. "If-a two years is a rush-a, I'd-a hate to see you take it-a slow."

"She's got a point, Francesca," my mother said, cradling her purse like the grandchild I hadn't given her as she stared sadly at her lap.

Nonna clasped her hands in a pleading gesture. "Listen to your nonna, Franki. Take-a the lemon." She reached into the fridge and pulled out a plastic bag full of the yellow fruit. "And look-a! Your mamma she buy extra for *la tavola*. She make it-a so easy."

I stood up and practically threw my cereal bowl into the sink. "Aren't you two supposed to be cooking for the poor?"

My mother let out a stoic sigh. "We're going to bake bread at Santina Messina's house. But first we need to start loading up some groceries we bought last night and take them to the church."

Desperate to get them out of the house, I said, "I'll take care of that. A guy I work with is collecting food for the event, so I can bring it to the office and have him deliver it for you."

A flicker of interest flashed in my nonna's eyes at the mention of a male. "Who is-a this-a guy-a?"

I leaned against the kitchen counter. "Don't even go there, Nonna. David's a college student, so he's too young for me."

My mother looked at her watch and rose to her feet. "Carmela, we need to get going. I told Santina that we'd be there by seven."

"If-a you want an older man, Santina's son-a Bruno is a catch-a," my nonna said as she retrieved her purse from the table.

I knew Bruno, and a catch he was not. In fact, the guy was as big a lemon as they came. He was a forty-one-year-old food stand manager who still lived at home with his mother. Not only that, when my nonna tried to fix me up with him a couple of years ago, he'd happily suggested that I cheat on Bradley with him. In other words, he wasn't exactly the kind of guy who swept a woman off her feet—unless you counted the fact that his reckless driving put his mother in a wheelchair.

"I hear Bruno's still single," my mother added in a singsong voice.

"I'm quite sure he is," I grumbled. "Anyway, if you guys don't mind," I began, pushing both of them into the living room, "I need to get ready for my appointment."

"Well, who's stopping you, Francesca?" my mother exclaimed in an exasperated tone as though I'd been stressing *her* out for the past hour. "Now, we'll be at Santina's until dinnertime," she said, pulling her keys from her bag. "We hope to see you then so we can have a nice meal together."

If dinner went anything like breakfast, I'd rather go on a hunger strike. And that was saying a lot coming from me.

My mother opened the front door, and I remembered my encounter with the masked man the morning before.

"Wait, Mom," I said, putting a hand on her arm. "You and Nonna be careful out there."

She closed the door and narrowed her eyes like Superman activating his X-ray vision. "What in the world would prompt you to say something like that?"

"Don't get all freaked out or anything," I began, "but someone's been following me."

Nonna's eyes lit up like a prayer candle. "*Un spasimante?*"

I sighed and looked at the ceiling. "No, not an admirer. In the United States, men who follow women are called stalkers."

"The bastard had better not mess with my daughter," my mother growled to herself as she stared at the floor.

I felt sorry for the masked man if my mom ever caught him. When you messed with her kids, she exhibited another one of Superman's powers—heat vision, i.e., the ability to shoot red-hot beams from her eyes.

"Have you called the police?" she asked, her voice dangerously low.

I nodded.

She put her hands on her hips. "What does Bradley think of all this?"

I glanced around the room, sensing that this was some kind of trap. "He doesn't know?"

"Francesca, honestly!" My mother threw open the door. "You're never going to have a meaningful relationship with a man if you don't confide in him."

Aaaand, I was right.

Nonna tilted her head back to look up at me. "You take-a the lemon. Or you start-a getting some cats."

"Don't waste your breath, Carmela," my mother huffed. "She's not going to listen to us." She motioned for my nonna to exit and then turned to me with a forced smile. "You have a nice day, dear."

After she'd closed door behind her, I stormed off to my bathroom to get ready. I had no idea how my having a stalker had turned into an indictment of my ability to have a relationship, but I shouldn't have been surprised. With my family, sooner or later every conversation turned to my *zitella*hood.

The thing that bothered me most was actually my mom's comment about me not confiding in men. I'd been keeping a lot from Bradley lately—my suspicions about Amber's killer, the business with Ruth and my reputation at the bank, and the fact that I had a masked maniac following me around town. Did this mean Veronica was right when she said that I didn't trust Bradley? Or worse, did it mean my mother was right when she implied that our relationship was doomed to fail?

As I picked up a bar of lemon verbena soap, my mind drifted to the St. Joseph's Day lemons. Then I splashed cold water on my face and scrubbed my cheeks hard.

* * *

"Give it to me straight, Dr. Lessler," I said, looking up at the forty-something dentist from my reclining position in the dental chair. "How bad is it?"

He pulled the mask from his face, and his full lips constricted as though he was struggling to suppress a smile. "The pain you've been feeling is because of a crack in tooth 30," he explained, pointing with a sickle probe to my lower right first molar on the X-ray image, "and you also have a cavity in tooth 31."

My stomach spasmed like it had been hit by my nonna's purse. It figured that the bum tooth would be number thirty, and I could only surmise that the cavity in thirty-one was a sign of things to come. "How could I crack my tooth?"

Dr. Lessler handed the probe to a petite blonde hygienist. "Well, unless you got hit in the mouth, the usual culprits are grinding or clenching your teeth, or chewing hard things like ice, hard candy, or nuts."

Although I'd definitely had occasion to clench my teeth lately, I blamed the salty snacks I'd been eating since giving up sweets for Lent. Desserts wouldn't have done me this way. "So, what's the plan?"

He leaned back in his stool and crossed his muscular arms across his purple and gold Louisiana State Universitythemed scrubs. "I can fill the cavity today, but you're going to need a crown on that cracked tooth."

As soon as he said "crown," Carnie popped into my head—and I quickly kicked her out.

"My assistant could probably work you in for a temporary crown later this week," he continued, "but you'll have to come back when we get the permanent crown from the lab."

I laid my head back on the chair and sighed. Three dental appointments in two weeks were a clear manifestation of the curse, as were my rotting and breaking teeth. "I guess the filling involves a shot, huh?"

"Don't worry." He smiled, revealing two perfect rows of teeth. "I administer a topical numbing gel first."

That was a small consolation. But I didn't have time to stress because I had a more pressing concern—getting in a few questions about Amber before the lidocaine shot. "So, I mentioned before that I'm a PI."

"Mm-hm," he said distractedly as he took a Q-tip from the hygienist.

"I'm actually working a case involving one of your clients." I watched his face for a reaction. "Amber Brown?"

If he was surprised by my announcement, he didn't show it.

"Dana," he began, turning to the hygienist, "can you give us a minute, please?"

"Of course." She hurried from the room.

"I heard what happened to Amber on the news," he said, turning to lay the Q-tip on the tray next to my chair. "It's tragic to see a life cut short so young, especially when she was getting ready to start over."

I pushed myself onto my elbows. "What do you mean 'start over'?"

"She came in last Friday, the day before she died." His bright blue eyes looked into mine. "Anyway, she said that she was planning to get an associate degree in dental hygiene."

I couldn't help but wonder whether her decision had been inspired by VIP Room visits from The Tooth Fairy. "Any idea how she was going to finance it?"

"That I don't know."

It occurred to me that Amber could've been intending to sell Carnie's necklace on the black market to cover the costs of college. On the other hand, her mom could've offered to fund her degree. "Did she ever mention a mother?"

"Not that I remember." He crossed his legs at the ankle. "But I see a lot of patients, so it's hard to keep track."

"Right," I said, glancing at my dental bib. "What was her demeanor like that last visit?"

He rubbed his chin with his thumb and index finger. "She seemed excited. You know, about going to school."

From the way Dr. Lessler spoke, it was starting to sound like Amber had been in a good place when she died. "Had she been a patient of yours for long?"

He nodded. "A couple of years give or take a few months."

I realized that he would have known Amber both while she was dancing and after she'd quit the business. "Did you notice a change in her during that time?"

"Yeah." He locked his hands behind his head. "It really seemed like she was cleaning up her act."

His comment reminded me of Amber's plan to *go clean.* "How so?"

"She used to wear some pretty risqué outfits in here," he replied with a knowing look. "But she'd toned down the dress lately, even if it was a little dark."

"Dark?" I repeated. "Like, Goth?"

"No, but the last time I saw her she was all in black, even her nail polish." He paused. "And she was wearing this strange charm."

"A pentagram?"

He shook his head. "It was silver—a diamond shape with a ball in the middle on top of an upside-down triangle. Between the two shapes there were scrolls on either side."

Dana returned to the room. "Sorry to interrupt, Dr. Lessler, but we've got quite a few patients in the waiting room."

"Back to work," he said, picking up the Q-tip. "Open, please."

I lay back on the chair. While he dabbed anesthetic on my gums, I tried to think of any questions that couldn't wait until my next appointment.

He discarded the Q-tip, and Dana handed him a syringe containing the local anesthetic. "You'll feel a slight pinch, and then your jaw and lips will start to go numb."

I nodded and opened my mouth. There was a small sting, and then a warmth spread through my jaw.

He removed a latex glove. "While we wait for the anesthetic to take effect, I'm going to pop out and see another patient."

"Before you go," I began, already noting a tingling in my lips, "why did you think Amber's charm was a symbol and not just some random design?"

He rose to his feet and ran his hand through his blondish-brown hair. "Oh. Because I asked her what it was, and she said it was a *veve*."

I looked up at him. "What's that?"

His mouth twisted into a smirk-smile. "Supposedly, it's a religious emblem that acts as a conduit for a voodoo god."

I wanted to return his sarcastic grin, but I couldn't. Not only was I losing control of my lips, I was also struggling to keep control of my nerves. In a town like New Orleans, a voodoo candle and some incense were one thing, but a voodoo conduit was quite another.

* * *

While I was heading for home to let the lidocaine wear off, my "Shake Your Booty" ringtone sounded. I wasn't planning on talking because my lips felt like lead, but then I saw David's name on the display. He usually only called if he needed a work assignment or had some information for me, so I tapped answer as I pulled up to a stoplight. "Hello?"

"Hey, Franki," David boomed into the receiver. "I finished that Etsy research, and Veronica told me to ask if there's anything you need me to do today."

Now that I'd finally questioned Dr. Lessler, the most pressing item of business on my agenda was finding Amber's mother. "I nee oo look hor Ammmer's odder."

There was a moment of silence on the other end of the

line.

"Uh, you need me to look for a whore and an udder," he repeated.

"No," I wailed, both because he was wrong and because I flashed back to Glenda and Bit-O-Honey's boobs bobbling over me. "I'll teksh you."

"Riiight." He paused. "You do that."

I was pretty sure that he hadn't understood me, but I figured he could just wait for my text. What I needed to know was what he had for me from Etsy about Amber's purchase. "Ut do you ha hor e?"

"Are you, like, speaking Italian?" he asked in a bewildered tone.

I slammed the back of my head into the headrest. Although the kid did have a point—I was using an awful lot of vowels. "No, Eshee."

"Yeah, so I'm good with programming languages, but foreign ones? Not so much. Anyway, this lady at Etsy emailed me a picture of what Amber bought. It's a necklace."

Given the significance of all the necklaces in this case, I was eager to get a look at that picture. "I nee duh icshure."

"Uh-huh," he said, clearly oblivious. "I forwarded the email to you, so, um… later."

"Anks." The light turned green, and I took the first right into the parking lot of Tulane University so that I could check my email. When I finally found the message and opened the picture, I gasped.

It was an exact replica of Carnie's amber necklace.

CHAPTER TWELVE

———

"It's Now or Never," I muttered, quoting The King as I climbed from my Mustang. It was ten thirty, and I'd been parked in front of my house for the past hour, dreading going inside. When I'd returned home from the dentist, there was no sign of the Taurus, but I found a flock of FIATs parked in and around the driveway. I knew instantly that my nonna had invited her friends over—after all, the FIAT was the Pope's preferred ride. So in the interests of self-preservation, I'd stayed in the car until the lidocaine wore off, because when dealing with a gaggle of Sicilian nonne it was imperative that you be able to speak.

As I strode up the walkway, my apartment door flew open, and Glenda darted outside like a prostitute fleeing a police raid.

"What were *you* doing in there?" I asked, not without a note of panic. I'd intended to introduce Glenda to my family gradually—you know, like when you add fresh pasta to a pot of boiling water.

She dragged off her cigarette holder like it was a lifeline. "I came here looking for you," she replied, exhaling smoke as she spoke. "But before I knew what'd hit me, the Lilliputians had tied me up in this straight jacket."

The "Lilliputians" were, of course, my nonna and her nonne friends, none of whom were over five feet in height. And the so-called "strait jacket" was an Italian-flag-colored bib apron that read, "If you like my meatballs, wait till you try my sausage." Obviously, the nonne had used it to cover Glenda's nudity but hadn't grasped the double entendre. "Sorry about that. I was getting a cavity filled at Dr. Lessler's office."

Her brow shot up and her hip jutted out. "*Mitchell

Lessler?"

I nodded and rubbed my jaw.

A sultry smile spread across her face. "That handsome hunk of man can fill my cavity anytime."

"Forget about Lessler," I said, because now I really wanted her to. "What are the Lilliputians doing in there?"

"At first I thought they were having a funeral, sugar, but they said that Miss Santina's oven broke." Glenda yanked at the halter of her apron as though it were a noose around her neck. "So your nonna brought everyone over here since there are three ovens."

The funeral part I could understand since the nonne were perpetually in mourning dress, but it took me a second to register what she'd meant by "three ovens." Then I figured it out—mine, Veronica's, and… "They're baking in *your* kitchen *too*?"

She took another deep drag off her cigarette. "They've invaded the entire fourplex, Miss Franki."

My jaw dropped, and I covered my mouth with my hands.

"Even your costume closet?" I whispered, referring to the forbidden fourth apartment, the sole purpose of which was to house Glenda's prized collection of stripper wear.

She shook her head. "I convinced them that the kitchen was out of commission."

"*Grazie a Dio*," I breathed. Letting the nonne go inside Glenda's costume closet would've been like sending Santa's Elves to an S&M dungeon. "Where are my mom and nonna?"

"They took an extra bag of lemons to the church." She flicked some ash from her cigarette. "Do they serve lemonade at this St. Joseph's Day soiree?"

"Something like that," I replied, my tone as acidic as the yellow fruit.

The door to my apartment flew open again, and this time Santina Messina, Bruno's mom, appeared in the threshold. "Francesca!" she cried, clasping her hands. "*Figlia mia*!"

I was surprised to see her out of the wheelchair, but there was no time to comment. Instead, I assumed the customary limp position as she pinched my cheeks and smashed my face into her ample bosom, cutting off my air supply and cramming her cross necklace into my forehead. Thanks to the suffocating embraces of Santina and others like her, when I was a kid I not only frequently bore the sign of the cross on my skin, but I could hold my breath longer than anyone in my elementary school.

When she finally released me, I was excited to find that I could've held out another thirty seconds. I might be thirty, but I still had the lungs of a child.

"*Venite, venite,*" Santina urged, gesturing for us to follow her.

Glenda stubbed out her cigarette, and we went inside.

Thanks to a slew of twenty-five-pound flour sacks, endless crates of eggs, and a squad of not-so-lean but definitely mean nonne, my apartment looked and smelled more like an old world Sicilian bakery than a seventies brothel. I was kind of excited about the transformation, even though I was disappointed to see that the only thing the nonne were baking was bread.

Santina led us to the kitchen, and while I greeted the other nonne, she began filling the table with food—*grissini*, bread, an antipasti plate, *lasagne*, sardines, veal cutlets, eggplant, bell peppers, and a bottle of Nero d'Avola.

Meanwhile, Napoleon, who'd grown quite fond of the nonne and their food, assumed his begging spot beside the table.

"*Mangia!*" she exclaimed, shoving Glenda into a seat.

Glenda, who'd never been seen eating, grabbed a *grissino* and held the pencil-sized breadstick like she did her cigarette holder.

I, on the other hand, dug in with gusto, glad that my mouth was fully functional. And as I popped a piece of prosciutto into my mouth, it occurred to me that besides the food, the best things about nonne were that they called you "my child" regardless of your age, they thought you were wasting away no matter what your size, and they let you drink wine with pretty much every meal.

Santina pulled a bag of Swamp Nuts from her apron pocket and pressed it into my hand, beaming as though the Cajun-flavored corn nuts were nuggets of gold. "*Da Bruno.*"

I forced a smile at Bruno's untimely concession-stand gift.

"Pass me those nuts, sugar," Glenda said, showing a rare

interest in an edible item. "Maybe if I have a few of these, Mitchell Lessler can do some drilling on me."

I rolled my eyes and, since we were in the presence of the nonne, tried to steer the topic away from sex. "How do you know Lessler, anyway?"

Glenda picked up the bag and began fondling it like a sex toy. "In the stripping business, we share doctors like we do body oil."

A rolling pin clattered to the floor as the nonne stopped baking and began furiously crossing themselves.

So much for a sex-free conversation.

"Was Mitchell able to tell you anything about Amber?" Glenda continued, contemplating the corn nuts.

I glanced at the nonne and leaned forward. "It seemed like he thought that Amber was into voodoo, but her waxer implied that it was witchcraft," I replied in a low voice. "What I don't get is why Amber would need to resort to either one of those things if she was a tough, no-nonsense feminist like Saddle and Bit-O-Honey say."

"New Orleans has a long history of exotic dancing and an even longer history of mysticism and black magic, Miss Franki," Glenda explained as Santina deposited an empty plate in front of her and pointed at the food.

She locked eyes with Santina as she grabbed the *grissino* again, this time brandishing it like a bat, and then she turned to me. "I've seen girls come from as far away as Slovakia to dance here, and sooner or later they all do some kind of ritual before going onstage. And most of them will tell you that they don't do the ritual in any other city."

"A ritual I can understand," I said, pouring myself a glass of wine. "For example, I always put my clothes on in the same order."

"I'm not talking about OCD." She pointed the *grissino* at me. "I mean an honest to goodness ritual. I know this dancer from L.A. who buys an altar candle to gods and goddesses like Chango Macho or Oshun every time she comes here to help manifest her intention."

When she said "Chango," my mind drifted to Changos Taqueria in Austin. "I'm sorry," I said, shaking myself from my

Tex-Mex trance, "but did you say 'manifest her intention'?"

"Stripping is all about bringing attitude, money, and intent, sugar, and strip clubs are dark places. To be successful, you have to bring light into the club. So a dancer may do a candle ceremony, anoint herself with oil, carry a gris-gris bag, chant a spell, or whatever else to set her intent for luck, money, or beauty."

I slipped Napoleon a slice of *soppressata*. "But some of those things are voodoo, and some are witchcraft."

Glenda hiked up her apron and crossed her glittered legs, provoking a "*Santo Dio!*," a "*Gesù mio!*," and an "*Oh, Signore!*" from the nonne.

"It's a matter of preference," she explained, immune to their exclamations. "But what it boils down to is this—there's a belief in the industry, and in the city at large, that the spirit of New Orleans has to bless you if you want to be here and do well."

"*Now* you tell me." I grabbed my wine and wondered if that was where I'd gone wrong on the curse front. "Do you think that's what Amber was doing in the bathtub?"

"It doesn't square up to me," Glenda replied, flipping back her hair. "She wasn't dancing anymore—at least not for strip-club patrons."

I looked up from my glass. "What do you mean by that?"

She shrugged and tugged at her bib. "Maybe she danced for the devil."

I gasped. "As in satanic worship?"

There was a clatter of bread pans as several of the nonne dropped to their knees and invoked the assistance of the Madonna.

"Just kidding," I announced, my face as red as the wine.

Glenda eyed the nonne over her shoulder as though *they* were devil worshippers. "All I meant was that maybe Amber crossed paths with a plain old psychopath."

I sat back and sipped my wine. After talking to Dr. Lessler and Glenda, I was more confused than ever about what had gone on inside Madame Moiselle's. What I needed was some clarity. "Can you do something for me?"

"Shoot, sugar," she replied, waving her *grissino* like a

wand.

"Go to the club and talk to Saddle and Bit-O-Honey," I said, reaching into my purse for my wallet. "I want to know whether they ever saw or heard Amber doing any rituals, and what rituals the other dancers at the club do. Also, find out whether anyone has heard from Curaçao."

"Consider it done," she said, bouncing her crossed leg. "Where are you off to this fine morning?"

I pulled a business card from my coin purse. "I'm going to track down a warped witch."

* * *

"Was it necessary to meet in a graveyard?" I asked as I followed Theodora through St. Louis Cemetery No. 1, New Orleans's oldest burial ground and the final resting place for some of its most famous and infamous citizens. Between the creepy crypts and her black caftan, I was getting a bad case of the heebie-jeebies. "There's a CC's Coffee nearby, you know."

Her lips twisted like an old tree root. "I don't drink coffee. Besides, I have friends to see."

I started to tell her that as a three-hundred-year-old woman she might benefit from the energy boost, but I was too fearful of those "friends" she'd mentioned. "They're not coming to meet you now, are they?"

"They don't have to." She stopped in front of a crumbling gray mausoleum dated 1792 and patted the façade as though greeting an old pal. "They're already here."

A shiver shot through my spine like a spell from a sorceress's finger. As usual, this witch was weirding me out, and somehow it didn't help that she'd covered her crazy cat eyes with cat-eye sunglasses.

Theodora gave the ghoulish grave one last caress and resumed walking, her caftan billowing behind her like a shroud. "Why'd you summon me?"

I pulled the collar of my pea coat around my neck and stepped carefully along the cracked and broken concrete walkway. "I'm investigating a murder, and I need to know whether witches and voodoo practitioners ever borrow each other's methods."

She stopped dead in her tomb tracks. "Not on your life."

Like my nonna taught me, I pointed my index and pinky fingers down to cancel the curse she'd cast my way.

She cackled Maleficent-style. "What was that little gesture?"

I blinked, wishing that she hadn't seen my hand. According to Italian custom, there was an alternative to the gesture—men could tap one of their testicles, and women could touch iron. But that presented a problem for those of us who didn't know our metals. "It's called *scongiuri.*"

"It's novices like you who mix witchcraft, voodoo, and hoodoo," she said, pointing at my forehead. "Around here they call that Old New Orleans Traditional Witchcraft."

I lowered myself a little—on the off chance that she could actually shoot spells from her fingertip. "Is that jazz-inspired or something?"

She sighed, and I would swear that I saw a puff of smoke come out. "It's the everyday kind of witchcraft that your great-great grandmother used to do, but with a touch of voodoo or hoodoo thrown in."

I was a little taken aback by her assumption that my *bis-bis-nonna* was a witch. But if my nonna was any indication, Theodora may have been onto something. "Can you elaborate on that?"

"It's just goal-oriented spell-casting."

"Oh, *goal-oriented,*" I stressed in an it-was-as-obvious-as-the-wart-on-your-face tone. "As opposed to your regular, slacker spell-casting?"

She glanced over her shoulder, and for a split second it looked like her green eyes glowed behind her sunglass lenses. "It's the kind of spell work you do if you want something, like a job or a mate, but you need a little help to make it happen. It used to consist mainly of traditional supplies, but these days you can get more specialized items at Erzulie's and at Hex Old World Witchery down on Decatur."

Decatur Street was where Private Chicks was located, and as you can imagine, I wasn't wild about the news of the witchery.

"Look at the voodoo queen Marie Laveau's grave, and you'll see what I mean." She led me to an old, Greek Revival-style tomb covered with large x's.

I gasped. The marks were like the ones in Lili St. Cyr's bathtub—some were even circled. "What are those *X*'s?"

"Years ago some fool started the rumor that if you want Marie Laveau to grant your wish, you have to draw an *X* on the tomb, turn around three times, knock on the tomb, and then shout your wish. If it's granted, you have to come back and draw a circle around your *X* and leave Marie a gift, like these," she said, leading me to the front of the crypt.

I looked down, and amidst lipstick tubes, Mardi Gras beads, coins, and various trinkets was a boa constrictor. "Sweet Jesus!" I shouted, jumping back. "Is that snake alive?"

"Shhht!" Her black arms flapped like the wings of a raven. "You'll wake the dead."

Like a psycho, I glanced around in case that was really a thing.

"It's clearly an animal sacrifice," Theodora said as though she were schooling a slow sorcery student. "Now, you can see from the burnt candles and incense that witchcraft was involved, but so was voodoo."

I looked again at the *X*'s. "Have you ever heard of a mermaid queen named Jurate or any mermaids in the voodoo culture?"

She straightened her caftan collar. "I keep my distance from water women. They're a bitchy bunch."

I wanted to tell her that it takes one to know one, but I held my tongue for fear that she would take it and use it for some macabre magic. "What about amber?" I asked, opting to keep the necklace and its copy quiet. "Is it used in any spells?"

"All kinds," she replied, proceeding with her cemetery stroll. "For luck, love, protection, purification, prosperity, sexual energy, healing."

My ears pricked up at that last word because Dirk had said that Jurate was the deity of healing. Had Amber actually been invoking the mermaid queen? If so, what did she need to heal from? The possibilities were endless, not to mention obscure.

Theodora stopped in front of another mausoleum with a cracked, copper plate that read *Madame Lalaurie, née Marie Delphine Maccarthy, décédée à Paris, le 7 Décembre, 1842, à l'âge de 6—*.

I could make out enough of the French to know that it was the burial site of Delphine Lalaurie, a nineteenth-century socialite and sadistic serial killer of slaves. Despite being dead for over a century and a half, Lalaurie was still one of the most notorious killers in history—so much so that the TV series *American Horror Story* had created a fictionalized version of her for its "Coven" season.

Theodora dropped to her knees. "Madame Lalaurie, may I collect dirt from your grave?"

I didn't know what she was going to do with the dirt, but I took a step backwards nevertheless. It was wise to be wary of this witch.

She cocked her orange-red head to the side and nodded as though Lalaurie were speaking to her from beyond. Next, she pulled a spoon and a small wooden box from her pocket and began digging dirt from a crack in the concrete at the base of the tomb.

The dirt reminded me of Glenda's comment about the glass vial I'd found at Madame Moiselle's. I pulled the plastic baggie containing the vial from my purse. "Is this part of New Orleans witchcraft?"

Theodora opened the baggie and sniffed it. "Smells like a mugwort and dragon's blood blend I use in my spell work. Where'd you find it?"

I hesitated for a moment, remembering Detective Sullivan's request for discretion on the specifics of the case. But I seriously doubted that this witch was a snitch, and I hadn't used Amber's name, so I decided to give her some vague details. "Next to the crime scene. There was also a candle, some incense, and an unopened bottle of liquor."

"It could be a spell, except for the booze. That's a voodoo offering to some loa or other. I never can keep those damn gods straight." She returned to her digging. "And I can't understand why people leave food and drink for them. It's such a waste."

My sentiments exactly.

She put a spoonful of dirt into the box. "Where was the oil used?"

"Uh, in bath water," I replied evasively.

"Well, why didn't you say so?" she asked snapping the lid shut.

Before I could reply, she held out her hand to silence me. I watched as she dropped a dime in the hole and covered it with the remaining dirt.

"As I have paid you in silver, Madame Lalaurie, so shall you pay me in labor!" she shouted, staring at the crypt like she was spellbound.

At this point, I was *scongiuri*-ing left and right. I didn't know what this labor was that Lalaurie was supposed to do for her, but I hoped that she either couldn't or wouldn't do it right then.

"So anyway," Theodora said as she stood up and brushed off her caftan like she'd been gardening instead of grave digging, "your victim was probably doing some good old-fashioned bathtub witchcraft."

"*Bathtub* witchcraft?" I echoed. "Whatever happened to the cauldron? You know, 'double, double toil and trouble' and all of that?"

She lowered her sunglasses and laid her eerie irises on me. "You've been reading too much Shakespeare."

Honestly, I'd thought that the rhyme was from a Disney film, but I just went with it. "Do you have any idea whether that was a healing spell the victim was doing?"

"Nah." She walked toward another tomb. "That would've involved a lavender and vetiver blend. Based on the oil in that vial, it was most likely an anti-hex spell."

I looked up in surprise. It didn't make sense for Amber to invoke Jurate for healing if what she was after had to do with hexes. "So, does this spell ward off the evil eye?"

"It undoes a curse that someone has already placed on you. And if your victim bought the spell, then he or she was definitely fighting witchcraft with witchcraft." She stopped to scowl at a pyramid-shaped tomb covered in lipstick prints with the Latin inscription *omnia ab uno*, all from one.

I recognized the kissed crypt from the local news as the one the actor Nicolas Cage had bought for his eventual demise. Suddenly, I longed for a shot. "But how does the bottle of booze fit in?"

"Like I said, Old New Orleans Traditional Witchcraft is often a mix." She plucked a weed from the exposed bricks of a deteriorated mausoleum and popped it into her mouth. "Your victim could've included a voodoo offering for good measure, or the killer might have put it there to throw you off track. But either way, you need to start by finding the witch who put the spell on your victim."

My stomach bubbled like a cauldron at the sight of her chewing that weed. "And how, exactly, does one find a witch?"

She turned and headed toward the exit. "One looks for the signs."

"Like, a third nipple?" I asked hopefully. I mean, that wouldn't be hard to spot given the nature of this case.

She spun around and removed her sunglasses as her feline eyes flashed.

I flinched, halfway expecting her to turn me into a big boob.

"I was talking about a pagan tattoo or jewelry," she said between clenched teeth. "Like a triangle or a moon or a goddess."

My blood ran as cold as a witch's teat. All this time I'd been focusing on Curaçao as the possible killer. But now I was wondering whether I'd made a potentially costly mistake. Because I'd seen someone at the club with a crescent moon tattoo.

And that someone was Saddle.

CHAPTER THIRTEEN

———

When I walked into Lucky Pierre's, a Bourbon Street gay bar as famous for its 3-for-1 happy hours as it was for its drag and burlesque shows, the old wooden door groaned in protest.

"Can't you read the *closed* sign, Hunty?" a Lucy Liu lookalike shouted from behind the bar.

"Mind your manners, Miss Gaysia," Glenda said as she stood up from her stool in black thigh-high boots and a belted cutout romper that was more cut than not. "Miss Franki's with me."

"What's a 'hunty'?" I whispered, hiding my mouth with my hand.

"A combination of honey and the *C* word," she replied and then turned to the bitchy bar queen. "She'll have what I'm having."

Gaysia gave me a glacial glare and grabbed a glass.

Ignoring the drag diva's dis, I tossed my bag onto the transparent, liquid-filled bar counter and spotted a holster on Glenda's thigh. "What are you dressed as, anyway? A frisky FBI agent?"

She looked at me like I'd pulled a gun on her. "This is my private-investigating suit."

If anything, she looked more like a slutty spy than a private eye. "You're not actually packing heat, are you?"

"I'm just using this holster to hold my PI supplies," she replied, returning to her seat.

Prudently passing on asking about those supplies, I took a quick look around instead. Lucky Pierre's had once been a brothel, and it showed. The two-story structure had a wide staircase that appeared custom-made for grand entrances, and it was decorated with sensual chandeliers, gilded crown moldings, sumptuous sofas, and a rainbow-shaped *Sinners* sign that served as a nod to the bar's *sexplicit* past and present. Thanks to the décor of my apartment, I felt instantly at home there.

Glenda scrutinized my face as she handed me the champagne. "You look like you've seen a ghost, sugar."

I took a sip and slid onto the stool beside her. "No, just a witch."

She didn't bat a feather false eyelash at my reply. "How'd you know where to find me?"

"I stopped by the club looking for Saddle, and Bit-O-Honey said you'd come here to talk to Carnie." I scanned the room and spotted a Céline Dion doppelganger at a table in front of the stage. "Where is she, anyway?"

"She'll be down in a minute." Glenda motioned to Gaysia for another glass of champagne. "She's getting ready to perform."

It was only one o'clock, and Lucky Pierre's didn't open until four. "It takes her three hours to get ready?" I asked. Then I remembered Carnie's fearsome five o'clock shadow. "Never mind. Are you here to talk to her about the case?"

"About arranging a funeral for Amber," she replied as she reached for her cigarette holder and lighter. "We entertainers take care of our own."

"Well, a few of the witnesses have said that Amber had a mother." I angled a glance at Gaysia expecting her to go off about the *no smoking* sign above the bar. "You might want to find out what her plans are."

"This is the first I've heard of any mother." She lit her cigarette and exhaled. "It seems odd that she hasn't come up before."

I had to agree. And it was even odder that she hadn't come forward despite considerable publicity about the case. "What'd you find out about the dancers' rituals?"

"So far I've only talked to the girls on the early shift," she replied as she adjusted a gadget on her belt. "Bit-O-Honey said that Amber used to light a candle before dancing, but that's all she remembers."

This was big news. If Amber had been into lighting

candles, then doing a spell wasn't out of the realm of possibility. "What about the others?"

"The usual things," she said with a shrug. "Anointing themselves with oil, rubbing a dildo, carrying a lucky condom."

I had some questions about that condom, but it was better not to ask. My stomach was already queasy from the lava-lamp-like counter.

"Hello my lovelies," a falsetto voice crooned from the second floor. "And Franki," it added in a low, flat pitch.

I smirked and looked up as Carnie sashayed down the staircase like a coquette at cotillion. Only, with her Mimi makeup, wig cap, and the lifelike latex breastplate strapped around her neck, she looked more like the Bride of Frankenstein.

Glenda raised her glass. "Ladies and lady-boys, Miss Carnie Vaul."

Carnie sauntered over and placed a manicured hand on her faux flesh. "Do you have an update on the case?"

Her boobie-bib was more embarrassing than Bit-O-Honey's bare bosom, so I was glad to have an excuse to turn away. "Gaysia, can you give us a minute?"

She gasped and stomped over to Céline, who was contouring her nose.

I started to lean in, but because of the boobs—live and latex—I opted to lower my voice instead. "After consulting with a local witchcraft expert, I think Amber was doing an anti-hex spell when she died." I shifted in my seat before asking the next question, realizing how silly it would sound. "Can either of you think of anyone who would've put a hex on her?"

"Curaçao, of course," Carnie said, putting her hands on her hoopskirt-sized hips. "I don't know if she was a witch *witch*, but she was definitely a witch *bitch*."

"Thanks for clearing that up," I said, shooting her a sideways glance. "I'll follow up on the witchcraft angle with Maybe."

"What about that Etsy charge?" Carnie asked. "Did you follow up on that?"

I tossed back the rest of my champagne. "It turned out to be for a copy of your amber necklace."

"That shady ho," she breathed. Then she stormed behind

the bar and helped herself to a shot.

Glenda leaned back on her stool and kicked her lipstick-heeled boots onto the counter. "I'll bet Amber planned to swap the copy with the original."

"That's what I'm thinking," I said. "But I should notify the police in case there's more to it than that."

Carnie lurched forward, causing her bib to bounce. "So you're going to turn me in for opening her credit card bill?"

"Down, woman," I said, holding up my hands in case she hopped the bar. "I don't have to reveal my sources."

Her blue-shadowed lids lowered to half-mast à la Herman Munster. "You'd better hope you don't."

Unfazed by Carnie's behavior, Glenda blew a couple of smoke hearts. "What makes you think this copy is relevant, Miss Franki?"

"Until we know where it is, I won't know whether it's relevant or not. What I need to figure out is whether the necklace is related to that mermaid on the tub." I turned to Carnie. "That reminds me, is there any chance that Amber was Lithuanian?"

"She was as Cajun as they come," she replied as she poured herself some Piehole whiskey. "Why?"

I put my forearms on the bar. "There was a drawing of a mermaid at the crime scene, and amber is associated with the legend of a mermaid who promotes healing."

"Amber wasn't sick or broken, okay?" Carnie said, pointing the bottle of whiskey at me. "Now I don't know why that mermaid was there, but we need to be clear on something— it didn't have a damn thing to do with fixing Amber."

I eyed the Piehole and wished that Carnie would shut hers.

"What about your necklace?" Glenda asked as she stubbed out her cigarette in the dregs of her drink. "Why do you think she was wearing it?"

Carnie slammed the bottle onto the bar. "Maybe she liked it, I don't know. But I can tell you this—she stole it because she wanted to sell it, not because she wanted to invoke some mermaid. That girl was about money and whatever it took to get it. End of story."

My sense was that she was right about the reason Amber

stole the necklace. But because Theodora had confirmed that amber was used in witchcraft, I had to consider all the possible angles.

The door groaned, and a Dolly Parton drag queen in an Elly May Clampett costume flounced into the bar. She took a seat next to Glenda and tossed a roll of Tuck Tape into Carnie's outstretched hand.

Carnie gave her the once over. "Pure country realness."

"Well, you know what I always say," Drag Dolly said as chipper as a chipmunk as she fluffed her breasts. "It costs a lot of money to look this cheap."

"Truth, gurl." Carnie turned and eyeballed my ten-dollar Target turtleneck. "Speaking of cheap, if you don't have anything else for me, then I need to finish painting."

"By all means," I said. And I meant it.

Carnie placed her whiskey on the bar and exchanged air kisses with Glenda.

I glanced at the amber liquid, and a thought occurred to me. "You guys—I mean, ladies—wouldn't happen to know of a voodoo god that drinks amaretto, would you?"

"Oh, I would," Dolly replied, tightening the bow in her wig. "The patron of gays and trans just loves amaretto, but her favorite is pink champagne."

"Now that's a voodoo goddess I can get behind," Glenda said before tossing back the last of her bubbly. "Which loa is this, sugar?"

Dolly toyed with the frayed ends of her rope belt. "Erzulie Freda."

As soon as she said the name, I thought of the painting at Erzulie's Authentic Voodoo. The sales woman had said that Erzulie Freda was the goddess of love, among other things. But it didn't make sense to invoke a love loa during an anti-hex spell. And yet I knew that's what had happened because the bottle said it all.

Amaretto di Amore.

* * *

As I made my way up Canal Street to Ponchartrain

Bank, I was met by an army of women in bodysuits, tights, and legwarmers. It was a terrifying sight, like an invasion of the '80s, but I forged through the fit females like a tank. All the talk about the goddess of love had made me want to see Bradley, and the fact that the goddess liked to drink had reminded me that I needed to invite him over to see my mom and nonna. If he didn't come there would be hell to pay, and my nonna would make sure that I was the one who paid it.

When I finally made it inside the bank lobby, I could see that Ruth was worked up about something. My first clue was the pursed look on her perpetually puckered mouth. The second was that the chains hanging from the sides of her black horn-rimmed reading glasses were swinging like swords at a fencing fight.

I eyed Bradley's closed door as I approached Ruth's desk. "Is everything okay?"

She tightened her gray-brown bun. "I've just been informed that I need to make last-minute travel arrangements for twelve board members—and during a national Jazzercise convention, no less."

That explained the warrior-like workout women.

"And I'll tell you what," Ruth said, pointing a letter opener at my gut. "If one more person comes in here and shakes their jazz hands at me, I'm gonna up and stab someone."

Given that I was ethnically inclined to gesture when I spoke, I took a step back. "Wait. Bradley just met with the board in New York. Why are they coming here?"

She bowed her head. "The bank lost two more big clients yesterday, and a third is threatening to follow suit. If I were a betting woman—which I'm not," she clarified with a flourish of her letter opener, "I'd wager that a certain bank manager named Jeff Payne was behind this business."

I happened to know that Ruth never missed Saturday night bingo at the Napoleon Room in Metairie and that she practically had a lifetime subscription to the Louisiana Lottery, but she called that "gaming," not "gambling," and I didn't dare disagree. "Why do you say that? Did you trace Jeff's restaurant receipt to Martin Slater?"

She put her hands on her thighs and jutted out her lower lip. "Mr. Slater's secretary confirmed that he had lunch with Jeff at Casamento's."

I was at a loss for words.

She grimaced, and the lines around her lips bled into her cheeks. "And that's not the worst of it."

I found my words. "Well, what is?"

"A few of the board members have been calling the clients who've abandoned ship." She paused and glanced around to make sure that no one was listening. "And apparently, every one of them has received the same anonymous letter."

I put my hand to my mouth. Anonymous letters abounded in the Sicilian culture, and they inevitably involved *le corna*, or bull horns, which were a symbol of infidelity in Italy. "What does it say?"

"No idea." She grabbed a peppermint from a candy dish and popped it into her mouth. "But that's still not the worst of it."

This time I took a step forward. "Would you just tell me what the worst of it is?" I asked through gritted teeth. "Or do I need to show *you* the worst of it?"

"Now don't go gettin' all pissy on me, missy." She sat back and raised her nose in the air. "I'm the one who's been trying to save your beau's behind while you've been out toodlin' around in a titty bar."

I clenched my fists one finger at a time. "How many times do I have to tell you that I'm working a homicide at Madame Moiselle's?"

"It's none of my never mind what a woman like yourself is doing in a gentlemen's club." She looked from side to side again and leaned forward. "But you should know that the anonymous mailer, aka Mr. Payne In The Rear, has also been sending out compromising photographs with that letter."

My mouth went as dry as her demeanor. "What do you mean by 'compromising'?"

Ruth threw her hands in the air. "Well, if I don't know what's in the letter, then I don't know what's in the photos, do I?" She arched an over-tweezed eyebrow and moved so close that I could smell her minty fresh breath. "But evidently they have something to do with Bradley."

"Bradley?" I shouted, wondering whether the type of compromising we were talking about was the *corna* kind. "What makes you think that?"

"Because the board is convening on Monday to discuss his future with the bank," she replied with a know-it-all nod. "That's what."

The news hit me like a pair of bull horns. If Bradley lost his job over a scandal, he'd have to leave New Orleans to find another bank position. On the other hand, depending on what was in those photographs, I might run him out of town myself.

Bradley walked out of his office, and I noticed that his face was drawn and pale. "Hey, babe," he said, sounding tired. "I thought I heard your voice."

I shook myself from my shock and forced a fake smile. I couldn't let him know that I knew the scoop. "You were right," I said as jolly as Drag Dolly at a square dance. "I'm here."

He pulled me into an embrace, and part of me wanted to hug him to make everything all better, but the other half of me wanted to hit him—just in case.

In the meantime, I locked eyes with Ruth over his shoulder. "*Get me that letter and those pics,*" I mouthed. "*ASAP.*"

Bradley released me and brushed a lock of hair from my cheek. "You seem stressed. What's going on?"

I resisted the urge to reply, "That's the sixty-four-thousand-dollar question, isn't it?" Instead, I said, "It's Mom and Nonna. They're expecting you to drop by tonight, and you know they'll be offended if you don't."

"Of course." He ran his hand through his hair and glanced at his watch. "I have to take care of some things here first. Would eight be too late?"

"Not at all," I said, sickly sweet. Then I scoured his face for clues to the content of those photos.

Bradley narrowed his eyes, obviously suspecting that something was up. "Franki—"

My ringtone sounded.

"I'd better take this," I gushed, pulling my phone from my bag.

"Okay, but we need to talk later." He gave me a peck on the lips. "Right now I've gotta get moving if I'm going to make it to your place on time."

"See you tonight," I said, wondering just what it was that we had to talk about. Then I glanced at the unknown number on the cell display and pressed answer. "Franki Amato."

"Is this Franki Amato?" a female asked.

I rolled my eyes. "That's what I just said."

"This is Bit?" she said in an up-talker tone. "From Madame Moiselle's?"

"Oh, right," I replied, realizing for the first time that she was using "O'Honey" as a surname. "What can I do for you?"

"Miss Glenda said that you're to get down here right away," she said, her voice descending like a dancer down a pole.

Apprehension filled my chest. "Can you tell me why?"

"Because we have a situation," she replied, matter-of-fact.

For some reason I got a sudden mental image of her boobs bobbing about and was instantly irked. "What kind of situation?"

She cleared her throat. "A few minutes ago I asked Iris to pull the honey pot from the storage room for my performance today."

I waited for her to explain the "situation," but apparently, she thought she already had. "And?"

"It wasn't full of honey!"

I sighed. Getting information out of Bit-O-Honey was like pulling pasties from a stripper. "What was it full of?"

"Curaçao."

My heart took a nosedive. I felt bad for suspecting her, and now I had to face the frightening possibility that there were more murders to come.

"Um," Bit-O-Honey hedged, breaking the silence, "you know I'm not talking about the liquor, right?"

"Yeah, I gathered that," I grumbled as I headed for the lobby exit.

"Good," she said sounding pleased as punch. "Because that pot wasn't made to hold real honey or liquid. But anyway, Miss Glenda said that I was to tell you one more thing."

I waited, but she said nothing. "And what would that be, exactly?"

"Curaçao is wearing an amber necklace."

My stomach joined my heart in a tandem free fall. "I'll be right there."

I hung up and hurried onto Canal Street. As I jogged through the Jazzercisers, I wasn't worried about whether Curaçao was wearing the original necklace or the copy, nor was I thinking about witchcraft or voodoo. Because all I could think about was the curse that supposedly followed those who hunted the Amber Room.

Was the curse what had done Amber and Curaçao in?

CHAPTER FOURTEEN

————

"The cops are going to have to break the pot to get Curaçao out," Glenda said as I entered the prop room. "She's as stiff as a male member."

I shot her a you-didn't-just-go-there glare. "Couldn't you go with something predictable, like 'crystalized honey'?"

"I call it like I see it, Miss Franki." She struck a stripper pose. "And, child, I see a lot of it."

I knew for a fact that she did. "How do you know about the condition of her body? You didn't touch her, did you?"

"Lord, no," she said with a flip of her hair. "Iris tipped the pot, but she wouldn't budge."

I glanced around the room, and nothing seemed out of order. "Were you in here when he came to move it to the stage?"

"No, Bit-O-Honey was," she replied, taking a seat on the hay bale. "Eugene and I came in when Iris started to scream."

It figured that the burly bouncer would be the one to get emotional. "Has anyone else been in here?"

"Eugene kept the others out." She put her hands behind her and stuck out her chest. "And as you can see, the police are taking their sweet time."

That was okay by me, especially if Detective Sullivan was coming. He would kick me out of the club faster than Carlos could say, "closing time." "Did any of you notice anything unusual?"

"Just that." She pointed the toe of her boot toward the other side of the honey pot.

I walked over to where she'd been standing and saw an unopened pack of Pall Mall cigarettes beside a bottle of rum. There were whole peppers inside the bottle, and I would've bet my soul that there were twenty-one of them.

"It's an offering to—"

"Baron Samedi, the loa of death," I interrupted. In one way or another, the voodoo god of the underworld had been involved in all the homicide cases I'd worked since moving to New Orleans. I tried to remember where I'd seen his image recently but couldn't.

Glenda removed a flashlight from her PI belt and placed it in my hand. "Take a look in the pot."

Anxiety ate at my gut as I peered over the edge. Curaçao was wearing a crimson Juicy Couture tracksuit, and on her feet were beige Uggs. She was in a seated position with her knees drawn to her chest, presumably because of the cramped space, and her arms were hanging at her sides. The worst part was that her head was thrown back and her eyes were frozen with fear, and it seemed like they were staring straight at me. I switched on the flashlight and shined it on her chest. The amber pendant came to life as though emphasizing her demise—and the purplish marks on her neck.

"How long do you think she's been in there, sugar?" Glenda asked in a pensive tone.

I studied Curaçao's scratched arms and the porcelain skin of her legs. "I'm not a medical examiner, but I'd say at least ten to twelve hours. That's how long it takes rigor mortis to set in."

"Well, it's around three o'clock now," she said, checking the clasp on her handgun earring, "and I'm guessing that the murder took place when the club was closed. So it could've happened as late as five by your estimation."

I stepped away from the pot unable to stomach any more of the sickening sight and handed the flashlight to Glenda. "Will you find out who worked last night and who was here after closing?"

"I'll get right on it." She returned the flashlight to her belt and pulled a penis pen and pad from her holster. "Do you think she was strangled like Amber?"

"Most likely," I replied, massaging my temples after seeing that writing instrument. "But the crime scene is different. For one thing, Curaçao's not nude in a bathtub."

"But she *is* inside a stage prop," Glenda said, pointing at the honey pot. "And there's a bottle of liquor beside it."

"True." I stood up and started to pace. "And she's wearing an amber necklace or the copy. The thing that's missing is the witchcraft."

She scribbled a note on the pad. "What's that got to do with it?"

"Witchcraft was a big part of Amber's murder." I looked at Lili St. Cyr's tub. "The killer knew about the spell and brought a specific brand of Amaretto to complete the scene."

"Are you saying that you think Curaçao was killed by someone else?" she asked, toggling the penis pen back and forth between her fingers.

"It's a possibility." I sat beside her on the bale. "But what I mean is that this doesn't seem like a killer who's targeting a coven. The Amaretto di Amore suggests that Amber's murder had something to do with love, but Curaçao was probably killed because she witnessed the killing. After all, we know that she was here the morning it happened."

Glenda tapped the pen on her lip. "Then she went into hiding, and he found her."

My mind went to the masked man, and I shuddered as I wondered whether he'd been hunting me. "It looks that way, doesn't it?"

She chewed the tip of her pen. "But if he was just killing her to cover his bases, why the offering to Baron Samedi?"

I stared at the rum and cigarettes. "Maybe just to let us know that the crimes are connected."

Police sirens sounded in the distance, and I leapt to my feet. That was my cue to get some last-minute questioning done before they made their way through the bacchanalia on Bourbon Street, and I knew exactly where to start. "Is Saddle here?"

"She's in the dressing room." Glenda stood up in her stiletto thigh-highs. "Eugene told the girls to wait there until the cops came."

"Good, because Saddle's got some splainin' to do," I said as I exited the prop room.

As I climbed to the second floor with Glenda in tow, I could smell the aroma of Eve's cooking. And my stomach—which remained steadfast in times of sorrow, strife, stress, even sickness—reminded me that it hadn't eaten lunch.

"You should say hello to Miss Eve, sugar," Glenda prompted, sounding worried. "She's devastated about Curaçao, but she's staying strong for everyone else. I tell you, that woman is pure Southern steel."

Although I was pressed for time, I wanted to show my support for Eve. "I'll meet you in the dressing room."

I popped my head into the kitchen.

Eve had her back to me at the stove, and Iris was at the table with his head in his hands.

"Oh, I'm so glad you've come, Miss Franki," Eve said, turning to greet me. "Isn't it just awwwful? We haven't even buried Amber yet."

I put my hands on her shoulders and looked into her grief-stricken eyes. "I promise I'll do my best to find whoever did this to her."

"Thank yewww." She clasped her face. "I can't wrap my mind around the fact that she's gone."

Iris burst into tears, and Eve rushed to his side. "There there," she cooed as she patted his back. "It's gonna be all right. You just sit tight while I git you some Hoppin' John."

For a second I considered crying to get some of the spicy black-eyed pea and rice mixture, but I had a dancer to question, and quick.

"Here you go, hon," Eve said, preparing Iris's plate. She put the food in front of him and then pulled a lighter from her apron pocket and lit a white candle.

I couldn't help but smile as I exited into the hallway. It was just like a Southern woman to worry about table ambience at a time like this, even if the candle was shaped like a nude woman.

The door to the dressing room swung open, and Saddle stepped out looking like a pole-dancer Pocahontas in a skimpy suede number with Native American jewelry. "Glenda said you were looking for me?"

Time was of the essence, so I got down to turquoise tacks. "You told me that Amber wasn't the superstitious type, and yet Bit-O-Honey said that Amber always lit a magick candle before going onstage. How is it that you managed to miss that?"

She smiled, but her eyes didn't. "I come here to work. I don't pay attention to what the other girls are doing."

I nodded to make her think that I believed her. "From what I hear, it's common for dancers in New Orleans to perform some sort of ritual for luck before a show. I take it you don't subscribe to that sort of thing?"

She gazed at me as she toyed with her long, black braid. "That kind of BS is for the weak."

"Is that because you don't believe in it, or because you're into something more powerful?" I paused for effect. "Like witchcraft?"

Her lips parted. "What are you talking about?"

"That crescent moon tattoo on your calf," I replied, pointing to the area that was once again covered, this time by moccasin boots. "It's a pagan symbol popular with witches."

"It's also the symbol of my company logo, Crescent Moon Saddles," she said, her voice slick with sarcasm.

Glenda popped her head out of the dressing room. "Miss Franki, we need you in here."

I gave Saddle a long, hard look. "For your sake," I said as I stepped into the room, "I hope that business brand checks out."

Before the door closed behind me, I stole a glance at Saddle.

Her face was expressionless, but the suede fringe on her costume was shaking.

* * *

"Uh-uh. No. Not a chance," I said, staring at my reflection in the dressing room mirror.

"But it's the perfect solution, sugar." Glenda looked up from her kneeling position at my feet. "The Saints, Sinners, and Sluts Revue is tomorrow night, and you have Amber's coloring and height."

"I don't care if I'm her clone. There's no way I'm going to strip to lure a potential killer." I tried to think of a solid justification—other than the extra twenty pounds I was carrying around my waist—but nothing was coming to me.

"You might want to reconsider," Bit-O-Honey advised as she tied a halter-top fashioned from scarves at my back. "Tomorrow's St. Patrick's Day, and those Irish guys lay out a lot of green." She met my gaze in the mirror. "You know I mean cash, not clover, right?"

"Yeah, I got that." I struggled not to roll my eyes and then seized on the holiday as my excuse. "But Catholics aren't allowed to strip on saint's days."

Bit-O-Honey leaned around my side, her bare breasts bumping into the back of my arm. "You should become a Unitarian. We can do whatever."

I fought off the urge to add, "like going topless in public, apparently." *I mean, I realized that I was in a strip club and all, but was it too much to ask for the woman to cover herself?*

"Shakey had a weakness for Amber, Miss Franki," Glenda explained as she wrapped an orange and black scarf around my hips. "If Madame Moiselle's advertises you as Amber's Texan cousin, Tiger Eye, I'm sure that would draw him to the club."

I didn't want to admit it, but her argument made sense. And now that I had a couple of homicide investigations under my belt I *was* starting to feel more comfortable in my own skin—but not so much so that I wanted to bare it onstage. On the other hand, I did need to question Shakey, especially since he'd been involved with both Amber and Curaçao. And if stripping could prevent another murder, I was in no position to refuse. "But I can't even dance. How could I perform a routine?"

"Don't think of it as dancing." Glenda inserted a pin into the fabric. "Stripping is a series of seductive poses set to music."

"Miss Glenda and I could teach you," Bit-O-Honey said brightly. "And since you've got the whole tiger thing going on, we could do a desert theme."

I didn't bother to correct her.

Glenda picked up her pincushion and rose to her feet. "This should give you an idea of what your costume will look like." She stepped back to admire her handiwork. "Keep in mind that I'll make a few adjustments when I sew it."

I stared at myself in the mirror. The skirt looked a lot like a loincloth, and based on the way my belly was bulging over it, I was glad that I hadn't had any of Eve's Hoppin' John. "Could you add a panel of fabric to cover my stomach? I look like a tubby Tarzan."

Glenda stuck out her hip and her lip. "Tarzan didn't have breasts like yours, sugar. At least, not the one on TV."

Bit-O-Honey giggled, and I looked from her to Glenda to get in on the joke.

"I was talking about one of our VIP Room regulars, sugar."

"Yeah, he's got big ol' man boobs." Bit-O-Honey cupped her breasts for emphasis. "But we call him Tarzan because he asks us to wear chimp masks and pound on our chests while he feeds us bananas."

My mouth fell open. If I didn't solve this case soon, these VIP Room escapades were going to drive me bananas.

Veronica opened the door. "Hey, ladies."

I covered my halter top with my hands. "What're you doing here?"

She looked at my loincloth and blinked hard. "Glenda called me. But the question is, what are *you* doing here?"

"That *is* a good question, Veronica." I glowered in Glenda's direction. "Why don't you ask the consultant you hired?"

"Never mind that now." Veronica motioned with her eyes to the hallway. "Detective Sullivan is outside, and he'd like to interview the dancers. Is everyone decent?"

"Let me check." Glenda inspected her posterior in the mirror.

Bit-O-Honey glanced at everyone's body but her own. "We're good."

"Speak for yourself," I said, reaching for my turtleneck.

Detective Sullivan entered and practically patted me down with his eyes. "Sorry to break up your little rehearsal, Amato, but I need you in the hallway—*before* you change out of your Great Pumpkin costume."

He strode from the room, slamming the door behind him.

Stinging from the squash comparison, I yanked on my sweater, which happened to be burnt orange, and glared at

Glenda. "Get to work on that stomach panel."

As I exited into the hallway, Detective Sullivan pointed a finger at my chest. "What the hell do you think you're doing playing dress up while there's a dead body downstairs?"

I couldn't tell him that I was preparing to set a trap for the killer, or he'd charge me with interfering in an investigation. Instead, I gave him my best blank stare.

"So that's the way it's going to be, huh?" His eyes locked onto mine like a pair of handcuffs. "Fine by me. Because I already have an idea of what's going on here. But for your sake, I hope I'm wrong."

A heavy-set officer came out of Eugene's office. "We're done with Stripper Sacagawea, Detective." He wrinkled his lips like he was suppressing a laugh. "Who's up next?"

Saddle pushed past the officer and flashed him a fiery look as she headed for the stairs.

"Bring in the manager. I'll be right there." Detective Sullivan turned to me. "You'd better be gone by the time I'm done with Mr. Michael, or I'll escort you to the door myself and maybe to jail."

I was so angry that I almost stormed from the club in my costume, but then I got a better idea. I had a couple of bargaining chips, and I intended to use them. "Before you do anything drastic, I suggest you hear me out. I've uncovered a couple of things that could be useful to you."

He studied my face like it was a piece of evidence. "I'm listening."

"Not so fast." I took a step forward to show him that I could play bad cop too. "I need some information from you first."

The detective's eyes did a Dirty Harry. "Such as?"

I swallowed and prepared to fire off a round of questions. "Eugene mentioned that the club doesn't use the surveillance equipment after hours. I'm assuming you verified this?"

"You assumed correctly." He crossed his arms.

"What about Amber?" I imitated his stance. "Have you been able to track down her last address?"

He pursed his lips. "She was living alone in a pricey

condo in the business district."

So Amber *had* been getting money from somewhere, possibly her mother. Or Shakey. "What about her next of kin? And her ex?"

"We have reason to believe the ex-boyfriend's in town, and we've verified that she was orphaned at the age of thirteen."

The news that Shakey was in New Orleans was even more reason to submit to Glenda's stripping scheme, but I wasn't willing to dismiss Maybe and Nadezhda's accounts of Amber's controlling mom. "That's strange, because two witnesses reported hearing her on the phone with her mother."

"Could be a close family friend." He leaned a shoulder against the wall. "Now what do you have for me?"

Evidently, my question-and-answer session was over. "A small glass vial I found near the main stage."

He tilted his head. "How do you know it's related to the case?"

"A hunch," I replied, already bracing myself for his reaction to what I was about to say. "I'm almost positive it came from a witchcraft spell kit Amber was using for protection."

A sneer unfurled across his face like a roll of crime scene tape. "That's rich, Amato. What else you got?"

I didn't care that he'd laughed off the witchcraft, because that only increased my odds of cracking the case before he did. Plus, I knew he'd take what I had to say next more seriously. "A credit card bill that links Amber to the purchase of a copy of the amber necklace."

His sneer faded. "I won't bother asking how you got that because I know I'd be wasting my breath." The steely glint in his eyes was menacing, like his tone. "But I expect you to turn it over immediately."

"It's at my place. I'll drop it by the police station with the vial." I paused as I thought of the pendant on Curaçao's neck. "Would you please do one thing for me?"

He snorted. "If you think I'm going to give you any more tips, you've flipped your jack-o-lantern lid."

I was pretty sure that my eyes flashed fire, and I imagined myself taking him down like I'd learned to do in police training. "Just keep the details of the necklace—and the copy—

quiet from here on out."

Detective Sullivan raised his chin like he was prepping to punch a perp. "I told your colleague, Ms. Maggio, that my men and I would keep the pendant out of the investigation, and I've kept my word."

"That's great," I said. But it wasn't.

"Now you get out of here and bring me that bill within the hour." He shot me a cold, cop stare. "You understand?"

I nodded even though I hadn't heard a word he'd said. I was too busy trying to figure out how a suspect could've known about the amber pendant if the police hadn't mentioned it.

And any way I looked at it, it didn't look good for Eugene.

CHAPTER FIFTEEN

———

My front door opened, and three white-haired women in black entered.

The nonne were increasing in number.

As Santina greeted the newcomers, I fed an *arancino* I'd plucked from a dinner platter to Napoleon and then looked across the kitchen table at Veronica. "How do you think Bradley's going to react to nine nonne under one roof?"

She tapped her cell display. "I don't know, but I wouldn't miss it for the world."

I scrutinized her bent head as I grabbed one of the fried stuffed rice balls for myself. Even though she was my best friend, it sometimes seemed like she had a serious case of *schadenfreude* where I was concerned.

"Crescent Moon Saddles looks legit." She held up her phone.

I leaned forward and studied the company's website on her browser. The brand image matched the tattoo on Saddle's calf to a T. "Well, it doesn't prove she's not a witch, but I have to admit that she doesn't strike me as one." I sat back in my chair. "And now that I know Eugene was aware of the pendant, I've shifted my sights to him. He doesn't have an alibi, and since he didn't run video surveillance after hours, he could've easily committed the murders."

She arched a blonde brow. "As a crime of passion?"

"For me, the Amaretto di Amore suggests that love was a factor, but he denies being involved with Amber or Curaçao." I bit into the *arancino*. "The thing I can't figure out is the part the necklaces play in all of this."

"What can I do to help?" She placed her phone on the table.

I wiped my hands on a napkin. "Do you know whether David has found anything on Amber's mother?"

She shook her head. "Not that I know of."

"Crap." I tossed the napkin on the table. "Then you look into the mom and have him pull any info he can find on Old New Orleans Traditional Witchcraft and the voodoo goddess Erzulie Freda."

"What about Baron Samedi?" she asked as she began typing a text to David.

For a split second, I almost remembered where I'd seen the Baron, but then the memory was gone. "I'm already way too familiar with him," I replied, chewing the rest of my rice ball as I grabbed another. "What I need to know is whether the amber had anything to do with the protection spell Amber was performing or with Erzulie."

"I may have to handle the research myself." She picked up a fork. "Your nonna's keeping David pretty busy."

I dropped my *arancino* and my jaw. "How the hell does she know David?"

Veronica piled prosciutto onto her plate. "Apparently, you told her about him and his fraternity."

My jaw fell open again. I was astonished at my ability to underestimate my nonna. I closed my mouth, but not before taking a bite of the *arancino*. "What's she having him do? Build a robot for me to marry?"

"He and his frat brothers are creating a computerized model of the St. Joseph's Day altar." She rolled a slice of the cured ham. "She wanted them to make it too, but they don't know how to build anything in real life."

That was hardly surprising. Comp-Sci geeks weren't known for their construction skills. "But the altar is usually just a bunch of card tables they push together. Why does Nonna need a special design?"

She picked at the prosciutto. "To make sure you have easy access to the lemons."

Rage rocketed through my body, and I squeezed the

arancino so hard that tomato-sauce-coated rice, mozzarella, and peas oozed between my fingers.

"Um, not to change the subject," she said, looking at my hand with eyes as round as ravioli, "but have you had any more run-ins with the man in black?"

"As far as I know, I haven't been followed." I stood up and went to the sink. "Maybe he came back over here, and the nonne scared him away."

Veronica didn't laugh because that scenario was all too possible—probable, even.

The toilet flushed, and my nonna shuffled into the kitchen chewing on a toothpick. She kept one in her mouth whenever food was around to spear herself the occasional olive or cheese chunk. "Franki, did-a you see? Santina can-a walk again!"

I scrubbed my hands to keep them from strangling her. "How'd it happen? Physical therapy?"

Nonna shook her head. "Bruno tell-a her that he was gonna leave-a home since she no cook, and-a Santina, she stand up and-a make him a four course-a meal!" She crossed herself. "It's a miracle!"

I suppressed a sacrilegious smirk as I dried my hands. The "miracle" would be if Bruno ever left. He was what Italians called a *mammone*, i.e., a mamma's boy-turned-man who was content to live at home and let his aging mother wait on him for life.

"That reminds-a me," Nonna said as she stabbed a salami slice with her toothpick, "Bruno asked Santina about-a you."

I grimaced as I sunk into my seat. "I hope she told him I was still seeing someone."

Nonna munched on the meat. "She tell-a him you work at a strip-a club."

I put my face in my hands. Bruno would be all over that information like white on pasta.

There was a knock on the door, and Bradley entered. "Hello, hello!"

I stood up to greet him, but my nonna got to him first.

"*Benvenuto*, Bradley." She kissed him on both sides of

his face in accordance with Italian custom and promenaded him into the kitchen.

He flashed a smile. "Evening, ladies."

The nonne gathered around as though they'd just been granted an audience with the pope.

"This is-a Franki's *fidanzato*," Nonna said, using the word for both *boyfriend* and *fiancé*. "But soon he gonna be-a much-a more than-a that. Eh, Bradley?"

His smile faltered, and my face turned as red as the ragù simmering on the stove. Before I could pull my voice from the pit of my sinking stomach, Santina approached Bradley and grabbed him by the cheeks.

"*Beddu comu lu culu de viteddu*," she cooed. Then she released his face and gave it a pat that was more like a slap.

Bradley rubbed his flushed flesh and looked at me. "What'd she say?"

Nonna beamed. "That-a you are as handsome as-a the ass of a calf."

He looked taken aback, but I put my hand on his arm to reassure him.

"It's totally a compliment," I said in a knowing tone. "Right, Veronica?"

When she didn't reply, I turned to look at her. She was grinning like a restaurateur who'd just booked an Italian family reunion.

"Can someone give me a hand?" my mother called as she entered the apartment carrying groceries.

Bradley rushed into the living room. "Let me get those bags, Mrs. Amato."

As soon as my mother's arms were free, she fluffed her hair. "Why, Bradley." Her shrill voice had taken on a breathy quality. "You know you can call me Brenda."

I rolled my eyes. Marilyn Monroe my mom was not.

"Of course, Brenda." He deposited the groceries on the kitchen counter. "Wow," he said, peering inside one of the bags. "That's a lot of lemons."

I gave my mom a sour look.

"Uh, Francesca," she said, averting her gaze to the plastic tubs of bread stacked against a wall, "have you shown

Bradley the bread?"

He tilted his head. "What bread?"

I removed the lid from one of the tubs. "Since the altar is to St. Joseph, they bake bread in the shape of carpenter's tools, staffs, crosses, animals—"

"And hands," Nonna interrupted from the kitchen. "Like-a this one."

She hurried into the living room with a loaf that looked like a left hand. "Oh!" she exclaimed in mock surprise as she pointed to a bump in the bread on the third finger. "It-a look-a like an engagement ring! It's a sign from-a God-a!"

The other nonne gasped and scurried from the kitchen to see the holy hand.

"Carmela is right," one of the newcomer nonne agreed. "It's a *fede*."

Fede meant wedding ring and faith, something I was running short on at the moment. I grabbed a hand-shaped loaf from the open container and tore off a finger, fully intending on doing some stress eating. As I brought it to my lips, Bradley's eyes widened.

"Is that a…?" His voice trailed off as his eyes opened a little wider.

I realized how phallic the finger looked and dropped it, to Napoleon's delight. "Good Lord, no!"

My mom and nonna both cocked a brow, so I dragged Bradley into the kitchen before they could comment. I mean, in his defense, it was only natural that he'd think the finger was a penis since my nonna had once served him a pastry shaped like a boob.

"Hey, Bradley." Veronica shot him a sarcastic smile. "How's it going?"

He ran a hand (that the entire house now knew was glaringly wedding-ringless) through his hair. "Pretty good."

I could tell that he was trying to be a trooper, but work was clearly weighing on his mind. "Are things settling down at the bank?"

His jaw tensed. "Actually, no. Before I left I found out that Craig Burns is thinking about going with another bank. If he does, the board'll have my head."

My stomach almost upchucked the *arancini*. Craig was a construction magnate who'd hosted the party where Bradley took me on our first date (and where my lips puffed up like a couple of puffer fish after Craig taught me to suck crawdad heads Cajun style). "I can't believe it. You two are more than business associates. You're friends."

"That's what I thought too." He gazed out the window. "I just can't understand what's happening."

"Bradley," I began, preparing to tread on dangerous ground, "have you considered the possibility that someone from within the bank is sabotaging you?"

"Have you tried the *arancini*?" Veronica gushed, pushing the platter in front of Bradley. "They're a Sicilian specialty, and the name means *little oranges* because of their shape and color. Isn't that adorable?"

He looked from Veronica to me. "Franki," he said, his voice lethally low, "is there something you need to tell me?"

"Nooo," I replied as innocently as my Catholic guilt would permit. "I'm just surprised that Craig of all people would go to another bank. It makes me think that something else must be going on."

He shoved his hands into his pockets. "Well, if this were sabotage, I can't imagine what anyone would have on me. It's not like I've been negligent or broken any laws."

I stood statue-still as I remembered Ruth saying that Bradley knew I was a *professional problem*. My thinking was that if I didn't move, maybe he wouldn't remember it too and think that I was somehow responsible for this mess.

He gave me a small smile and kissed my cheek. "Don't worry. I'll deal with whatever's going on. As for Craig, I'm sure he has his reasons for wanting to leave."

And I knew exactly what those reasons were: Jeff and Payne. Evidently, the Machiavellian manager had paid Craig a visit like he had that other client Ruth told me about. The good news was that I knew Craig well enough to pay him a visit too— and to get to the bottom of this bank business.

My mother walked into the kitchen, tying an apron she'd brought from home around her waist. "Bradley, can Franki fix you something to eat?"

She gave me a serve-your-man stare, which I countered with a get-off-my-back glare.

"I'm good, thanks," Bradley said, sliding his arm around my shoulders.

A loud knock preempted my mother's protest about his refusal of food.

The shortest of the nonne opened the door and leaned her head back to see who it was.

"Evening ma'am," Detective Sullivan said. He had one hand on the doorjamb, and the other was in the pocket of his black, form-fitting suit pants. "Is Franki available?"

The baking ceased, and the nonne's eyes grew to the size of tortelloni. From their Old-World-Sicilian standpoint, the fact that a man had come to my home and uttered my name was tantamount to a declaration of undying love and also a sure sign of my betrayal of my not-yet-betrothed.

Stunned, the nano-nonna stepped aside and motioned toward the kitchen.

Detective Sullivan strode into the apartment and straight to my seat at the table. "I need a word with you outside."

The nonne's eyes darted from me to the detective and then fell on Bradley like a meat tenderizer on a veal cutlet.

"And you are?" Bradley asked, rising to his full six feet three inches.

I jumped up and knocked over my chair, which did nothing to allay his suspicions. "Uh, Bradley Hartmann, this is Detective Wesley Sullivan," I said as I picked up my seat. "He's in charge of the homicide investigation at Madame Moiselle's."

"Investigations, *plural*," the detective corrected, making no move to shake Bradley's hand.

Bradley looked at me. "There's been more than one murder?"

"Another dancer was killed this morning," I said in a hushed tone, hoping it would minimize the massive damage unfolding before me.

"*Madonna mia!*" the nonne shouted.

Bradley's face lost all expression, kind of like the calm before the storm. "And you didn't tell me about it?"

"Oh, Francesca!" My mother threw her arms into the air.

"You really should confide in your boyfriends."

"Boyfriend, *singular*," I stressed. I wasn't surprised that my mom was more worried about my relationship than the homicide, but I was completely unprepared for her contribution to the "plural" party.

"Now everyone stay calm," I semi-shouted as I stomped around Detective Sullivan and headed for the door. "This is just business."

The detective followed me out, and the second we were alone on the porch I spun around to face him like a Tasmanian devil in a tornado. "What're you doing here?"

He squared his stance. "I came for the credit card bill and the vial."

I crossed my arms. "I told you I'd bring them by the station."

He leaned into my face. "And I told you I needed them within the hour."

I pointed at his pecs. "No, you didn't."

"Yes, I did." He gestured toward the door. "Now hurry up. I've got something you'll want to see."

I lowered my lids. I wasn't sure I trusted him to share evidence with me, but I needed all the breaks in the case I could get. "Be right back."

When I went inside, all nine nonne jumped away from the window, while Bradley, my mom, and Veronica pretended to be busy the kitchen. Without a word, I ducked into my bedroom and pulled the plastic bags containing the items from my nightstand, and then I rushed back to the porch.

"Here." I thrust the bags into his hands. "This is everything I've collected."

"Make sure you don't collect anything else." He turned and headed down the walkway.

"Hey!" I ran after him. "What do you have for me?"

"Right. My bad." He stopped and pulled a wad of fabric from his back pocket.

It took a second for my brain to register what it was. When it did, I felt my chest and realized that I was still wearing the scarf halter-top that Glenda had made for me at the club.

"Looks-a like you got-a some competition," my nonna

announced from behind me.

A tightness wrapped around my torso like the bra I wasn't wearing as I turned and saw her and Bradley standing in the doorway.

Bradley's eyes were fixed on the bra dangling from the detective's hand.

I snatched the offending undergarment. "I can explain."

"Just business, eh?" Bradley said as he set off across the yard toward his car.

"Wait!" I yelled. "I know this looks bad—"

The door to his BMW slammed, and the engine roared.

I watched helplessly as he sped away.

"It may look-a bad to Bradley," Nonna said as she sized up Detective Sullivan, "but from-a where I'm-a standing, it's-a lookin' pretty good-a."

* * *

Bradley's phone went straight to voice mail.

In the ten minutes that I'd been locked in my bathroom, I'd called him at least twenty times with no luck. Reluctantly, I opted to heed Veronica's advice and give him some space—but only until tomorrow.

To drown out the noise of the nonne, who were all abuzz about the *scandalo* that had gone down between Bradley, Detective Sullivan, and me, I put in my earbuds. Then I tossed back half of my highball of Lazzaroni Amaretto, desperately wishing that Lent were over so that I could top off my drink with a little chocolate cheesecake. In times like these, stress drinking alone wouldn't do. After all, I'd been trained to eat my emotions since birth.

With my laptop in one hand and my drink in the other, I climbed into the claw-foot tub fully clothed. I leaned my head against the back and felt something rubbery and cushiony, like an inflatable plastic bath pillow, so I settled in and got semi-comfortable.

Then it occurred to me that I didn't own a bath pillow.

I turned to take a look, and the screechy *Psycho* music went off in my head.

It was my nonna's enema bag.

After I'd scrubbed my hands for five solid minutes, washed and dried my hair, and lined the tub with towels, I got back inside and prepared to do some online research. Since sleep was out of the question and my nonna was monopolizing David's time, I decided to try to find out for myself whether the amber necklace was a component of the spell or the voodoo.

A half an hour passed. Various search combinations of *amber* and *Old New Orleans Traditional Witchcraft* and *New Orleans voodoo* produced nothing. Frustrated, I entered *amber amaretto* to see if I could find anything to connect the two items.

To my surprise, I got a hit—*Amaretto Amber*.

I clicked the link, and what I saw prompted me to drain my highball glass.

Now I knew how Amber had been making her money.

CHAPTER SIXTEEN

———

"Amber was *what*?" Veronica asked, her phone voice gravelly with sleep.

"Sugaring," I whispered into my cell, glancing across the dentist lobby at a twenty-something tech nerd absorbed in an issue of *Wired*. "You know, Lisa Ling, CNN?"

She was silent. "Did Dr. Lessler give you laughing gas?"

"I haven't even seen him yet," I replied, annoyed. "I was talking about a TV show on sugaring."

"Oh." A cabinet door slammed. "Is that the thing where young women date wealthy men for money?"

"Uh-huh." I picked at a crack in my thumbnail. "The women get rent or tuition or whatever, and in exchange the men supposedly get *companionship,* i.e., sex."

The man's head snapped up, as did his bushy brows.

I gave him a get-a-life glare, and his eyes lowered to his magazine.

"How do you know Amber was doing it?" Veronica asked over the banging of pots and pans.

"I found her profile on a sugaring website, sugarshack.org. And get this—" I shifted the phone to my other ear and shielded my mouth with my hand. "She went by *Amaretto Amber.*"

Veronica gasped. "Do you think that's why the amaretto was left at the crime scene? As a clue that she was sugaring?"

I scooted to the far end of the couch to get out of earshot of the gawking geek. "I still think the *Amore* part of the brand name is significant, but, yeah, I've been wondering if it was some kind of statement from a jilted sugar daddy."

The man peered at me over the top of his magazine, and

I narrowed my eyes into an I-can-see-you stare.

"Wait a second." Silverware jangled as she closed what I assumed was a kitchen drawer. "Didn't Carnie say that Amber was leaving the sex trade?"

"I know what you're thinking—this sounds like prostitution." I paused and shot the man a preemptive dream-on smirk. "But in the eyes of the law it's not because both parties consider it to be dating."

"Yeah, that would be tough to prosecute." She yawned, and I heard water running. "Have you tried calling this company?"

"I can't because they don't have any contact info listed. I did a *Whois* search on the website, but nothing came up."

"They're using a masking service, obviously." The water sound stopped. "Your only option for information is to infiltrate the company somehow."

"If you're suggesting that I pose as a sugar baby, you can forget it." I crossed my ankle over my knee. "Stripping is as far as I'm willing to go."

The man's mouth dropped open and, to my dismay, stayed that way.

"Read your magazine, will ya?" I yelled, waving my arm Italian-style for emphasis.

He leapt up and left the lobby.

"I don't get it," Veronica said in a bewildered tone. "Why do you want me to read a magazine?"

"Never mind," I muttered. "Anyway, what would you think about me asking David to investigate the company? He could create a fake profile as a prospective sugar daddy to see what he can find out."

"I don't have any problem with that, but your nonna will if it interferes with that altar." She giggled.

"You let me handle her," I said, even though we both knew that I couldn't.

"Listen," she began, "have you talked to Bradley yet?"

I frowned at my broken nail. "No, but it's only seven thirty. If he hasn't surfaced by lunchtime, I'll call him."

Dana, the hygienist, entered the lobby holding a patient file. "Franki?"

I stood up, and my stomach fell. "They've come for me."

"Have fun," Veronica said as though I were redeeming her spa gift instead of getting a crown.

I was tempted to reply with a choice word or two, but I would've felt dirty swearing in front of a hygienist. So I tapped end—hard.

As soon as I was settled into the dental chair, Dana sat on a stool and clipped a bib around my neck. Then she rose to her feet and pulled a bleach wipe from a Clorox canister.

"Dr. Lessler will be here in a few minutes," she said as she disinfected the seat.

"Wow." I watched her swab the stool. "Now I get why they call you a hygienist."

She laughed. "Dr. Lessler's kind of a germophobe."

The doctor entered the room, pulling on a rubber glove. "I see how it is," he said in a joking tone. "I'm a few seconds late, and you two talk about me behind my back."

Dana's face turned a shade shy of the purple on the doctor's LSU scrubs.

I smiled as I semi-sat up. "We were discussing what a clean freak you are."

"Well, we see an awful lot of spit around here." He winked and pulled a surgical mask over his face. "How's that filling?"

"Fine, I guess." I reclined, resigned.

"Let's take a look before I start the crown." He took a probe from Dana's hand.

I opened my mouth and stared at a poster on the ceiling of a dolphin that was leaping carefree from the sea as if to mock me.

"How's the investigation going?" he asked, poking my tooth.

"Uh, ohay," I replied, mainly because it was only thing I could safely say with a pick between my lips.

"I have some information for you." He prodded my gums.

My eyes widened. "Reary?"

He placed the probe on an instrument tray. "I just talked to my office manager, and she said that a woman called a couple of times over the past year to make sure Amber didn't have any outstanding bills."

I rose to my elbows. "Does she know her name or her relation to Amber?"

The corners of his mouth turned down. "The only thing she remembers was that the woman had a strong Texan accent."

At the mention of Texas, Shakey came to mind. It was possible that he had a secretary paying Amber's bills, but the woman could have also been an associate of a sugar daddy Amber had met through the website. Either way, someone had to be covering her expenses, especially the rent on that Uptown apartment she'd moved into. "Is there anything else you can tell me about Amber? Or about that necklace you saw her wearing?"

A memory dawned on his face. "I can't believe I almost forgot." He turned to Dana. "Can you give us a minute?"

She nodded and exited the room.

"Yesterday was my daughter's fifth birthday, and my wife gave her an Ariel doll. It reminded me that Amber had said something about the *veve* being associated with a mermaid."

I was so excited by this revelation that I almost forgot the reason I was in Dr. Lessler's office. If there was a voodoo mermaid, that would explain the one on the bathtub since the Lithuanian legend had never quite fit with the crime. "You might've just provided me with a missing link I needed."

"Glad I could help." He picked up a Q-tip.

"What's that for?" I asked, holding up my hand to keep his at bay.

His shoulders relaxed. "I have to anesthetize your tooth so that I can prepare it for the crown."

If I'd known about this part of the procedure, I would've anesthetized myself to prepare *me* for the crown. I sighed and gripped the arms of the chair. "All right. Let's get this over with."

He swabbed my gums with the topical anesthetic. "I take it you're not surprised that she was into voodoo and witchcraft given the, uh, sordid life she'd been living."

I turned my head to look at him. "You mean, the stripping?"

He gave an apologetic grimace. "I knew about the prostitution too. If her attitude hadn't given it away, her outfits would have." Dr. Lessler glanced at the clock and picked up the syringe. "I'd better get a move on. We've got a full schedule today. Ready?"

"No, but shoot." I opened my mouth but squeezed my eyes shut.

As the needle pierced my flesh, my eyes popped open. But it wasn't because of the prick. It was because I finally remembered where I'd seen the image of Baron Samedi.

It was on the top of King's cane.

* * *

I opened my eyes, and a slack-jawed face came into focus. Fearing that the dude from the dentist had followed me to Private Chicks, I bolted upright from the lobby couch and knocked him in the nose with my noggin.

"Ooof!" His head flew back, and he pinched his nostrils.

I blinked and realized that he wasn't the nosy nerd but rather "the vassal," a fraternity brother of David's who'd earned the feudal nickname when he'd been appointed as a pledge to serve David the year before. "Sorry I hurt you," I said, rubbing my forehead. "But why were you staring at me like that?"

"You were breathing all weird, and then you stopped," David replied, removing a tissue box from the reception desk. "We thought maybe you'd died."

"I almost did," I muttered, recalling the horror of having my bad tooth filed down for the crown.

"Whoa." He handed the box to the vassal. "What happened?"

"The dentist appointment from hell." I touched my tongue to my temporary tooth. "Anyway, I have an urgent assignment for you."

David glanced at the vassal, who was inserting a tissue plug into his nostril. "But Standish and I are working on a St. Joseph's Day project."

I snorted. "Standish? Who's that?"

The vassal inserted a wad of tissue into the other side of his nose. "Mbe."

Trying not to peer at those plugs, I said, "First of all, you should stick with the vassal. And second, I know all about my nonna and that altar, but Veronica and I agree that the case takes priority. So, I need you to create a fake profile on a website for sugar babies."

The vassal's already Coke-bottle-lens-magnified eyes grew even larger. "I'm not allowed to eat caramel. Mother says dairy isn't good for me."

"It's not for the candy," I said dryly as I looked from him to David. "It's called Sugar Shack, and it advertises young women seeking platonic and sexual relationships with men in exchange for money or goods."

David doubled over, and the vassal exhaled so hard that the tissue plugs shot from his nostrils like rockets.

I curled my lips as I contemplated David's collapsed form. "Maybe you're not the man for the job."

He held up a hand. "Just...give me a second."

"No, now that I think about it," I said, shaking my head, "this won't work. To get the kind of info I'd need, you'd probably have to attend one of the meet-the-girls parties that prospective sugar daddies are invited to."

David's back seemed to give out, and he placed his hands on his thighs for support.

"And since you work for Private Chicks," I continued, "that could expose you unnecessarily."

The vassal clenched his fists at his sides and took a step forward. "I know how to party with girls."

I bit my lip. I'd been to a so-called "party" at the vassal's dorm the previous year, and the only women in sight were the ones on the surveillance video I'd brought for him to analyze. "I can't let you do that since you're not our employee."

My message tone chimed from my office.

"I need to see who that is." I pushed myself off the couch. "You two go ahead and work on that altar design, and then David, you get me anything you can find on a voodoo mermaid."

"Can't we at least do the profile?" David croaked.

He looked so broken that I decided to throw him a bone.

"Why not?" I said and then hurried down the hallway for my phone.

As I'd hoped, the text was from Bradley.

We need to talk. Can you come by my place at 8?

I started to confirm, but then I remembered that I had to strip at around that time. Of course, there was no way I was going to tell him that, so I opted for a kinder, gentler version of the evening's event.

I have a stakeout at the club. Is 10 too late?

While I waited for him to respond, I unlocked my lower desk drawer and pulled out my emergency bag of Elmer's Green Onion CheeWees *and* my crisis can of Zapp's Spicy Cajun Bean Dip.

I used a cheese curl to scoop a dollop of the dip and tossed it into the good side of my mouth. No sooner had I begun to chew than my "Shake Your Booty" ringtone sounded.

Tapping *speaker* to keep my hands free for snacking, I answered, "Hey, Glenda."

"Miss Franki." She exhaled what had to be a puff of smoke. "What are you doing right this minute?"

"Oh, just stress eating." I chewed another CheeWee. "Why do you ask?"

"Because we've got prep work to do before your performance."

I licked dip from my lip. Something in her inflection sounded ominous. "I've got to learn the routine, right?"

"Not only that," she said, sounding stressed. "I imagine we have quite a bit of waxing to do."

I almost choked on a cheese curl. "And why would you imagine that?"

"Are you or are you not Italian, sugar?"

"Not all Italians are hairy," I huffed, keeping it general. If I got into family specifics, I'd be busted for sure.

"Far be it from me to stereotype." She sucked in some more smoke. "But based on the way your front fluff filled out your panties during your costume fitting, I'd say you fall into the hirsute group."

I cradled the bean dip can for comfort. I didn't mind being outed by my underwear, but the implication that I had back fluff really stung.

"Now, normally I wouldn't concern myself with what

grows in your grove," Glenda assured, "but for tonight, I need to make sure those pubes get pruned. Luckily, I was able to get you a noon appointment at Vaxing for Vomen."

I swallowed, stunned—not because I had to have my vagitation *vaxed* but because I didn't remember telling her about the salon or Nadezhda. "Why are we going there?"

"Because all the salons on Yelp were booked solid, and it was the only place I could find with an opening on such short notice."

Given its austere ambiance, that was certainly understandable. "If it wasn't on Yelp, how'd you hear about it?"

"I ran across Miss Nadezhda's card…at the club," she added evasively.

I dropped the dip. "*Where* at the club?"

"Don't tell Eugene," she said in a low voice, "but I found it when I was looking for a pen in one of his desk drawers. Why?"

That was exactly what I wanted to know.

* * *

"Could we at least leave a landing strip?" I pleaded, clutching my just-waxed inner thigh.

"Not with your tiger costume, sugar." Glenda adjusted her green, white, and orange feather boa to make sure that it wasn't covering her shamrock pasties. "That hairkini of yours is going Hollywood."

I got a visual of my vajayjay in bright lights. "What do you mean, 'Hollywood'?"

She raised her skirt and pulled her gold-sequined thong to the side, and I stared at her hairless hoohah in horror. Now not only was my skin searing, my eyes were too.

To overcome the awkwardness, I asked, "What's that rainbow on your skirt got to do with St. Patrick's Day?"

She pursed her lips into a pout. "A leprechaun hides his pot of gold at the end of a rainbow, Miss Franki."

I rolled my eyes and then my head to the other side of the waxing table and watched as Nadezhda mixed the wax in the warmer. It occurred to me that she looked a lot like a witch stirring a cauldron.

She turned and ripped a muslin strip from my bikini line without warning. "I do mustache and goatee too. Yes?"

Glenda nodded, and I was in too much pain to protest.

Nadezhda looked at my upper lip and curled hers. "I get more vax."

As soon as she'd stepped out, I sat up and seethed. "FYI: I don't have facial hair—just a little peach fuzz. But we'll table that conversation for the time being, because we need to find out how the Wicked Witch of the Wax knows Eugene."

Glenda blinked eyelashes that matched her boa. "He could be one of her clients."

"How do you figure?" I whisper-shouted. "The guy's hairier than Tom Selleck in a gorilla suit."

"Well, I wouldn't know." She gave a haughty hair flip. "Maybe he's into manscaping."

"So, he tends the briar patch but leaves the weeds all over the rest of his body?" I asked in keeping with her gardening theme. "I doubt that."

She crossed her arms, covering her clover. "Then what do you suggest we do?"

"I don't want Nadezhda to think I'm questioning her, so when she comes back, get her talking about herself—you know, where she's from, what her hobbies are." I returned to my supine position. "Maybe she'll say something that'll help us connect her to Eugene."

Glenda tapped an Irish-manicured finger to her cheek. "This calls for some old-fashioned flattery."

Nadezhda entered with a block of wax and stole a sideways glance at Glenda and me as though she suspected that we'd been talking about her. She dropped the block into the warmer and began breaking it up with a wooden stick.

"Did you ever do any modeling, Miss Nadezhda?" Glenda asked. "You have such a striking face."

"Tank you." She gave a modest grin and touched her maroon spikes. "I was actress in Borscht Western."

I pulled myself onto my elbows. "A *what* western?"

Her grin turned to a grimace. "Like Spaghetti Western, only Russian."

"How exciting!" Glenda exclaimed, shaking her shamrocks. "Which one were you in?"

She did her signature sneer-smile as she turned up the heat dial on the warmer. "*Caviar Cowboy*."

Glenda plopped down onto the waxing table, perching her pot of gold next to my face. "Did you have a speaking part?"

"I play saloon girl." Nadezhda put her hand on her hip and struck what I presumed was a seductive pose. "Larissa Lockhart," she drawled. "From Texas."

I tilted my head like Napoleon did when I said a word that sounded familiar to him. Only it wasn't a word that got me— it was Nadezhda's Texas accent. It wasn't good, but it wasn't bad either. In fact, unlike her English, it was pretty darn passable.

As she smeared wax around my mouth, our eyes locked. And even though I couldn't tell whether she was the woman who'd called Dr. Lessler's office asking about Amber's account, there was one thing I could detect.

Guilt.

Nadezhda was involved in the Amber Brown case, and I would've bet my bottom lip that Eugene was too.

CHAPTER SEVENTEEN

───────

"What the—" I flinched at my reflection in the dressing room mirror at Madame Moiselle's. And it wasn't because of the tiger-striped Lycra costume, the purple-and-gold platform pumps emblazoned with the LSU tiger, or even the tiger ears and tail. It was because of the big red bumps around my mouth and thighs. "Someone please tell me that you can't get herpes from a waxing salon."

Glenda squatted and scrutinized my crotch. "It's just a rash, Miss Franki."

"Or an allergic reaction," Bit-O-Honey added as she pressed the costume snap closed at the nape of my neck.

I bent over and examined my inflamed inner thighs. "No, it's a burn. I saw Nadezhda crank up the heat on that wax warmer, and she did it on purpose."

Bit-O-Honey pulled up one of the black thigh-high fishnet stockings of her sexy saint costume. "Why would she do something so cruel?"

"Because she knows I suspect her of being involved in the murders." I straightened and scowled at the redness around my mouth, which made me look a lot like a crazed clown. "Someone with a Texas accent called Dr. Lessler's office asking about Amber's bills, possibly this mother figure we've been hearing about, and it could've been her."

Glenda sealed the Velcro closures at my hips. "But why would she tell you and Carnie about Amber's mother if it was her?"

"Because Amber talked to the mystery mom on the phone in front of Maybe, too," I said, eyeing the Velcro with concern. "And if Nadezhda is this mom, she's probably trying to deflect suspicion from herself."

"Could be." Glenda stood up and checked to make sure that her apple-pastied breasts were still barely tucked inside her blue lace-up bustier.

"Hey, uh, I know you're a slut," I prefaced to preempt any protest. "So why would you dress as Snow White for The Saints, Sinners, and Sluts Revue?"

Her lips puckered into a playful pout. "She lived alone with seven men, sugar."

Now that I thought about it, that *was* suspiciously slutty.

"What do you think of your costume?" She stepped away from the mirror, and I got a full frontal of my tiger getup.

My first reaction was to suck in my breath—then my belly. Glenda had reduced the halter to the size of a string bikini top, and the skirt barely covered the thong I had on underneath. Even worse, the fabric panel she'd added to cover my gut consisted of an upside down triangle that essentially functioned as a giant arrowhead pointing to my lady bits.

"You call this 'a few adjustments'?" I asked, yanking my tail for emphasis.

She smoothed her yellow skirt. "Well, I had to sexy it up."

"Sexy it up?" I turned back to the mirror. "I look like a Mardi Gras tiger. With mange."

Bit-O-Honey snapped her fingers. "I know what you need. Tiger balm!"

I gave her a pre-pounce-on-the-prey gaze.

"There's no time for that. She's on in thirty minutes." Glenda pointed to a makeup case on the counter. "Get me the Dermablend."

I crossed my arms over my breasts. I didn't know what Dermablend was, but I already knew that I wasn't a fan of the spirit gum she'd used to glue on the pasties that the club required me to wear under my top.

"Relax, sugar," she said as she took a cosmetic tube from Bit-O-Honey. "It's body concealer."

"In that case, could you cover the spare tire I'm carrying around my stomach?" I leaned into her face. "Because that fabric panel isn't doing the trick."

"Oh, it won't cover fat," Bit-O-Honey gushed. "Just your rash."

I shot her a silent roar.

"A-anything else I can do to help?" she asked, pushing open the door as she backed away from me.

I caught a side view of myself in the mirror and winced. "Get me a stiff drink, will ya? And find out if Eugene is here yet."

Eugene appeared in the doorway as though he'd been standing outside trying to eavesdrop. He leaned against the jamb, striking a pose in his black-and-white Adidas tracksuit. "What can I do for you?"

"I need to speak to you privately." I tried to look him in the eyes, but they were otherwise occupied with checking out the exposed flesh in the room.

"We can talk in my office," he said coolly.

Glenda pointed the Dermablend tube at me. "You don't have time to talk, Miss Franki. You've got to be on that stage at nine o'clock sharp."

"This won't take long." I turned to follow Eugene, but I hadn't practiced walking in the six-inch heels yet. So, instead of the stealthy stride of a tiger, I had the spastic step of a chicken. By the time I got to his office, he was already seated behind his cheap metal desk.

"Guess I'm gonna get my wish," he said as he opened an Altoids tin.

I crossed my arms and frowned. "What wish is that?"

He dropped a mint onto his tongue. "To see a fiery Italian strip."

I was fiery, all right—as in angry and, if you counted the burning bumps on my mouth and thighs, on fire. But Eugene hadn't noticed those because he was focusing on the bumps on my chest.

"I gotta say…" His eyes traveled down my torso. "…based on what I know about your people, I'm surprised you didn't go for leopard."

I chose to ignore the Italians-wear-animal-print stereotype. I *was* wearing tiger stripes. "While we're on the subject of animals, I'm trying to figure out whether you're a wolf

in sheep's clothing." I glanced at his gold collar-style chain.
"Make that dog's clothing."

His breathing seemed to stop. "What are you getting at?"

"Your relationship to Nadezhda Dmitriyeva." Now my
eyes focused on *his* chest—specifically, on the hair tufting from
his unzipped jacket. "And don't tell me you're one of her clients."

"Okay. I won't." He placed his hands behind his head.

I waited for an explanation, but one didn't come. "You
might want to tell me how you know her, because right now it's
looking like you two are accomplices."

"Accomplices in what?" he asked, sitting forward in his
chair.

"Which one of you told the other about the amber
necklace?" I shot back, trying to catch him off guard.

Anger erupted in his eyes. "Just what the hell are you
trying to say?"

I bent over and rested my hand on his desk. "You knew
about that necklace even though the police didn't make it public."

He opened his arms, feigning innocence. "They told me
about it at the station."

"Not according to Detective Sullivan." I stood up and
stared, waiting for his body language to betray him.

His arms relaxed at his sides, but his hands gripped the
chair. "Well, he's wrong."

"I don't think so." I started to pace in my platform pumps
but promptly abandoned that plan. "What I do think is that
Amber told Nadezhda about the necklace, then Nadezhda told
you. And the two of you decided to steal it."

He exploded from his desk like a Molotov cocktail, and I
leapt backwards, stumbling slightly in my stilettos.

"Nadezhda was a friend of my mother's from the old
country," he said through clenched teeth. "And since my mom
died, she's been like a second mother to me."

My ears pricked up at the *mom* mention. *Had Nadezhda
also been a second mom to Amber—one who betrayed her?*

Eugene and I faced off across the desk, and something
told me to pursue the connection between Nadezhda and his
mom. "Where, exactly, were they from?"

"Some small town," he muttered. "I don't know the

name."

"You don't know where your own mother was from." I made it a statement rather than a question because I didn't buy it for all the vodka in Russia.

He looked down, and it wasn't because he was embarrassed. It was to hide the fear that flashed across his face.

And although Eugene claimed not to know the name, I had a feeling I did.

Yantarny.

Because anyone from the Russian amber-mining town would know about the Amber Room, its significance to the people of Russia, and, of course, its incalculable value on the black market.

* * *

"No sign of Shakey yet," Glenda said as she peered at the crowd through the curtains around Madame Moiselle's main stage.

"Welp, if he's not here, I guess there's no point in me dancing." I turned to go back to the dressing room—and I couldn't get there fast enough.

She grabbed my shoulder and spun me around. "We don't know that Shakey had anything to do with these murders, Miss Franki, so the show must go on. Remember, your dancing could help us catch the killer." She let go of me and reached for my cell. "Now give me your phone."

I pulled back and glanced at the display. Bradley had never responded to my text about meeting at ten o'clock, and I was worried that he'd had a change of heart about discussing the Detective Sullivan situation—just like I'd had a change of heart about the stripping situation. "Um, first I need to make a quick call."

"It's too late for that." She wrested the phone from my grip. "We hired a top DJ for this event, and he's about to announce you."

Bit-O-Honey bounced up and shoved a drink into my empty hand. "Carlos made you a tiger goddess."

"Thanks." I didn't feel like a tiger or a goddess—more

like a combination of a chicken and a monster. But I chugged the drink, hoping it would give me a confidence boost.

It didn't.

"I can't do this." I thrust the empty glass at Bit-O-Honey and turned tail and ran—well, plodded, thanks to my platform pumps.

"You can, and you will." Glenda grabbed my arm and dragged me back. "Just remember your routine—crouch, roar, pre-pounce wiggle."

My legs started trembling so hard that my tail shook, but somehow in my hysteria I thought of another reason that I couldn't strip. "Wait! My costume doesn't fit with The Saints, Sinners, and Sluts Revue theme. I'll ruin the whole show."

"How silly of me," Glenda said in a blatantly false tone. "I forgot a key accessory."

I cocked a glittered brow. "What accessory?"

"One sec, sugar." She strutted to the prop room, and I seized the opportunity to peek through the curtains.

Madame Moiselle's was a zoo, and I was a caged animal. The club was standing room only, and there were so many men in green that it seemed like half of Ireland had flown in for the show. I scanned the room looking for a Stetson, but I spotted a Sullivan instead. And the dastardly detective was making his way toward the stage.

"Don't move," Glenda said from behind me. "I need to drape this over your shoulders."

I assumed she was referring to her Irish flag boa, but the accessory was heavy—and cold and slick. I looked down and froze. It was definitely a boa, but of the live constrictor variety. My eyes darted from the snake to Glenda, because I was too afraid to move anything else. "Wha...wha...wha?"

"St. Patrick drove the snakes from Ireland," she replied as though I'd formulated a complete question. "The idea is that the Irishmen in the crowd drive the snake—and the rest of your costume—from you."

I stared at her, stricken. Snow White wasn't only a slut, she was a *strega* too.

Morris Day and the Time's "Jungle Love" began to play, and my legs turned to jungle juice.

"Coming to the stage," the DJ intoned into a microphone, "Tiger Eye, the late, great Amber's Irish-Italian porn star cousin."

Porn star?

The crowd roared, and before I could strangle stripper Snow White with the snake, she shoved me onstage.

The lights were blinding, so I couldn't see the steps to exit. I couldn't faint, either, because I was too afraid of what the snake would do to me if I fell on it. So, I stood still and made like a jungle tree.

"Woo-hoo!" A man yelled. "Look at her shake that money-maker!"

Bewildered, I looked down and discovered that I was vibrating like Tina Turner on a treadmill.

"Come on, guys," the DJ boomed. "Make it rain for Tiger Eye—like in a rain forest."

"Crouch, sugar! Crouch!" Glenda yelled.

I inched sideways toward the sound of her voice, and then someone pulled my tail. My costume constricted, and a rush of air whooshed over my skin as the audience hooted and hollered.

Now I knew the reason for the Velcro and the snaps—Glenda had made me a tear-away tiger costume, and she'd just torn it off me.

"Reeeeemember, fellas," the DJ bellowed, "tip when they strip. If you want to see her flashin', you've gotta slide some cash in."

The snake, probably as annoyed by the damn DJ as I was, reared its horrifying head.

Terrified, I recoiled and fell backwards onto my hands, and the cheering turned to jeering.

"What the hell kind of move is that?" a man shouted.

"A crab walk?" another offered.

Ignoring the catcalls, I focused on the tasks at hand—getting myself off the stage and the boa off my boobs. Fortunately, in my crustacean position I was out of the glare of the lights. I glanced around for the exit and came face-to-face with another snake—Detective Sullivan.

He grinned and held up a five-dollar bill. "You might

want to put this in the bank," he said as he slid the money into my thong. "Because it looks like your stripper career is going belly up, pardon the pun, just like your PI career."

A camera flash went off in my face, and when the light spots cleared my tiger's blood ran cold.

Bradley was making his way to the stage, and his eyes were darker than Iris's tattooed scleras.

I scuttled toward Glenda, but I slipped and collapsed. I watched in alarm as the snake slithered to the stage and as Bradley took a swing at Detective Sullivan.

The crowd went wild. Within seconds, green beer and top hats began to fly as a bar brawl broke out.

Iris swooped down and scooped up the snake and me and whisked us off the stage, depositing us in front of Glenda.

She crossed her arms and tapped a yellow-bowed stiletto. "Caught a tiger by the tail, didn't you, sugar? Too bad it wasn't the killer."

* * *

"They don't call us the Fighting Irish for nothing, eh, Sullivan?" A ginger officer joked as he loaded three handcuffed club patrons in shamrock suits into a paddy wagon outside Madame Moiselle's.

The detective laughed. "Ain't that the truth, Sean?"

I clutched my coat lapel to stop myself from going all *Raging Bull* on them and kept my eyes trained on the squad car that they'd loaded Bradley into fifteen minutes before. I hadn't spoken to anyone since he'd been arrested—not even to Bradley. And like the Irishmen in the club, I was fighting mad—at Glenda for suggesting that I strip, at myself for agreeing to the stupid scheme, at Bradley for coming to the club after I'd told him I had a "stakeout," and at Detective Sullivan for arresting him.

Sensing my animosity, the detective strode over to me. "Speaking of the Irish, you must have some of our luck. Otherwise, you'd be sitting in the back of that squad car with your boyfriend."

"This isn't about luck," I seethed as I rubbed my right fist, which was aching to punch him. "I didn't do anything wrong, and neither did he. You provoked him when you put that bill in my...uh...thong."

A corner of his mouth lifted. "Well, he's going to have to get used to that sort of thing now that you've taken up stripping. Fortunately for him, your business partner's an attorney, because he's going to need one." He paused and gave me a penetrating stare. "And you will too if you interfere in my investigation again."

He spun on his heel and climbed into the passenger seat of the squad car. Moments later, the engine roared to life. As the car pulled away, I watched numbly as Bradley disappeared into the night and, I feared, from my life. We'd been through a lot, but I wasn't sure how we'd survive this. Because when the bank got word of his arrest, heads were going to roll—his first and then mine. And the more I thought about it, the more I realized that it might be in his best interest if I rolled right out of his life.

"I thought we could use a drink," a squeaky female voice said.

I turned and found Maybe Baby standing next to me with two Hurricanes from Pat O'Brien's Bar. She was wearing a long, black nightgown with a fuzzy pink coat, a green wide-brimmed hat, and red heart-shaped sunglasses. Anywhere but Bourbon Street she would've looked conspicuous.

"Thanks." I took a go-cup from her hand and gulped down half of the red liquid. "But this won't take the sting off seeing my boyfriend get arrested."

"Gee, I'm sorry." She put a hand on my arm. "I didn't know."

I looked at my drink. "Then what's this for?"

She fished the cherry garnish from her cup and popped it into her mouth. "I saw you dance."

Tilting my head in concession, I raised my glass, and we made a silent toast to my epic stripping failure. I was no Blaze Starr, but for the record, I'm sure Blaze's landlady never slipped a snake on her seconds before she took the stage. "You haven't told me why *you* need a drink."

Maybe pushed stray blonde locks from her face with the back of her hand. "Somebody broke into my house last night, and I had to climb out my window in my nightie."

My gut lurched to alert me—in case my brain hadn't already—that this was probably no random break-in. "You haven't been home since?"

"Well, yeah." She gestured to her ensemble. "I went back this afternoon to change."

I glanced again at her gown and took another swig of my drink to prime me for the rest of the conversation. "Do you know who it was?"

"It could've been the maniac who killed Amber and Curaçao." Her brow furrowed as she chewed her straw. "Or my landlord."

My head jerked forward. "Does your landlord break into your house often?"

"Only when rent is due," she replied in a matter-of-fact tone.

Glenda was looking a lot better as a landlady—stripping, snake, and all. "What did the police say?"

Maybe looked at me and closed one eye, like she was trying to bring me into focus. "What've the cops got to do with this?"

"Um, their business is solving crime?" I suggested.

"You're funny, you know that?" She sat on the curb in the middle of the partying pedestrians and spread her legs.

Against my better judgment, I took a seat beside her on the filthy sidewalk—the partiers were known to puke, and who knew what else. As we sat in silence, I sincerely hoped her seafood platter wasn't showing. On a street like Bourbon, that would be like offering an open tab to a serious drunk, and I didn't need any more trouble. "So, did they take anything?"

She swallowed a half-gallon of her Hurricane. "Who?"

I sighed and stared at the pavement. "The person who broke into your house."

"Not that I could tell," she replied, swishing her drink in her cup.

That struck me as odd. But given Maybe's less than stellar housekeeping skills, I wasn't sure whether she would've noticed if an actual hurricane had blown through the place. Also, the intruder could've been scared away, especially if he or she hadn't expected her to be home. "What did they do? Jimmy the door?"

She put her drink down and frowned. "Who's Jimmy?"

"Oh, no one in particular." I pursed my lips and pondered how to rephrase the question. "What did this intruder do to actually get inside your house?"

"They broke the window in the room where Curaçao had been staying."

I bit my lower lip. Maybe was in serious danger, because the killer was looking for something, and my money was on the amber pendant. "Maybe, if Curaçao did steal that necklace from Amber, where would she have hidden it?"

She wrinkled her mouth and widened her eyes. "Your guess is as good as mine."

I folded onto my knees, thinking that the pendant might never be recovered. "Can you think of any reason that she would've been wearing the copy of the amber necklace when she died?"

"Beats me." She looked down at her clear plastic stilettos. "Curaçao told me that real amber would protect you since it was the stone of the mother goddess, but obviously that fake amber didn't do any good."

My back straightened. "What mother goddess?"

"It's got something to do with that hocus pocus stuff she was into," she replied as she grabbed her drink.

Shocked, I sat my cup on the sidewalk. "Why didn't you tell me about this the other day?"

Her fuzz-covered shoulders raised into a shrug. "Because I was drunk, I guess."

I gave her the onceover, marveling at the implication that she was sober.

"Also because I'm not sure how much she really believed in that witchcraft business." She drained her drink and wiped her mouth with her wrist. "Her mom is the one who got her into it."

"Her mom?" My gut was no longer lurching—it was doing a lap dance. "Do you know her name?"

She crunched a piece of ice. "Mama."

This time I wasn't annoyed with her reply. I was bewitched. "Maybe, what else can you tell me about Curacao's mother?"

She yawned and pulled her phone from her pocket. "Well, she wasn't her real mom," she replied, sounding bored as she checked her display. "Just some lady."

My head began to spin—but only partly because of the four ounces of rum I'd imbibed. *Was there a witch acting as a mother figure to Amber and Curaçao? If so, was it Nadezhda?*

As hard as it was for me to imagine, she was like a mother to Eugene. Plus, she'd refused to answer my question about Amber being a witch that day at the salon. But if she had been a mother to the girls, I doubted that she would've let them call her by the Southern *mama*. Something about the affectionate term didn't jive with her harsh personality.

"You okay?" Maybe asked, nudging me in the side.

I nodded, even though I wasn't okay at all. "Can I use your phone?"

"Be my guest." She entered her passcode and handed me the device.

Out of curiosity, I pulled up her browser and googled the Russian word for mother. As I'd suspected, it looked somewhat severe—мать, pronounced *mought*. But what I hadn't expected to see was the more commonly used informal version of the term.

Мама, the pronunciation of which was all too clear.

CHAPTER EIGHTEEN

———

"Francesca Lucia Amato!" a deep voice bellowed.

I started to come to, still in a crab crawl position. *Why was I onstage again? And how did that guy in the audience know my real name?*

The boa constrictor began to slither on my belly, and my eyes flew open. I wasn't at Madame Moiselle's—I was lying in my claw-foot bathtub in my pajamas with my arms and legs hanging over the sides.

And the cord from my nonna's enema bag was on my stomach.

I hurled the bag across the room as I hopped from the tub.

But wait. I cocked my head to the side. *If that wasn't a strip club customer heckling me, who—*

The bathroom door burst open with a bang, and my mother marched in.

"Is it *true*?"

She had venom in her voice.

"Did you sss…sss…sss…?"

She even hissed like a snake.

"*Strip*?"

I was too terrified to move. When my mom was this mad, she was Medusa incarnate.

"Answer me, young lady," she commanded through clenched teeth.

I averted my gaze because, like her Greek mythology alter ego, I was pretty sure she could turn me to stone. "Mom, I'm investigating a case—"

"Don't try to deny it," she interrupted in a kind of low

growl. "Bruno saw you."

My fear was replaced with contempt. The second I'd heard that Santina had told him I was working at Madame Moiselle's, I knew there'd be fallout. And thanks to that rat, I was backed into a corner—er, a bathroom—by a gorgon. "All right." I sighed, resigned. "I had to strip for work."

"*Mamma mia, che disgrazia!*" Nonna screamed from the doorway.

I started, unaware that she'd snuck up on us like that.

"Look at what you've done!" My mother gestured to my nonna, who chose that moment to fall to her knees and hold her hands up to heaven.

"*Che Dio ci aiuti!*" Nonna wailed, asking God to help us—for emphasis.

An assortment of supportive shrieks and laments ensued from the nonne in the kitchen.

"This is just great." I threw my arms in the air. "I'm a grown woman in trouble with her mom for doing her job. Tell me," I said, resting a finger on my cheek, "did Bruno get in trouble for going to a strip club to check out my semi-nude bod?"

My mother gasped as more cries came from the kitchen, and someone started moaning.

Nonna did the only thing she could do—whip out her rosary and begin to recite.

"He went there to try to talk you out of ruining your reputation and our family name," she rasped. "Get your mind out of the gutter, Francesca."

I was beginning to smell a double standard, which, in addition to garlic, was a common odor in Italian households. "Oh, of course." I sneered. "Because Santina's son is a saint."

It was no doubt my imagination, but I would've sworn that my mother's face turned a greenish hue. And I was halfway expecting snakes to sprout from her head.

"The fact that you would disrespect that nice man tells me that you're not the person I thought you were." She jabbed her finger in my chest as a preface to her classic closer, "Just wait till your father hears about this."

I sunk onto the edge of the tub as she stormed past my nonna, who stopped praying and glanced toward the kitchen.

Then she clambered to her feet and rushed into the room.

"Franki," she whispered, "did-a that detective really give-a you a five-a dollar bill-a?"

"Uuuuhhhh," I uttered, wondering whether it was a trick question. "Yes?"

"*Evvai*!" she cheered with a fist pump. Then she retrieved her enema bag from the floor beside the sink and stepped into the hallway, making sure she was in full view of the other nonne. "You take-a your clothes off in-a public again," she said, shaking the bag at me for show, "and I'm-a gonna wrap-a this thing around your neck-a, *capito*?"

I stared blankly at the bag because, by this time, it had basically been all over my body. "I understand, Nonna."

With a satisfied nod, she tossed the bag into the sink and returned to the kitchen.

I closed the door and climbed back into the tub. My heart ached about the situation with Bradley, and my head ached from arguing with my mom—and from a hangover. After I'd collected my stripping money (twenty-four bucks counting the nineteen singles dropped during the brawl, which was better than that dollar I'd gotten for my birthday), I drowned my sorrows in a second round of Hurricanes with Maybe. Then I asked Glenda to let Maybe stay with her until the murders were solved, a decision I was starting to regret. Now I was going to have to deal with my Medusa Mom and Ninja Nonna until St. Joseph's Day was over, because the odds of me getting Maybe out of a giant champagne glass were slim to none.

The door burst open again, and I sat up in the tub.

Glenda ran into the room and latched the lock behind her. With a pink polka dot ruffled apron tied around her waist and another around her chest, she looked like something from a fashion-forward 1950s mag—except for the stripper shoes that said *Pay Me.*

"What's happened now?" I nestled back into the tub. "Did the Lilliputians tie you up in the kitchen curtains?"

"Miss Ronnie asked me to come get you because you haven't been answering your phone." The aprons rose and fell with her breath. "But right after I got here, Santina showed up with the strippergram, and the mood turned ugly in the kitchen.

You see what happened to me," she said, gesturing to her apron dress. "So, you'd best shake a leg, sugar."

I shot her a look. "My shaking days are over."

She shot me a look right back. "I'm telling you, we have got to go. Besides, Miss Ronnie has news about Bradley."

My pulse perked up. "She's spoken to him?"

"It's 9 a.m., Miss Franki." She put her hand on her hip. "She's already been to the jail and had him released."

I sprung to my feet. "Let me change out of my pajamas."

"There's no time for that," she said, pulling me from the tub by the arm. "The way those women are slapping and pounding that dough makes me think that our buns are the next things they're gonna bake."

Glenda had a point. Nine nonne conferring in a kitchen about a fallen female family member was a recipe for disaster—in this case, mine. And I had an idea of the type of rehabilitation plan they'd cook up.

I grabbed her by the biceps in the grip of panic. "We've got to get out of here before they call in a priest for an exorcism."

* * *

The plain *pain perdu* seemed to mock me from my plate. French toast without syrup was like a life without love, which was what I was facing at the moment. "Sullivan's really going to press charges against Bradley?"

"I'm afraid so." Veronica pushed the butter dish toward me across her rattan kitchen table. "Battery against a police officer."

Glenda, who'd forgone French press coffee in favor of champagne, slammed her flute onto the glass tabletop. "How long a stretch in the jug are we talking?"

My head snapped in her direction. Sometimes she reminded me of Ruth—and of an ex-con.

"Typically, six months," Veronica replied as she pressed egg-battered bread into the skillet with a spatula. "But because an officer is involved, he could serve up to a year."

I put my face in my hands as I imagined Bradley back

behind bars. *How would he hold up? How would I hold up? And what if he were cellmates with a spitter or a skin slougher? Or worse?*

"How was he supposed to know Sullivan was a detective when he was in plain clothes?" Glenda rose from her rattan chair. "And while we're on the subject, get me out of this bondage suit."

I untied the aprons and immediately understood why the nonne had covered her. She was wearing a red spaghetti strap dress that was all straps and no dress.

"Bradley knew who Sullivan was." I picked up my fork and stabbed my *pain perdu*. "The good detective came to my house the other night to collect some evidence—and drop off my bra."

Glenda gave me a shame-on-you smirk. "You little wildcat, you."

I was so mad that I could've mauled her. "I forgot it at the club when you were fitting me for my costume, which, incidentally, is what started this whole nightmare."

"Looks like you've forgotten your bra again," Veronica said with a pointed look at my pajama top.

"That's not fair. I just escaped from the nonne nuthouse." I stopped and shot Glenda a sideways glare. "And our seasoned stripper here forgot to tell me about pastie remover. So, like me, my boobs need a break."

Glenda, who'd also forgone food in favor of false eyelashes, opened a tube of adhesive.

I scooted my chair—and my pair—away from her. "Veronica, Bradley doesn't think I cheated on him, does he?"

She plated her *pain perdu*. "Of course not. But he does think Detective Sullivan is interested in you."

I breathed a sigh of relief—and two lungsful of eyelash glue.

"And, between us," she added as she took her place at the table, "he doesn't regret hitting him."

"*Roar*, sugar," Glenda said, elbowing me in the side. "Bradley's a tiger, just like you."

"Would you quit with the cat references?" I snapped.

She hissed and made a paw-swipe gesture.

I rolled my eyes and turned to Veronica. "Did you explain to him that Sullivan and I have a mutually antagonistic relationship?"

"I tried." She stirred Sweet'N Low into her coffee cup. "But he's convinced otherwise."

I dropped my fork and stood up. "Well, I'm going to go set him straight." *And maybe break up with him*, I thought. But I didn't say it. I wasn't ready to commit to the idea yet, much less communicate it.

"You'll do no such thing." Veronica narrowed her eyes. "Sit."

I stared at her, shocked, and did as I was told.

"As his attorney," she began, spreading a napkin in her lap, "I've advised him to lay low until after the bank board meets on Monday, and that includes staying away from you."

"What?" I grabbed my fork like a weapon. "Who are you, Jeff Payne?"

"I don't think you're a liability to Bradley, if that's what you're suggesting." She poured syrup on her food. "But for the time being, the only things he needs to worry about are staying out of jail and saving his job. Fortunately, the charge is just a misdemeanor, and the incident happened outside of work. But he can't afford to get into any more trouble."

"Oh. So you think I'm trouble, then." I shoved a forkful of dry French toast into my mouth to keep from saying something I'd regret.

She put the syrup down. "I think that right now you'd be a distraction."

"She's right about that, Miss Franki," Glenda said, gluing a red, spiked lash to her eyelid.

I swallowed so that I could snort. "Theodora told me I was cursed, and she was right. My boyfriend's going to jail, my family's ruining my life, and despite the fact that I gave up sweets for Lent, my teeth are falling out."

"Curses are nonsense," Veronica said as she cut her breakfast into bites.

"Are you sure about that?" I asked. And I was serious. "Look at Amber and Curaçao. There's a curse on people who hunt for The Amber Room, they both stole a piece of it, and they're dead."

She leaned across the table. "Franki, I'm not going to argue with you about this. I just need for you to let Bradley and me sort out his situation while you and Glenda focus on solving the murders. Okay?"

I stayed silent. I wasn't ready to make any promises.

"This case is getting scary," Veronica said, waving her knife. "We've gone from a murder to a possible serial or spree killing. Meanwhile, you're being followed by a masked man, and this morning Glenda told me that Maybe spent the night because the killer might be after her too. The way I see it, you can't afford to concern yourself with Bradley's problems because we have serious issues of our own."

She was right. I had to keep my head in the crime game. More lives might depend on it—possibly even my own. "Don't worry, I know. And we are making progress on the case. Last night I learned that both Amber and Curaçao were into witchcraft, and that Amber probably wore the necklace to invoke protection from some mother goddess."

"You mean, Erzulie Freda." Veronica took a bite.

"Actually," I said, reaching for my coffee, "since she was doing witchcraft, I think it's some pagan earth goddess."

She shook her head. "According to the research I've been doing, Erzulie's the mother goddess. Even witches conjure her."

I flashed back to Drag Dolly telling me that Erzulie loved amaretto. "That makes sense. Amber could've been summoning her for protection with the help of the amber necklace."

Veronica swallowed a sip of coffee. "I'm glad you understand it. There's a lot of information about the loas in the New Orleans context, but it's complicated because they all have so many different aspects. For instance, Erzulie isn't just a goddess of love. She's also a mother figure and a protector of lots of different groups, like children and prostitutes."

Dolly hadn't mentioned that, but the prostitute part fit in Amber's case. It also meant that she could've been appealing to Erzulie for assistance with an angry ex-john.

My cell began to vibrate on the table. David's name was on the display, so I put him on speaker. "Hey, man. Veronica and

Glenda are here with me."

"Hello, ladies." He cleared his throat. "It's good that you're all there because I kind of have a situation."

Veronica frowned at the phone. "What's wrong?"

"Standish—I mean, the vassal—and I set up a fake profile on sugarshack.org for a twenty-five-year-old tech millionaire. And I found out this morning that he stayed up all night messaging with this chick from the site. I mean, girl." He coughed. "Woman."

"We get the picture," I said, trying to hurry him along. "What did he find out?"

"That this woman knew Amber." His tone sounded as astonished as Veronica, Glenda, and I looked. "She said Amber hooked up with the first guy she met at something called a sugar bowl party."

"Any chance she remembers the guy's name?" I prodded.

"I wish," he replied. "But I could tell the vassal to ask her to describe him."

Veronica furrowed her brow, probably calculating Private Chicks' legal liability. "This is great information, David, but we can't have him doing any work for us. Thank him and let him know that Franki will take it from here."

"But that's the situation," he said, his voice breaking slightly. "The woman invited him to a martini mixer at lunch today, and he's going. I told him it wasn't a good idea, but he's a man on a mission."

I couldn't help but smile. The sugar babies on that website were probably hotter than anything the vassal had seen since he'd been introduced to the Bunsen burner in high school science class. "Do whatever you have to do to keep him away from that mixer, you understand?"

He exhaled as though trying to stop the smitten Standish would be like taking on Mike Tyson. "I'll do my best."

I tapped *End*.

"Sounds like the killer could be Amber's sugar daddy," Glenda said, swirling the champagne in her glass.

"Or Nadezhda, or Eugene, or Shakey." I drummed my fingers on the table.

Veronica gazed at me over the rim of her mug. "What're

you thinking, Franki?"

I looked her in the eyes. "That we might not figure out who the killer is until we make sense of the crime scene."

Glenda batted her lashes, looking like she was ready for a geriatric rave. "We already know what it means. It's an anti-hex witchcraft spell and a request to the voodoo goddess, Erzulie, for protection."

"Maybe. But there's one clue at the crime scene we haven't cracked—the mermaid that Amber carved into the tub." I glanced at the *Pay Me* message on Glenda's shoes. "And I think I know just the person to help me decipher it."

* * *

"It's just your imagination," I said to myself as I looked into the rearview mirror of my Mustang. Ever since I'd arrived in the French Quarter, I'd felt like I was being followed. Of course, my paranoia could've had something to with the fact that Veronica had mentioned the masked man. Nevertheless, I couldn't shake the sensation.

I turned onto Bourbon Street and checked the mirror again. Still nothing.

"Told you so," I intoned as I searched for a place to park and seriously considered psychotherapy.

Across the street from King Nation's corner, I spotted a rare parking space. When I pulled up, I discovered that it was occupied—by the wino who'd tried to steal from King's tip jar.

"Excuse me, sir," I called as I leaned from the car window. "Could you please move to the sidewalk so I can park here?"

He lifted his head from the stuffed black trash bag that he was using as a pillow. "Can't you see I'm trying to sleep off a hangover, lady?"

I blinked. "Actually, I *can* see that."

He lay back on the bag, and I laid on the horn.

After jumping a good three feet in the air, he shouted out a string of obscenities that would've made Glenda blush. Then he did as I'd asked.

"Some people are so grouchy in the morning," I

grumbled as I parallel parked.

My phone began to ring as soon as I stepped from the car. I bit my lower lip when I read Ruth's name on the display. If she'd heard about Bradley, then the wino's diatribe would seem pleasant in comparison to this conversation. But on the off chance she'd spoken to him, I tapped answer.

"Hey, Ruth. What's up?" I held my breath and waited.

Silence.

I looked at the display to make sure the call hadn't dropped and put the phone back to my ear. "Hello?"

Then I heard it—the sound of heavy breathing, bull-about-to-charge style.

Clearly, Ruth had found out about Bradley. But based on her huffing and puffing, it didn't seem like the time to ask if she'd talked to him.

I glanced at King and saw that he'd started to roll up his red carpet.

Now, I knew that parishioners were hard to come by in the Quarter, not to mention at eleven thirty on a Friday morning. But judging from the way King was stealing sideways glances at me, I had a feeling that I was the reason he was closing up shop, i.e., church.

"Listen, Ruth. It's been great breathing with you," I said, keeping an eye on King, "but I've gotta run." I closed the call and crossed the street.

King saw me coming and rose to his feet, practically glowing in head-to-toe peach. In theory, his fruit-colored suit should've been an improvement over his purple, green, and gold getup, but the pastelness of it all would've taken even Ruth's breath away.

I strode up to him and stared into his gold sunglasses. "I guess you heard that another dancer was murdered at Madame Moiselle's?"

He frowned and clutched his linen lapel. "Shame about that."

"Her name was Curaçao," I added, watching his face for any sign of recognition. "I don't suppose she was one of your girls?"

"We was not biniss associates, no." He hoisted his

keyboard. "But with a name like that, I could've made her a star."

Of the porno screen.

"Now, if you'll excuse me." He brushed past me. "I have an engagement elsewhere."

"Hold on a second." I started after him. "As a man of God, I know you'd want to help me find Amber and Curaçao's killer."

"You would think that," he said as he rounded the corner. "But the good Lawd doesn't want no misfortune ta befall me while I'm spreadin' his word." He stopped beside a Cadillac Seville that looked factory-made to match his ensemble, or vice versa, and popped the trunk.

"Wow." I shielded my eyes from the glare of his car and his gold teeth. "Someone's ready for Easter."

He stowed the keyboard inside the trunk and slammed it shut. "Peach is my favorite color."

"Huh," I said in a sarcastic tone. "I would've guessed green."

"Now that you mention it, I do enjoy green." He lowered his sunglasses so that I could see his eyes lower to my purse. "Particularly when I'm bein' pumped fo' information by a PI."

I could've kicked myself with one of his peach leather wingtips. I'd set myself up for that one.

"Without no cash, I've got to dash." He turned and headed back to his pulpit.

I trailed behind him and rummaged through my bag for my wallet, wishing I'd saved some of my stripping money to pay him off—and contemplating how sad that scenario sounded.

When we got back to his corner, he tossed the carpet over his right shoulder and grabbed his cane.

By some miracle, I found a twenty-dollar bill tucked in my coin purse—something that never happened when I needed money to spend on myself. I made sure King saw it, but I didn't want to hand it over until I'd asked a few more questions. "I noticed Baron Samedi on your cane. Do you practice voodoo?"

"Girl," he said, pulling down the brim of his peach pimp hat, "you been watchin' too many movies."

I was surprised that he would deny it, especially since it was common practice to mix voodoo with Christianity in New

Orleans. I decided to offer him the cash to see whether that inspired some brotherly love.

When I held out the twenty, a breeze blew it from my hand. As I stepped into the street to retrieve the bill, a thought occurred to me. I turned and looked at King. "Amber learned voodoo from you, didn't she?"

His hands went to his face, and I read *Lawd* and *Gawd* on his rings at the same time I heard tires squealing.

Then I was down.

And out.

CHAPTER NINETEEN

———

The first thing I saw when I opened my eyes was a large crucifix. I would have thought I was in heaven, but I was fairly certain that the crosses in paradise weren't encrusted with cubic zirconias.

I raised my eyes and realized that the crucifix belonged to King, who was stooped over me. With his wide-brimmed hat and distinct front teeth, he looked like the Mad Hatter, only in peach and gold. In that moment, I knew exactly where I was—down the rabbit hole.

"What's going on?" I asked, pulling myself onto my elbows.

He squatted beside me. "You done had yo' bell rung."

It all came flooding back—the twenty-dollar bill, the squealing tires. I looked around for a paramedic or a policeman, but the only people in sight were tourists. "Didn't you call an ambulance?" My tone reflected my anxiety. "I got hit by a car!"

He lowered his gold sunglasses. "There's no need for nervous postrations, now. That car didn't touch a hair on yo' head. But you did get a nasty bump when Apollo pushed you out the street."

Of course, I knew he wasn't referring to the Greek god, but I was kind of holding out hope for a fireman. "Who's Apollo?"

In reply, the wino walked up and waved.

Talk about a misnomer.

"Sorry 'bout that lump, lady," Apollo said, pulling his faded "Tales of the Cocktail" festival T-shirt over his exposed beer belly.

"No problem. Thanks for coming to my rescue." I felt

the side of my head and looked at my hand. There was a trace of blood. "Did either of you get a look at the driver or any information about the car?"

The two men exchanged a look that I'd become all too familiar with since moving to New Orleans—one of a complicit silence that reined supreme among the Kings and Apollos of the city.

"It happened so fast." King spread his hands in a helpless gesture.

Apollo pushed matted brown hair from his puffy face, presumably so that I could see how honest he was trying to look. "And we were worried about you."

"Tha's right." King tipped back his hat. "After you hit yo' head, Apollo carried you ta safety. I couldn't do it myself, you understand, because this suit is dry clean only."

Apollo nodded as though saving the suit was the logical concern.

"Uh-huh." Clearly, I wasn't going to get anywhere with these guys. But if the driver of the careening car was the masked man, he was going to get away with attempted murder.

As I pulled myself to my feet, both men offered their hands. After weighing the two options, I took King's hand, albeit with reluctance. When he let go, I wobbled.

"Hold on ta this." He handed me his cane.

The Baron Samedi topper glinted in the sunlight, and I remembered what I'd asked King before losing consciousness. "We still need to talk about Amber and voodoo."

He turned to Apollo. "Why don't you get the lady somethin' ta calm her nerves? You'll find a selection of beverages in my Caddy."

Apollo's eyes lit up like a neon bar sign, and he hurried around the corner.

Although I couldn't see King's eyes through his dark lenses, I stared straight into them. "I was right about you teaching Amber voodoo, wasn't I?"

"F'true, but it wadn't no big thang." He adjusted his suit coat. "Tha's jus' how we do in New Awlins."

He was right about that—voodoo was an integral part of the local culture. "What did you tell her about a mermaid voodoo goddess?"

"La Sirène?" He pulled a gold toothpick from his pocket. "She's the goddess of the sea and all its treasures. But she's also the goddess of love, motherhood, and protection."

I remembered my earlier conversation with Veronica about Erzulie's three aspects. "Are you sure you're not talking about Erzulie Freda?"

"La Sirène *is* Erzulie," he said, pointing the toothpick at me.

My head was starting to throb—both from the accident and from this conversation. "I don't get it."

He sucked his teeth. "You know how tuna is the Chicken of the Sea?"

I blinked, unsure if he was really referring to the fish or if that bump was getting the best of me. "Uh, I guess?"

"La Sirène's like that." He slipped the toothpick into a corner of his mouth and smiled. "The Erzulie of the sea."

Okay, so it wasn't the bump. "Is it possible to appeal to the gods for more than one thing at the same time? Or maybe to use witchcraft to ask for one thing and voodoo for another?"

His lips protruded. "It's not advisable, no. You got ta put all yo' energy into a request for it ta work. Plus, if you axe fo' mo' than one thing, the gods might think you bein' greedy."

That corresponded to my suspicions about the crime scene. Amber hadn't left that amaretto—the killer had. "If someone is invoking a god, can another person undo it with their own voodoo?"

"F'sure." He nodded. "It's called red magic."

The color red got my attention since the Amaretto di Amore label was red and even the amaretto was a reddish-amber. "Not black magic?"

"Tha's Hollywood." He clutched his bedazzled cross. "In real voodoo, we don't have no black nor white."

I hated to mention the amaretto to King, especially since I'd already asked him about it once before, but he was the best chance I had of deciphering the killer's message. "What if a red magic practitioner gave La Sirène a bottle of amaretto?"

"She'd drink it." He collapsed with laughter and slapped his knee.

While King cracked himself up, I glanced around for Apollo, wishing he'd hurry up with my drink. In the meantime, I decided to try another tack. "If I wanted to ask La Sirène for help, how would I do that?"

He rubbed his eyes beneath his sunglasses. "Lots o' ways—pray to her image, light a candle, hold her *veve*, or jus' take a baf."

I leaned forward. "A what?"

"A baf. You know." He lowered his lenses and winked. "Rub-a-dub-dub?"

I tightened my grip on the cane both because Amber had been taking a bath with La Sirène's image etched into the tub and also because I wasn't sure what that wink was about. "What does her *veve* look like?"

"It's shaped like a diamond about yay big." He rings sparkled as he approximated the size. "And it sits on top of an upside down triangle—"

"With scrolls on each side?" I interrupted.

"You seen it?"

"No, but I've heard about it," I replied, recalling my conversation with Dr. Lessler about the *veve* Amber had worn.

"Tha's good." His head bounced up and down as he straightened his suit coat. "Because you don't want ta mess around with La Sirène."

I thought about Erzulie D'en Tort, Erzulie Freda's Petro manifestation. "Does she have a vindictive side?"

"Her Petro nation aspect is La Baleine, a whale disguised as a nice piece o' tail." He broke into a glittering gold smile. "Like what I did there? The rhyme and the tail thang?"

I wrinkled my lips. It was as close as I could come to faking a smile. "Why does she disguise herself?"

He snorted. "To trick the ones that offended her. She lures 'em inta the deep and drowns 'em."

The drowning didn't quite fit with Amber's murder. Even though she was in the bath, she didn't drown—she was strangled. And Curaçao wasn't anywhere near water when she was killed.

Apollo rounded the corner carrying a black chalice that looked a lot like a pimp cup—except for the word *preacher* written in rhinestones. "This'll make you feel better."

"Is it wine?" I asked as I took the cup from his hand. I wanted to know because I was worried that it had come from Apollo's personal stash.

He smiled, revealing purple-stained teeth. "It's red drink."

"Ah." Red drink was the local name for Barq's Red Creme Soda.

"I tol' you to get her somethin' ta calm her nerves, and you get her creme soda?" King pulled the hat from his head and whacked the wino who stepped backward and knocked the *preacher* cup from my hand.

"Boy!" King stomped a peach wingtip on the sidewalk. "Now look what choo done."

I watched with dismay as the red liquid trickled into the gutter. Make no mistake—I was glad that I didn't have to drink it. But as it drained away, I felt like my hopes of understanding the meaning behind the Amaretto di Amore were draining away with it.

*   *   *

Once I was safely in the Mustang, I pulled a bottle of aspirin from my purse. The headache from my hangover was kid stuff compared to the post-accident migraine assailing my brain.

While I wrestled with the child safety cap, I glanced at my phone. Bradley hadn't called, but Ruth had. Twelve times. I wondered if she'd ever calmed down enough to find her voice, but I didn't really want to find out.

When I finally got the cap off the bottle, Ruth brought the call count to unlucky thirteen.

I put her on speaker and placed the phone on the center console. "You still mad at me?"

There was no heavy breathing, just a series of choking noises.

"I'll take that as a yes." I popped four aspirin and started to chew. Now I had two reasons to need pain relief.

The gagging turned to gurgling.

"Maybe try saying just one word," I suggested as I gingerly laid my head against the headrest.

"Jeff," she gasped.

My head shot up, along with my pain level. "What about him?"

Silence.

"Speak, Ruth," I urged. "You can do it."

"Acting president," she said through clenched teeth.

I grabbed the phone. "Was Bradley fired? Spit it out, woman!"

"On leave."

More choking noises followed, but this time I was the one making them. Jeff might've gotten Bradley's job temporarily, but if he thought that he was going to keep it, he had another thing coming—from me.

Gripping the steering wheel, I ground out, "Get me Craig Burns's phone number ASAP."

* * *

After convincing Craig to meet Ruth and me at ten a.m. the next morning, I was on my way home to treat my head wound and wash my hair. Craig had been reluctant to agree, but luckily Ruth had told me that his favorite restaurant was Cochon Butcher on Tchoupitoulas Street. It had taken considerable coaxing—the promise of a Le Pig Mac and a Cajun Pork Dog as well as a vow of silence if his health-conscious wife ever got wind of the forbidden feast—but in the end his hankering belly had beaten out his hesitant brain.

I could understand why Craig wouldn't want to meet his banker's girlfriend and secretary for breakfast, but there was one thing that I couldn't wrap my hurt head around—he hadn't once reminded me about my lips blowing up like two blowfish at his crawdad boil. And if you knew Craig, then you knew that he was the guy who was going to jokingly remind you of that thing you'd rather forget every time you talked to him for the rest of your life. And his silence about that sensitive subject spoke volumes. Craig was upset with me.

But why? Did he think that I was a professional problem for Bradley too? If so, where would he have gotten such an idea? No matter how upset Bradley got with me, he would never talk about me behind my back. And Ruth wouldn't betray me, either—not because she was loyal to me, mind you, but because she wouldn't want to jeopardize her job. The obvious source was Jeff. But what could he have told Craig about me that would cause him to sever his friendship with Bradley and pull his money from Ponchartrain Bank? Was it about me breaking into the bank's security room the year before and those other minor incidents that Ruth mentioned? Or was it something else?

As I pondered this puzzle, my phone began to ring. To my relief, it wasn't Ruth. But it wasn't Bradley.

With a sigh, I pulled up to a stoplight near Tulane University and pressed answer. "Hey, David. Whaddya got for me?"

"An epic fail."

My gut tensed. David didn't use gaming terms lightly. "This isn't about the vassal and that sugar baby, is it?"

He took a couple of deep breaths, frat-boy-prepping-to-chug-a-forty style. "They hooked up at the martini mixer."

I slammed my fist on the dashboard. "I thought I told you to stop him from going?"

"I tried," he whined. "But he had, like, meta strength. I stood in front of his door to block him, but he picked me up and moved me out of the way."

My eyes almost popped from my head. The vassal was at least a foot shorter than David, and thanks to a lifetime of computer programming and video games, he had the muscles of a newborn babe. "Where is he now?"

"In his dorm room." He cleared his throat. "That's where I'm calling from."

The tension in my belly relaxed somewhat. "So what's the problem?"

"Yeah. About that." He paused. "He wants to clean out his college account to pay for the sugar baby's boob job."

My stomach bounced like a silicone breast implant on a strutting stripper. Not only was the vassal jeopardizing his own future, he was also laying Veronica's and mine on the line because his parents would surely sue. "This time you've got to stop him."

"Uh, I have," he said in an uncertain tone. "But I don't

know how long it's gonna last."

That didn't sound good. "What have you done to the vassal, David?"

"Oh, uh, me and a couple of his dorm mates tied him to his Emperor Palpatine throne with a fifty-foot Ethernet cable."

The light turned green, and I hooked a U-turn. "I'll be right there."

* * *

"Open up!" I yelled as I stood outside the vassal's dorm room in Tulane's Monroe Hall. I was in a hurry to get inside—not so much because I was worried about the vassal, but because the hallway smelled like dirty socks.

The door opened to reveal a pasty-faced boy that I recognized from the first time I'd come to the dorm. Actually, it wasn't so much him that I recognized as his orthodontic headgear. "What's your name again?"

"Shorty." He was as solemn as a soldier as he stepped aside.

The room was so jam-packed with computer equipment and video consoles that it smelled like a Best Buy. But compared to the hallway, it was like perfume to my nose.

As I crossed the threshold, I spotted David sitting beside the vassal's *Star Wars*-themed throne. "Untie him this instant."

"But he'll try to escape," he protested as he rose to his feet.

I strode over to the throne and spun the vassal around to face me. Despite the stress of being bound, he still had his usual slack-jawed stare. "We can trust you to stay put, right Vassal?"

"Honestly," he began, "I'm probably going to make a break for it."

I bowed my aching head. *Why were men so difficult?*

"I know how to handle this," Shorty announced. He reached for the crystal-studded Godric Gryffindor sword hanging on the exposed brick wall above the gaming console.

"Slow down, Shorty." I pulled him away from the sword by the back of his Dumbledore's Army of Tulane T-shirt. "There's no need for weaponry. Now is there, Vassal?"

He shrugged. "Well, if I'm gonna run…"

I pursed my lips. By this point, I was pretty sure that I was getting a headache on top of my migraine.

David looked from the vassal to me. "What should we do?"

"Don't worry. I got this." Resting my hands on the throne armrests, I bent over and leaned into the vassal's face. "You can't throw away your college degree on this girl because you're going to need a lucrative career to keep her in breast lifts. Trust me when I tell you that those implants are eventually going to drop." I straightened and added, "Not that I would know anything about that."

His magnified eyes blinked behind his thick lenses. "You make a valid point."

"All righty, then." I patted him on the thigh. "David's going to untie you, and then we're going to have a chat about the martini mixer. And if you try to run, or if you blow your college money on breasts at any point after I leave here today, then I'm going to get that Ethernet cable, hog-tie you with it, skewer you with your sword, and roast you over a spit like we do in Texas. Sound good?"

His slack-jaw slackened, and Shorty slipped from the room.

David dropped to his knees and began untying the cable at the vassal's feet.

I took a seat on the vassal's twin bed and opened a pizza box. I hadn't eaten a thing since the *pain perdu*, and seeing the vassal tied up like a roast reminded me that it was well past lunchtime. "What's this girl's name, anyway?"

"Sugar Cherie." The vassal sighed. "She's really sweet."

"I'm sure." I bit into an ice-cold slice of pepperoni. "So," I began, covering my full mouth with my hand, "did this, uh, Cherie give you any more info about Amber's sugar daddy? Like a name or a description?"

He shook his head, which was the only part of his body that he could still move. "She never saw the guy because she wasn't at the sugar bowl party Amber went to. Cherie only heard about him after the fact when she ran into her at the mall."

"Crap." I gnawed off a piece of crust.

David began to work a knot behind the vassal's knees. "Didn't she tell you that the guy turned out to be someone Amber already knew?"

The vassal started, as though coming out of a Sugar Cherie-induced stupor. "I almost forgot. Amber said that her sugar daddy was a man she'd known for a while. Apparently, she wasn't aware that he'd been in the market for a sugar baby."

It wasn't much of a lead given that Amber had regularly come into contact with men who spent money on her, but Shakey did come to my mind. "Did she tell you anything else about him? Any little detail?"

The vassal rubbed his freed knees. "Only that he rented her an expensive apartment."

So, the apartment was courtesy of the sugar daddy, and not the mystery mom. "Did you learn anything at all about how the business works?"

"Not really." He stood up so that David could untie the cable at his wrists. "You create an account, and then you can browse the sugar babies' profiles and exchange messages with them. Plus, they have the parties."

"Cherie invited you to the mixer today, right?" I popped a piece of pepperoni into my mouth.

"Yes, but I also got an email invite from the owner—some guy who goes by the name Peach."

I started choking on the pepperoni, and the vassal, whose hands were now free, whacked me on the back, knocking the food from my throat. Personally, I suspected that he was paying me back for my earlier threat, but I couldn't worry about that at the moment.

Because all I could think about was King and his favorite color.

Peach.

It was a long shot, but it wasn't out of the realm of possibility that the preacher was the owner of the sugaring service given his pimp past.

Was it?

CHAPTER TWENTY

———

"If you ask me, Craig escaped through the bathroom window," Ruth said, looking in the direction of the men's room at Cochon Butcher where Craig had gone a good fifteen minutes before.

"Well, I didn't ask you." I rested my elbows on the butcher-block table and massaged my temples. After doing some fleeing of my own—from my family—and spending the night on a couch at Private Chicks, my migraine was gone. But breakfast with Ruth was bringing it back.

She slurped through her straw and jabbed it in the ice. "You probably ran him off with the way you've been beating around the bush about the business at the bank."

I glared at her through my hands. "That's ridiculous, and you know it. He just overdid it with the meal."

The old-world market-style restaurant was a butcher shop, sandwich counter, and wine bar, and within forty-five minutes of arriving, Craig had taken liberal advantage of all three.

I glanced at Ruth's empty whiskey glass—the third of the morning. "That cherry bounce is alcoholic, you know."

"Oh, pshaw." She shooed me and swayed slightly on the tall metal stool. "It's made from cherries."

"Uh, and brandy." I widened my eyes for emphasis.

"And that's made from grapes, which makes this a fine fruit punch." She raised her glass in a salute. "It was one of George Washington's favorite drinks. He used to make it all the time."

"That explains the cherry tree—and the false teeth." I looked around the renovated warehouse and spotted Craig en route to our table.

I turned to Ruth. "Here he comes. Remember, I'm doing the talking."

"All right, but if you don't find out why he's closing his account in the next five minutes..." She made a slicing motion across her neck with one of her plastic cocktail swords.

I rubbed my sweaty palms on my jeans as Craig took his seat.

"I thank you ladies for the nice meal and the pleasant company." He pulled a handkerchief from the pocket of his beige button-down and wiped sweat from his brow—courtesy of the pint of Covington Pontchartrain Pilsner and side of hot boudin sausage he'd had for dessert. "Now why don't you tell me what it is that you need my help with?"

"Actually..." I paused and licked my lips. "Bradley's the one who needs your help."

Craig looked from me to Ruth. "Are you sure this is about him?"

That was an odd question. "Of course I am." I hesitated as I weighed whether to mention Jeff, but then I decided that it was best to be vague in case he and Craig were friends. "Someone at the bank is intentionally sabotaging Bradley."

"And outside the bank too." Ruth pointed her sword at me.

I was tempted to kick her, but it was too much of a risk. She wasn't known for keeping her lips locked, especially when she was liquored up.

"Franki, I don't think anyone at the bank has it in for Bradley." Craig folded his hands. "If he's in trouble, he's either brought it on himself or..." His voice trailed off.

"Or what?" I pressed.

"Well, maybe Ms. Walker's right." His normally booming tone had grown subdued. "Bradley's troubles could be due to someone outside of work."

Ruth grinned behind her glass.

Of course, I suspected that he was referring to me, so I decided to turn the tables on him. "If you're referring to longtime clients like yourself taking their money elsewhere, then yes, his problems stem from the outside."

He pursed his lips. "That's not what I mean."

My eyes narrowed. "What exactly *do* you mean?"

Craig looked down at his empty plate. "A man in Bradley's position needs—"

He stopped short as the bald, bespectacled bartender hand-delivered Ruth's fourth cherry bounce.

When the bartender had left, I asked, "Needs what?"

"A good secretary behind him," Ruth replied, raising her glass and drinking to herself.

I snorted and rolled my eyes.

"You laugh," Craig said in an admonishing tone. "But Ms. Walker's onto something."

"Ain't that the truth, Ruth?" She cackled and drank to herself again.

It took me a second to figure out what he was getting at, but it soon became painfully clear. What Bradley needed wasn't a good secretary—it was a good woman. And, apparently, I wasn't one. "Why don't you just come out and say it, Craig?"

His ruddy complexion turned as red as Ruth's cherry bounce. "You know I've always liked you, Franki—"

"But what?" I interrupted as I crossed my arms.

He slid off his stool and pulled a manila envelope from the side pocket of his briefcase. "It's only right that you know. I got these pictures in two emails—the most recent came last night."

My hands were shaking as I took the envelope and pulled out the pictures. As I flipped through them, so many things began to make sense, starting with the reason I'd been followed. Based on the images, I gathered that the photographer could've also been the driver of the car that had almost clipped me and possibly even the man in black.

There were seven photos in all—me being released from Central Lockup, holding a pentagram at Erzulie's Authentic Voodoo, drinking booze from a bag in front of Vieux Carré Wine & Spirits, hanging out with a preacher who looked like a pimp on Bourbon Street, wrestling with a drag queen outside a drunk stripper's house, stripping with a snake at Madame Moiselle's, and, the coup de grace, lying unconscious in the arms of a wino.

With each picture, Ruth's breathing had grown heavier.

But I refused to look at her—or at Craig, for that matter. Instead, I took a minute to fight back the angry tears stinging my eyes. I couldn't imagine what I'd done to deserve such a hateful attack, or how I was going to undo the damage to Bradley. Because even though I could explain the pictures, they were still proof enough that I was a professional and personal problem that Bradley needed to wash his hands of if he wanted to save his job and salvage his career. It was time for me to walk away so that Bradley could make things right at work and move on.

When I finally had my emotions in check, I looked at Craig. "I'm assuming that the sender of those emails was Jeff Payne?"

He bowed his head in reply.

Ruth bowed her head too, but she wasn't mad. She was as juiced as a jackrabbit on a wheatgrass farm.

* * *

Glenda opened her apartment door strutting her stuff to the RuPaul song "Supermodel (You Better Work)." Even though it was past noon, she was still in her pajama pasties. "Hello, Miss Franki." She shook her *Playboy* bunny tail. "Do we have investigating to do?"

"It's St. Joseph's Day, so I'm calling it a mental health day," I replied, fully conscious of the fact that I had to carry out the lunatic act of stealing a lemon from a church that night. "But I was hoping to talk to Veronica. Is she around?"

"She went to lunch with Dirk, sugar." Her eyes narrowed as she scrutinized my face. "Why don't you come in so we can chat?"

I really wanted to vent to Veronica about what Jeff had done, but if I had to choose between talking to Glenda and the nonne, it was a no-brainer. "Okay, but are you having a party or something?"

"A few of the girls from Lucky Pierre's are here," she replied as I stepped inside. "And Miss Carnie's on her way."

That explained the music selection.

Glenda closed the door behind me. "We're cooking for

Amber's funeral tomorrow. And between you and me," she said in a low voice, "those women are slave drivers. I've worked on my feet, knees, and hands for years, and I can barely keep up with them."

Probably because they're really men. "Hey, where's Maybe?"

"Still asleep." She gestured toward the giant champagne glass in the center of her all white living room, and I could make out Maybe curled up in faux fur blankets inside.

"Must be nice," I muttered, thinking about my bedtub and that blasted enema bag as I followed Glenda into the kitchen.

After days of seeing the nonne baking in black at my house, the scene at Glenda's was disorienting. With Céline in a sheer Cher-style number, Dolly in a crystal country costume, and Gaysia in a geisha-inspired gown, I felt like I was backstage at Cirque du Soleil—or The Grand Ole Opry—instead of in a kitchen. "Hey guys, er, gals. What're y'all making?"

"A chocolate-cherry piecaken," Dolly chirped as she stirred cherries in a saucepan. "It's a drag dessert."

I opened the cabinet and got a champagne flute—the only glassware Glenda kept in the house. "How is that drag?"

Céline cocked a silver-glittered brow as she kneaded dough. "Because it's a pie baked inside a cake."

"Okay?" I turned on the faucet and filled my glass.

Glenda lit a cigarette in a pink holder. "It's all in the imagery, Miss Franki. Think of it as beef cake but with cherry pie."

For the first time I was grateful that I'd given up sweets for Lent. I took a sip of water and pulled out a chair, but there was raw poultry on the seat cushion. "Ugh! Who put these chicken cutlets here?"

Gaysia turned off the mixer and picked them up with her bare hands. "Uh, *hello*, Hunty! It's not like they're the kind you eat."

"What other kind is there?" I asked, bewildered.

"The kind you make boobies with," she replied, stuffing them into her bra.

I poured out my water and grabbed an open bottle of champagne.

"What's eating at you, sugar?" Glenda sat on the kitchen table trucker-girl-mudflap-style. "Are you having more man troubles?"

"You could say that." I flopped into the chair. "Jeff Payne, the manager at Bradley's bank, has been sending pictures of me in compromising positions to the bank clients."

Glenda gave me a half-lidded look. "You took nudie pics?"

"Werk it, girl," Céline said as she rolled out the piecrust.

Gaysia licked chocolate cake batter from her finger. "Sounds like Ms. Cheesecake could teach us a thing or two in the dessert department."

"It wasn't like that." I filled my champagne glass to the brim. "Out of context the pictures look incriminating, but they're not."

"Mm-hmm," the queens intoned in unison.

"I'm serious," I protested. "Jeff set me up so that he could get Bradley fired and take his position as president."

Dolly stopped stirring. "Now why in the heck would this man sabotage you to get your beau's job?"

"Because women have been exploited by men throughout herstory," Gaysia replied, jabbing the mixer at an invisible enemy.

Céline shook her rolling pin. "Someone needs to make this Jeff guy RuPaulogize."

"He'll get what's coming to him, girls." Glenda took a deep drag off her cigarette. "'Whatsoever a man soweth, that shall he also reap.'"

My jaw dropped as my injured brain wondered whether it had hallucinated that Bible quote. If it hadn't, then forget Cirque du Soleil and The Grand Ole Opry—Glenda's kitchen was *The Twilight Zone.*

As if to reinforce my theory, Carnie entered the room sporting a blonde pixie wig and a shift dress with long, puffed sleeves covered with pink, yellow, and orange daisies. She looked like the 1960s model Twiggy, only trunky.

"Sorry I'm late." She spotted me and put a hand on her chest. "Well, look what the tiger cat dragged in. I haven't heard from you in so long that I thought you'd run off to the jungle to live among your kind—the snakes."

I sighed. Carnie was no hippie at a love-in, no matter what her outfit implied. "Um, I saw you three days ago, and I've been working on your case ever since."

She sniffed and eyeballed my champagne. "Doesn't look like you're working now."

"It's Saturday, Miss Carnie." Glenda gave her a reproachful look. "Miss Franki's taking a well-deserved day off."

Carnie glanced at her mod Mary Janes and managed to look quasi-contrite. "I was shocked when I saw the news about Curaçao's murder. Glenda said she was wearing an amber pendant. Do you think it was mine?"

"I'm no Dirk, but I'd say it was the fake," I replied. "Real amber doesn't sparkle the way that pendant did when I shined my flashlight on it."

Céline placed a platter of pigs in a blanket in front of me and winked. "The weenies are tucked extra tight."

"Awesome," I said, because it seemed like the appropriate reply.

"You know," Carnie began as she took a seat, "I can't say I'm surprised that Commie waxer is a killer."

"We don't know that Nadezhda killed anyone." I helped myself to a pig in a blanket. "Eugene is still a suspect, and so is Amber's ex-pimp."

Glenda exhaled a puff of smoke. "This is the first I've heard of you suspecting King. What gives?"

I blew on the piping hot pig. "Yesterday I found out that he might be the owner of the sugaring company Amber was working for."

Carnie shrugged her psychedelic shoulders. "So, he found a new way to exploit her. That doesn't make him the killer, either."

"I know, but preaching for tips on Bourbon Street has to be the world's worst way to make a living—second only to begging at a homeless shelter." I pulled the pig from the blanket and popped it into my mouth. "He needs another source of income, and your necklace could've set him up in suits for a long time."

Glenda stubbed out her cigarette. "Miss Eve did tell us

that King has been upstairs at Madame Moiselle's, so he knows his way around the place."

"Right." I swallowed and bit into the blanket. "I just have to verify that he goes by the nickname Peach."

"Peach?" Carnie echoed. "Gurl, I heard Amber talking on the phone to someone by that name about a month ago. That's why I thought she was hooking again."

I almost choked in mid-chew.

"Why?" Glenda slid seductively off the table. "What did she say?"

Carnie pressed flower-power fingernails to her pixie. "She said something about not being able to take on another client while she was in school. I figured it had to be a regular john."

I swallowed. "Or a second sugar daddy."

Either way, it was time to pay another visit to the pulpit.

* * *

Semi-convinced that I was being punked, I glanced in the rearview mirror and then turned to stare at my mother from my Mustang window. "Are you guys seriously going to watch the St. Joseph's Day parade from Madame Moiselle's balcony?"

"Well, what do you expect us to do, Francesca?" She flailed her arms like a drowning woman. "Santina just started walking again, and your nonna doesn't like crowds. It's the perfect place."

Sure, except for the nude women, the horny men, the simulated sex acts, the excessive drinking, the foul language, and the occasional fist fights. "Uh, does this mean that you're okay with me stripping there?"

My mother's lips grew as thin as a switchblade. "I didn't drive all the way from Houston—with your nonna, no less—to have you smart off to me. Drop the attitude before you get back from parking the car."

"So much for the mental health day," I said as I pulled away from the curb, and I didn't care if she'd heard me. I wasn't big on parades, especially after I'd gotten arrested at the last one. And now not only did I have to go to a parade, but I had to watch it with my mom and the nonne from lap dance chairs on the balcony of a sex club.

If I ever made it back, that is. The parade was due to start at six, which wasn't for another hour. But the Quarter was already packed, and I had to make it the mile to the Private Chicks parking lot.

As I inched my way up Burgundy Street, I started to think about Bradley and the fact that he hadn't called. Attorney's orders or no, he should've contacted me by now, and I couldn't understand why he hadn't. He wasn't the type to blame me for his own actions, so the only thing I could guess was that he was embarrassed about punching Detective Sullivan. *Or...*

My blood ran so cold that icicles pierced my heart.

...Jeff had sent him those pictures.

I shuddered and shook off the thought. Even though it didn't matter if he had seen the pictures since I was planning to break up with him, I couldn't go there, not now. To distract myself, I looked out the window at some members of the Italian-American Marching Club who were standing by their traditional ATV-drawn chariots. I took one look at their signature black tuxedoes with flashy red and green bowties and stacks of matching Mardi Gras beads around their necks, and I swerved onto St. Ann.

Forget the freakin' parade, I had a pimp-preacher to call on.

It took twenty minutes to travel the two short blocks to King's corner, but I was rewarded for my travail. He was standing in the pulpit in a silk dollar-bill suit—not with bills pinned to the fabric like Glenda did to me on my birthday but with solid dollar-bill print fabric.

And on the subject of bills, a buxom fifty-something woman in a bodacious blue spandex minidress was in the process of handing him a wad of them. It was too much to be a donation for a street sermon but enough to be a payout from a long day of hooking.

King looked over his shoulder when he pocketed the cash, as though making sure no one had seen him. By chance, our eyes locked through the windshield, and he broke into a run.

On autopilot, I whipped into a customer-service zone

and hopped from the car. As I gave chase, he dashed up the street and darted to the right.

When I rounded the corner, he ducked into the last place I would've expected—Cathedral Academy, an old convent chapel that served as the site of St. Louis Cathedral's altar to St. Joseph.

I ran inside and saw David and the vassal standing by the altar as King hoofed it up the aisle on the right side of the building.

"Stop that preacher!" I yelled as I pointed at King.

Not known for their physical prowess—unless sugar baby boobs were at play—David and the vassal began pelting King with lemons, presumably those that my mom and nonna had bought to ensure my engagement.

At least they're serving some purpose, I thought, *because my engagement odds aren't looking good.*

King stopped running and shielded himself with his arms, and I shoved him stomach-down to the ground.

"You're Peach, aren't you?" I ground out as I straddled his back and twisted his arms behind him.

"What choo talkin' 'bout, woman?" he demanded with one side of his face pressed to the floor.

"You own the sugar baby company that Amber signed up with. Admit it," I ordered as I gave his wrists a twist.

"Ow!" He kicked his leopard-spotted shoes. "I don't own no damn comp'ny."

"Then what was that woman paying you for?" I leaned close to his ear. "And don't try telling me it was for a sermon, because if you do, you'll be preaching that song and dance to the police."

His body went slack. "I cain't be arrested. I'm in a sanctuary."

That explained the choice of the chapel. I turned to David and the vassal. "Arm yourselves."

"That won't be necessary, now." King drew a deep breath. "If you mus' know, I'm often called upon by the female doubters in my congregation to help them find the divine— through sacred unity."

"I don't understand."

He grinned revealing his gold teeth. "I help them find Gawd with sex."

I cocked a brow as the reality of what he'd said dawned on me—and as I tried to comprehend how any woman could get past his suits. "You're a *gigolo*?"

"If you don't mind, I prefer the term *spiritual escort*."

I climbed off of him. "No more questions."

King stood up and straightened his pink dollar-sign tie. "I'd like to say it was a pleasure, but instead I'll wish you all a blessed day." He looked at me and winked. "And may the Lawd be with you."

For once, the vassal wasn't the only one with a slack-jawed stare. David and I watched equally open-mouthed as the pimp-turned-preacher-gigolo strolled from the chapel like a king leaving his castle.

"We'd better pick up those lemons," I said as I noted the whispers and scowls of a few churchwomen. "What're you guys doing here, anyway?"

David scratched his head. "Uh, your nonna said we had to test out the altar before you guys got here from the parade."

I rolled my eyes. "Thank God it's finally St. Joseph's Day so I can get back to my life, and you can get back to working on the case."

"Oh, I have something for you." He pulled a piece of paper from his back pocket. "I looked up Old New Orleans Traditional Witchcraft, but it's, like, lame."

"Why do you say that?" I asked as I bent over to retrieve a lemon.

The vassal pushed up his glasses. "Because the practitioners rely mainly on different colors of the same candle for all their witchcraft needs."

"Huh?" I stood up and looked at the color printout in David's hand, and my face turned as white as the image he was pointing to.

It was the candle of the nude woman I'd seen in the kitchen at Madame Moiselle's on the day Curaçao's body was discovered.

The one that Eve Quebedeaux had lit.

CHAPTER TWENTY-ONE

———

"Why did we have to visit this altar again?" Glenda asked as she wrestled with the blue and white tablecloths that the nonne had draped over her. "I'm sweatin' like a whore in church in this getup."

I refrained from commenting on her second statement given that a) the Cathedral Academy was owned by the Catholic Church, and b) she was dressed like the Virgin Mary. "You heard the nonne—because we're stripper sinners, you need to eat, and I have to steal a lemon."

"Oh, for heaven's sake." She grabbed a grissino off the table, bit off the tip, and chewed it like she was eating a dead cricket. "There." She choked down the breadcrumbs. "I've eaten. Now I'm heading back over to Madame Moiselle's."

I grabbed her by the garments. "Not without me you don't. You're my ticket out of this hell."

She rolled her eyes. "Then swipe a damn lemon already."

By this point, I was more than ready to steal a lemon if it meant getting my mom and nonna on the road back to Houston. The problem was that people were milling around all three tiers of the altar. "I have to wait until no one's looking."

Glenda frowned at a fig pie next to a platter of lemons. "Then you might want to gouge out the eyes on this pie."

The only eyes I wanted to gouge out were Bruno Messina's, because they'd been glued to my chest ever since he'd arrived with Santina to see the altar. "That's a St. Lucy's eye pie," I explained as I gave Bruno a go-to-hell glare. "They put eyes on it because she was blinded for refusing to renounce her Christian faith."

She blinked blue lashes. "That's an odd tradition."

What could I say? Obviously, since I was about to steal a lemon from the church to get a husband, the oddities in the Sicilian-American culture abounded.

"And what does '*prega per noi*' mean?" she asked, referring to the words written in crust on the pie.

"'Pray for us.' And frankly, I could use some prayers right now." I looked longingly at a bottle of Pinot Grigio on the altar. "Between my crazy family and this case, I don't think I'm going to make it to thirty-one."

As though reading my mind, Glenda picked up the bottle and popped the cork. "Well, your mom and nonna are leaving the day after tomorrow, and you're making progress in the case. You've practically ruled out Saddle and King as suspects."

"But I've added Eve, I think." I picked up a wine glass. "I mean, she's the house mom, so it makes sense that she could be Amber's mother figure. I just can't believe she's a witch. She seems so normal."

Glenda filled my glass. "Appearances can be deceiving, Miss Franki."

"I'll say." I glanced at her Virgin Mary look. "The thing is, Nadezhda could be a witch too."

"Why don't you call Witchiepoo?" she asked as she poured herself a drink.

I almost gagged on my wine. "Theodora?"

"No, sugar," she replied drily. "The witch from *H.R. Pufnstuf.*"

I looked at her like she'd lost it. "Why would I want to call that whacked witch?"

"Because she might be able to tell you whether Eve is a witch." She tipped her glass toward me. "And Nadezhda too, for that matter."

As much as I wanted to avoid Theodora, I knew she could help. After all, she was a *witchcraft consultant*, according to her business card. "I guess I could ask her to stop by Amber's funeral in the morning. I'm sure Eve and Nadezhda will be there."

"Perfect." She took the wine from my hand. "Why don't you go pick your fruit and then give her a call?"

"All right. Here goes nothing." Glancing from side to side, I approached the lemons. When I reached the table, the platter raised to the level of my hand. Astonished, I looked around and spotted my nonna—holding a remote control.

Now I knew why she'd had David and the vassal design the altar.

"Franki, baby!" Bruno shouted from behind me.

I jumped as though my hand had been in the collection plate instead of the lemon platter.

He lowered his mirrored shades. "Or should I call you *Tiger Eye*?"

As smooth as his slicked back hair, I thought. "You don't call me anything after throwing me under the bus to your mother."

"Hey, it was nothing personal." He straightened the black collar of his *Saturday Night Fever* shirt. "I had to tell her something after she found a receipt from the club in my pants pocket."

No doubt when she was doing your laundry.

"By the way, Mamma said you liked those peanuts." He gave a self-assured sneer. "Consider them a belated birthday gift."

I rolled my eyes. The peanuts reminded me that I still had to go back to the dentist to get my permanent crown, which was yet another reason to dislike Bruno. "Yeah. Thanks."

He nudged me with his shoulder. "I hear you're gonna swipe a lemon."

"Why would I do that?" There was no way I was going to let this creep think I was looking for a proposal.

His beady black eyes widened. "Because you're not getting any younger, and I've seen you strip."

Before I could react, Glenda stepped between us and pointed at a platter with twelve whole fried trout, symbolizing the twelve apostles.

"Move it on along, mister, or you'll be sleeping with the fishes." She picked up a loaf of bread shaped like a cross and held it like a club. "You got me?"

Bruno backed away and ran to his mother.

"Now's your chance, sugar." Glenda pointed the cross at

the altar. "Go get yourself a lemon."

I saw my nonna and a short, dark-haired woman headed in our direction. "I can't. My nonna's on her way over here with someone."

Nonna shuffle-strutted up wearing a tricolored sash that one of the parade marchers had bestowed on her, as well as the "Kiss me, I'm Italian" beads that she'd wrenched from the grip of Swedish tourist. With her black mourning dress, the red and green accessories made her look like Miss Elderly Italian-America.

"Glenda," Nonna began as she took her by the arm, "my friend-a Mary, she want-a to meet you."

I smirked and wondered if it was because of Glenda's Virgin Mary garb.

"How nice." Glenda smoothed her tablecloths.

"She say you bake-a the best-a man hands she's-a seen," Nonna said with an approving nod.

Mary put a hand on her bosom. "The detail! I don't know how you do it."

Oh, I did. Glenda had intimate knowledge of the male hand.

Mary turned to me, wide-eyed. "If you haven't seen her work, you really should take a look at it."

"Eh, she's-a no gotta time for that." Nonna shoved me toward the altar. "She's-a gotta get a lucky fava bean. Right, Franki?"

Of course, lucky fava bean was code for lemon. But, I figured I could use a fava bean too since it was supposed to give you good luck in the coming year. "Sure, Nonna." I sighed. "Whatever you say."

While they continued to talk man hands, I made my way around the altar looking for a bowl of the beans. I passed the *pasta milanese* topped with *mudica*, which was browned breadcrumbs representing Joseph's sawdust, the fried *pignolatti* pastries reminiscent of the pine cones that Jesus played with as a child, and, my favorite, the *pupa cu l'ova* bread baskets baked with dyed eggs inside as a reminder of the coming of Easter.

I found the fava beans next to the *cucchidati* fig cookies at the base of the life-sized statue of St. Joseph holding the baby

Jesus, which was on the main tier of the altar. I pocketed a bean, hoping that it would undo the effects of the curse I'd been living under.

Thinking of the curse reminded me of the one allegedly on those who hunted for the missing Amber Room. Logic told me that the people who had died searching for the priceless treasure had probably been killed by accident or by the hands of greedy individuals, and not because of any curse. Was that what had happened to Amber and Curaçao? Had they been killed for the amber pendant? Or were their murders tied to a love gone horribly wrong, as the bottle of amaretto suggested?

And where was the pendant? I had a hunch that whoever had broken into Maybe's house had been looking for it. But was it there?

I gazed up at the statue of St. Joseph and the baby Jesus. As I looked to them for divine inspiration, something whizzed past me and knocked a statuette of the Virgin Mary to the floor. Startled, I looked down.

It was a lemon.

I looked back at St. Joseph as another lemon shot from between his feet and hit me hard on the arm.

Then I clenched my teeth. Either St. Joseph was trying to tell me that the answers to my questions lay in finding a husband, or Nonna had David and the vassal put an air cannon underneath the statue that she was now using to pelt me with lemons.

Clearly, it was the latter.

Crouching into my old softball outfielder stance, I caught the next lemon and slipped it into my pocket. Then I turned and looked around. Incredibly, no one seemed to have noticed.

Cursing my nonna all the while, I knelt to pick up the statuette and saw that it had broken. I was pretty sure that breaking an image of the Virgin Mary negated the effects of the lemon and the fava bean and ensured more years of bad luck than a broken mirror. But hey, I'd been living this way for thirty years. What was ten or so more?

The statuette had broken in half, and it was hollow. I fit Mary's upper and lower half together to see whether they could be glued, and I flashed back to another hollow figurine I'd seen.

A jolt went through me as though God were striking me down. And no, I hadn't been hit by another lemon. I'd been struck by a shocking realization.

I knew exactly where the amber pendant was hidden.

* * *

From my stool at the Madame Moiselle's bar, I rubbed my eyes and looked at the stripper pole clock. It was ten forty a.m., and I'd spent a sleepless night thinking about Bradley and the case. Now everyone I'd questioned was gathered near Amber's casket in front of the main stage—Carlos, Iris, Bit-O-Honey, Saddle, Maybe, Eugene, Nadezhda, Eve, King, and even Dr. Lessler. It felt like the culminating scene in an Agatha Christie novel. I just wished that Miss Marple or Hercule Poirot would show up and solve the murders.

Other guests included Detective Sullivan, who, like me, was keeping an eye on the situation. He was seated at a table in the middle with his men, as was Carnie with hers. My mother was sitting in the back with the nonne. She'd insisted on attending to show her support since Amber didn't have any immediate family. And the nonne had come because that's what little old Italian ladies did in their spare time.

One thing that struck me was the mood in the room. No one was sad, and everyone was tense. The dancers didn't know what to make of the cops being there, the cops didn't know what to make of the drag queens being there, and none of them knew what to make of the nonne being there. But the nonne didn't seem bothered by the odd assortment of people. They were too busy trying to cover all the exposed flesh with their shawls, and I, for one, was grateful that they'd bundled up Bit-O-Honey and her boobs good and tight.

Out of the corner of my eye, I spotted Glenda coming downstairs from the dressing room in a black cage dress and a matching mourning hat with a veil. She paused and placed her hand on the closed casket and then strutted up to me. "Is Glinda the Good Witch here yet?"

"Pfff," I scoffed. "She's more like Elphaba with a healthy

dose of Endora. And I left her a voice mail, but I haven't heard back from her."

Glenda slid onto a stool. "Well, I hope she flies in on her broom soon, because we have to start at eleven o'clock sharp. The jazz band has another funeral after this."

I took a sip of the obituary cocktail that Carlos had prepared for me. "What's the agenda?"

"We'll process with the hearse to the cemetery for the burial, and then we'll process back to the club for the food and stripperoke." She pulled a pair of black funeral gloves from her bag. "You know, a proper funeral."

I tilted my head to one side and then the other, unsure where to start. "What's stripperoke?"

"Karaoke with strippers," she replied as she pulled a glove onto her hand. "They strip to try to distract the singer."

By this point, I knew better than to question Glenda's logic, but I had to ask. "How is that proper at a funeral?"

She slipped on her other glove. "Amber was a stripper, sugar. And the mourners need some form of release."

Oh, they'll get it, I thought as I took another drink of my cocktail. "Any word from Shakey?"

"Not so far." She lit the cigarette in her *Breakfast at Tiffany's*-style holder and exhaled. "But he's still got fifteen minutes."

Someone tapped me on the back, and I turned to see Nonna and Santina armed with shawls.

"Ciao, Franki." Nonna turned to Glenda. "I see you got-a your face all-a covered up." Her gaze lowered to the straps that barely covered her body. "But it look-a like you forgot-a your dress again."

Santina shoved a shawl at Glenda. "*Dai, prendilo!*"

"She's telling you to take it," I explained in an apologetic tone.

"No ma'am." Glenda gestured to her cage dress with one hand while holding her cigarette with the other. "This is proper attire for strip clubs and jazz funerals. I draw the line at a habit."

Nonna raised her chin, and Santina lowered her lids.

Sensing a Sicilian storm on the horizon, I said, "They're not habits. They're mourning dresses."

Glenda forced a smile. "I'm not saying I don't like them. In fact, I think they're…well…*convenient.* You didn't even have to change for the funeral."

"You know us-a," Nonna said, pointing a thumb at herself and Santina. "At-a our age, we're always-a mourning something!" She chuckled as though enjoying her grieving status. And from the way she talked about my late nonnu, I was pretty sure that she was.

Santina nudged my nonna. "*Il limone.*"

"Oh, that's-a right!" Nonna turned to me. "Show us the lemon that you stole-a last night."

Refraining from an eye roll, I fished the fruit from my purse and noticed that it was bruised.

Nonna planted her hands on her cheeks with a smack. "*Oddio!* You stole a *lemon* lemon?"

A bitter taste filled my mouth like I'd just bitten into the bad lemon. "Is that a problem?"

"Sorry to interrupt," Carnie boomed as she bounced up in a black Elizabethan bustle dress and a hat with a bulky black bow. "But we need to chat."

I glanced at my nonna, anxious for her reply. With my luck, the bum lemon meant that Bruno would be the one to propose to me instead of Bradley.

"*Pronto,*" Carnie pressed, yanking me from my seat to the end of the bar.

Prying my arm from her manly grip, I huffed, "What's the matter with you?"

She crossed her big biceps over her bigger bosom. "Glenda says you know where the pendant is, so I'm wondering why I don't have it. Are you trying to squeeze a few extra paychecks out of me or something?"

"No one wants to squeeze you." *Least of all me.* "When you hired me for this case, you said you wouldn't feel right if you didn't try to find Amber's killer. I think I have a way to do that."

The muscles in her jaw relaxed. "I'm listening."

Even though she seemed calm, I took a few steps back to keep a safe distance between us. "Since the funeral is closed casket, you start the rumor that your amber pendant has been found, and you say that given the tragedy now associated with it, you've decided to let Amber be buried in the necklace. Then we wait and see who tries to open the casket before it goes into the ground, and we have our killer."

"It's morbid, but I like it." She put her hands on her hips. "Is there someone specific you want me to tell?"

"The queens," I replied without missing a beat.

Her blue lids dropped like metal shutters. "Are you implying that we're gossips?"

"Yes, I am."

She nodded, and the bow on her hat did too. "Fair enough."

I exhaled as she turned and bustled back to her table.

When I returned to my stool, a tiny, forty-something man dressed in a dark green suit, black boots, and a black Stetson entered the club.

I patted Glenda's shoulder. "Is that western-style leprechaun Shakey?"

She turned and lifted her veil. "Sure is, sugar. I've never met him, but I've seen him around."

Shakey's spurs jangled as he approached the bar. "Miss Glenda O'Brien?"

"The one and only." She extended a gloved hand, and he didn't have to bow to kiss it.

"Pleased to make your acquaintance," he drawled in a high-pitched voice. "Milton Presacco, but my friends call me Shakey."

Glenda gave a sly smile. "As in, *The Shakiest Gun in the West*?"

"With all due respect, ma'am," he replied, removing his hat, "there's nothing shaky about my gun."

She cocked a brow. "Duly noted, cowboy."

"Um," I interjected to break the awkward sexual-weapon vibe, "why do they call you Shakey?"

He placed his Stetson on the bar counter, which was as tall as he was. "Because I used to own a chain of Shakey's Pizza Parlors. Now I'm in olive oil. Got a grove outside o' Austin."

Texas oil baron, my eye. "Well, my name is Franki Amato, and I was contracted to investigate Amber's murder with Glenda."

He ran a hand through his reddish wisps of hair. "I heard through the grapevine that Miss O'Brien was working with a PI, so I wanted to tell y'all what I told the police."

"You have information about the case?" I asked as I reached into my bag for a pad and pen.

"Indeed I do, ma'am." He straightened his bolo tie. "Like I told that detective, Amber got mixed up in some bad business on account o' her mama—not her real mama, mind you, but kinda like a stepmama."

I glanced at Glenda. "What kind of bad business?"

"She went and got herself a sugar daddy," he said in a low tone.

Glenda crossed her legs. "We know all about that, Shakey."

"Hang on, though," I said, holding up my hand. "What does her mother have to do with the sugar daddy?"

He tucked a thumb inside his silver-buckled belt. "She had a rough view of relationships. Told Amber that all women exchanged their bodies for money, even wives with their husbands. Said she might as well get a man to pay her bills and keep her freedom."

Precisely the kind of thing I could imagine Nadezhda saying. "Do you know anything about her mother or her sugar daddy?"

Shakey scratched his clean-shaven cheek. "I can't say I know anything about the man, but her mama goes by the name o' Peach."

I sunk onto my stool.

Amber's mother owned the sugaring company.

CHAPTER TWENTY-TWO

"Did you see that?" Gaysia shrieked as she stood in the cemetery with her hands pressed to her wig cap. "That hoochie mama ho pulled off my hair!"

The jazz band abruptly halted their rendition of "The Stripper" as Saddle waved Gaysia's black-and-blonde wig like a handkerchief.

"*Your* hair?" Saddle laughed like a coyote. "You got this fur piece off a German Shepherd."

Gaysia gasped and swiped at Saddle with panda-adorned claws.

A scuffle broke out between the queens and the dancers. And as Detective Sullivan and his men set about breaking up the brawl, feathers and sequins began to fly.

"So much for a 'proper' funeral," I said under my breath, although nothing about it had been proper. Before the procession had gotten underway, the dancers announced that they would be the "first line," traditionally reserved for family, and that the queens would be the "second line," reserved for friends and passersby. A catfight ensued, and rather than "processing" to the cemetery, the strippers and queens had scratched, slapped, and shoved each other the entire way—that is, when they weren't voguing and vamping for onlookers.

"I've had enough of this nonsense," Glenda huffed as she high-stepped onto a tomb in black stripper shoes that said *Pay Your Respects*. "Ladies! Where are your manners? We're in a place of rest."

The scuffling ceased.

Gaysia retrieved her wig from the ground and arranged it on her head. "I know Amber was a stripper, Miss Glenda, but we queens feel that the strippers should walk in the second line on the way back to the club." She smoothed her mofuku kimono. "We belong in the first line because we have style." She turned to Carnie. "Except for you, Lady-boy Macbeth. With those garage doors, you belong in the second line."

"Garage doors?" Carnie's face turned purple. "This blue on my eyelids is a blend, not a single shade."

King stepped between the querulous queens. "There's no need ta fight, ladies…" He turned to Carnie and her crew. "…and gentlemen. Cuz, like our Lawd and savior hisself, King Nation is here ta save the occasion." He grasped the zebra-striped lapels of his black velvet suit. "If it's style y'all want, then I'll lead the procession back ta the club."

I halfway agreed with him. He *was* wearing red leather shoes reminiscent of a previous pope—but his were crocodile, not cow.

"You and I need to talk," Detective Sullivan growled over my shoulder. "Now."

Although I had no intention of speaking to the detestable detective, I followed him down a path, away from the gossip-prone guests. "Until you drop the charges against Bradley, I've got nothing to say to you."

"Well, I have something to say to you." He placed a hand above his holster. "There's a rumor circulating that the missing pendant is on the body. You wouldn't know anything about that, would you?"

As a former cop, I knew that he would be obliged to open Amber's casket if I didn't tell him the truth, and I didn't want it to come to that. "I started the rumor to flush out the killer."

His ice blue eyes turned stone cold. "And you have no idea where the amber is."

I hesitated, and he stepped forward.

"Save your breath," I said, holding up my hands. "I'll tell you where the pendant is when the funeral's over."

Glenda strutted down the pathway with her cigarette holder. Scowling at the detective, she flicked her ash and turned to me. "The service has started, Miss Franki."

"We'll resume this discussion at the end of the

ceremony, Amato." He straightened his tie and stalked off toward the gravesite.

She thrust out a hip. "You all right, sugar?"

"Yeah, thanks for coming to get me," I said as we headed back. It wasn't that I didn't want to deal with the detective—I just didn't want to miss the eulogy. Bit-O-Honey had obtained ministry credentials online for Amber's funeral, and it wasn't every day that you got to see an ordained stripper minister.

As we made our way back, Theodora emerged from a burial vault like a zombie from a grave.

I swallowed a scream to avoid causing a scene.

Glenda gave her the onceover. "You must be the witch."

"My name's Theodora." She brushed dirt from her black caftan. "It means God given, which is kind of ironic, don't you think?"

On a couple of levels. I cleared my throat. "Uh, we need to get back to the service. Theodora, I'll point out the two women I left you the message about."

"Sounds like a plan." She extracted a root protruding from a broken crypt and took a bite.

My belly began to bubble like a cauldron. "Do you have to eat here?"

"Yes, we're serving pigs in a blanket and piecaken after the service," Glenda said in a helpful tone.

Theodora spat, and it was red from the root—at least I hoped that's what it was from. "I can't come to the club." She wiped her mouth with her wing-like sleeve. "Tonight's a full moon."

Not wanting any details of her lunar exploits, I hurried toward the attendees and started scouring the seating area by the casket for Nadezhda.

The first two rows of folding chairs were occupied by my mom and the nonne, who'd convinced Shakey to sit with them not only because he was their same size but also because he was now their olive oil contact in the "new country." The strippers were in the last two rows, and King had planted himself among them since they comprised a whole new crop of women that he could help to "find Gawd." The queens stood behind the seating area, this time voluntarily taking a backseat to the strippers, because it meant they were with all the men.

I spotted Nadezhda near the queens, leaning on a mausoleum topped with a stone cross. And I was surprised to see that she was deep in conversation with Drag Dolly, who was presumably spreading the necklace rumor. "That's one of the women right there."

Theodora lowered her sunglasses and fixed her feline eyes on Nadezhda.

Unaware that she was being watched, Nadezhda sidled up to Eugene and whispered something in his ear.

My heart raced when I saw Eugene's gaze lock onto the casket. Even though I was unable to prove it, I was positive that the pair had plotted to steal the pendant.

Theodora pushed up her sunglasses. "That one's a witch, but the kind that starts with a *b*."

At least I'd been right on that count.

"Where's the other woman?" she asked, scanning the crowd.

"Over there." I pointed at Eve, who was standing by a tree to the left of the seating, red-faced, and wringing her hands.

Theodora removed her sunglasses and chewed on the tip. "There's something earthy about her, yes."

I scrutinized Eve, who'd been getting more distraught as the day progressed. "Why do you think that?"

"Have you missed the fact that I'm a witch?" she snapped, pointing her creepy pupils at me.

"D-definitely not," I stuttered, moving backwards a step.

She turned and looked at Eve. "Did you notice that she's wearing amber?"

My head jerked in Eve's direction. Sure enough, it looked like she had an amber pendant around her neck, but it was round, not rectangular like the missing piece. "Maybe in honor of Amber?"

"Or to invoke the mother goddess." Theodora narrowed her eyes like a cat contemplating a mouse. "She seems like an amateur. Is she from New Orleans?"

I shrugged. "Her last name is Cajun, but I just assumed from her accent that she's originally from Georgia."

"Hm." Theodora's red-stained teeth bit her lip. "A Georgia peach."

I froze at the reference. And then I remembered seeing peaches on one of Eve's aprons.

Eve was Peach—Amber's mother and the owner of the sugaring website!

I looked toward the tree, but Eve was gone. Frantic to find her, I glanced around the grounds and realized that she was standing right in front of the casket.

"Farewell, Amber," Bit-O-Honey said as the coffin began to lower into the ground. "We'll see you in that big strip club in the sky."

A murmur of disapproval arose from the queens, most likely because of the strip club reference.

An anguished wail followed.

"You can't take my girl!" Eve screamed and threw herself on the coffin.

A murmur of approval arose from the nonne, since casket diving was a thing among elderly Italian women.

Detective Sullivan rushed to the casket and pulled Eve to her feet, while the ginger officer I'd seen the night of Bradley's arrest began to handcuff her.

"Eve Quebedeaux," the detective announced, "you're under arrest for the murders of Amber Brown and Curaçao."

She gasped. "You can't be serious." As the detective read Eve her rights, she looked from him to me. "Miss Franki, you're an investigator," she shouted over him. "Tell them I didn't murder those girls! You know I could never do such a horrible thing."

I stared at her, unsure what to think. It wasn't clear whether the officers had arrested her because they thought she was making a play for the necklace or because they had evidence against her that I was unaware of. Nevertheless, when Detective Sullivan stopped reciting, I approached her and put my hand on her shoulder. "It's all right, Eve. If you're innocent, you have nothing to worry about."

"I loved Amber," she explained. "Curaçao too, although I did *not* like her behavior. That's why I told Amber to do the spell—to undo the hex that Curaçao had cast on her." She began to sob. "I wanted to make things riiight."

So, it had been an anti-hex spell. I was tempted to ask Eve about the Amaretto di Amore and Amber's sugar daddy, but I couldn't risk compromising the investigation or her defense. She'd said too much already.

Detective Sullivan looked at the ginger officer. "Let's get her to the squad car."

"I loved those girls like they were my own," Eve shouted as they led her away. "I was trying to help them. Why, I even found men to take care of them so they could get out of the stripping business. You have to believe me."

The funny thing was, I did believe her.

But if Eve hadn't killed Amber and Curaçao, who had?

* * *

Veronica sighed into the phone receiver. "I feel awful that I missed Amber's funeral because of work. I might have to go ahead and hire a part-time investigator."

I shot straight up in the dental chair. "Swear on your life that it won't be Glenda," I practically shouted into my cell. I lay back down and then sat up again. "Or anyone associated with the Amber Brown case."

"Don't worry, Franki," she breathed. "I swear on my life that if and when I hire someone, it'll be a professional PI."

Still vaguely unsettled, I clutched my phone and scooted deeper into the dental chair.

"Anyway," she continued, "judging from what I've seen on the news this morning, it was quite a ceremony."

"Veronica, even if Federico Fellini, Wes Anderson, and Tim Burton were all directing the same film, they couldn't have created a scene like that." I shook my head at the memory. "When I get to the office, I'll fill you in on all the outlandish details."

"Oh, I'm still at the house." She slammed a cabinet door. "What time will you be in?"

I glanced at the clock and saw that it was already seven thirty. "I thought I'd be out of here by eight or so, but Dr. Lessler's hygienist called in sick, and his receptionist is running late, so he's having to make some calls to try to find a sub. No telling how long that'll take."

"It's a Monday," Veronica said. "While you're there, I'll call my contacts at the police station and try to find out whether there's any chance of Eve being granted bail."

"I would give my eye teeth to be able to question her right now." I glanced at the dental instruments on the tray next to my chair. "On second thought, no I wouldn't."

A knocking sound came from the other end of the line.

"I think your mom and nonna are here to say good-bye," Veronica whispered. "I'll let you go."

"Make sure they actually leave, will you?" I urged, but she had already hung up.

Still holding my phone, I looked at the poster on the ceiling. Seeing the dolphin frolic among the waves made me think of the sea goddess, La Sirène. Even though King had laughed off my question about La Sirène and the amaretto, I still suspected that there was information out there somewhere that could help me connect the liqueur to the crime—and maybe even clear Eve's name.

"Sorry about the wait," Dr. Lessler said from behind me.

From my reclining position, I looked back and saw him in the doorway in his LSU scrubs.

His blondish-brown brow furrowed. "I'm going to call a temp agency for dental hygienists, then I'll be right with you."

"No problem, doc." I held up my phone. "I can do some case research while I wait."

"Great." He flashed his dazzling dentist smile. "Be right back."

Once he was gone, I opened my browser and googled La Sirène. After scrolling through several links, I clicked one that had an alphabetical list of the various voodoo gods and their functions. Baron Samedi was at the top, and the first thing it said was that he was called upon to heal sexual diseases.

I curled my lips. *That explains why King has the Baron as his cane topper.*

The entry for La Sirène referred the reader to the entry for Erzulie. I scrolled up and discovered that the entity known as Erzulie was actually a family of voodoo goddesses divided into four categories, one of which caught my eye—Petro Manifestations. The woman at Erzulie's Authentic Voodoo had implied that Erzulie D'en Tort, who sought vengeance for wronged women and children, was Erzulie Freda's sole Petro aspect. But according to this article, there were three others— Erzulie Mapiangue, who protected newborn babies, Erzulie Toho, who aided those who were slighted in love, and Erzulie Yeux Rouges, who took revenge on unfaithful lovers.

The unfaithful lovers line got my attention. I'd suspected all along that love was a factor in Amber's murder given the bottle of Amaretto di Amore at the crime scene. I figured that either she had some boyfriend who'd found out about her sugar daddy, or she'd cheated on the sugar daddy with someone she really cared about. What I needed to know was whether Erzulie Yeux Rouges was so evil that her acts of revenge included cold-blooded murder.

As tension mounted in my gut, I performed a search on the vengeful Erzulie. And I discovered that when Erzulie Freda's desires as the goddess of love weren't met, she turned into the fierce and fearsome Erzulie Yeux Rouges, which was French for Red-Eyed Erzulie. Apparently, the red eyes referred to crying and anger. And not only was she merciless, but her wrath knew no bounds.

I chewed my thumbnail as I contemplated the reference to the color red. Was there a connection between Erzulie's eyes and the label on the Amaretto di Amore? It was tenuous, but I had to try.

With my heart in my throat, I typed *Erzulie* and *amaretto* into the browser. It took a few minutes, but I located a source in Italian, of all languages, that confirmed what I'd suspected.

Erzulie Yeux Rouges preferred gifts that were red in color, and like Erzulie Freda, she loved to drink amaretto.

"All right," Dr. Lessler said with a clap of his hands.

I jumped at the sound.

He laughed as he took a seat on his stool. "You know, I'm used to people being scared of me, but I've never had a patient jump when I entered the room."

"Oh, it wasn't you. I guess I got spooked by some

information I came across." I put my phone beside my left leg and lay back in the chair. "Did you find a hygienist?"

"Ugh." He threw his head back. "The agency's sending someone over, but she won't be here for at least an hour. So, I'll have to go it alone with your crown. Speaking of which," he said, holding up a tooth with a gloved hand, "this is a porcelain-fused-to-metal crown. Pretty cool, huh?"

"I guess," I said, unaffected by his enthusiasm for a fake tooth. "What I'm really interested in is the shot situation."

He smirked and placed my crown on the tray. "Most patients are fine with a topical anesthetic, but if you experience any pain I can administer a local."

I hid my disappointment at the needle news as he placed a bib around my neck.

He pulled up his surgical mask and selected a tool from the tray. "Open, please."

I did as I was told and felt him prodding my gums.

"That was quite a funeral yesterday, wasn't it?" His eyes met mine as he sat up and reached for another tool.

"Uh-huh." I looked at the dolphin to avoid further eye contact.

"I'll tell you what," he said as he began working the tool between my gums and the crown, "the last thing I expected was to see the murderer arrested at the ceremony."

"I O," I replied, which was dentalese for, "I know." Of course, I didn't think that Eve was the killer, but I couldn't tell him that.

He snorted. "Did you believe all that stuff she was saying about loving Amber and Curaçao like they were her own children?"

"I O O," I said, which was the negative, "I *don't* know."

"If she did love them," he said as he tugged at the crown with his fingers, "she sure had a funny way of showing it."

My tooth felt cool, and I watched as he tossed the temporary crown onto the tray.

"Now I'm going to remove the cement." He picked up another instrument. "Let me know if this hurts, okay?"

I nodded and opened wide.

"The part that got me was when she said she had Amber

do an anti-hex witchcraft spell," he said as he scraped the surface of my tooth. "What a psycho."

Prior to this case, I would've agreed with his assessment of Eve. But after my crazy encounters with Theodora, Eve just struck me as a sweet but naïve woman who grasped at whatever straws she could—namely, spells—to try to control the uncontrollable.

Dr. Lessler returned the tool to the tray and grabbed a Q-tip.

I focused on the dolphin as he dabbed the anesthetic on my tooth.

He gave a sardonic laugh. "Only in New Orleans."

"Ut?" I asked, the meaning of which was obvious.

"This is the only city I know of where even the witchcraft involves alcohol." He tossed the Q-tip into the trash. "Like the amaretto."

"Oh," I said.

Then my eyes dropped from the dolphin to the doctor.

And the room seemed to rock like I was seasick.

Because the only way Dr. Lessler could have known about the amaretto was if he'd been at the crime scene.

CHAPTER TWENTY-THREE

———

Dr. Lessler's bright blue eyes turned icy gray, like two frozen lakes. "You're going to need that shot now."

A chill spread through my veins like a lethal injection. He and I both knew that I wasn't in pain and that the shot would be my death sentence. "If I die in your office, it'll be obvious you killed me."

With his gaze glued to me, he reached for a packaged syringe. "Not if I make it look like an accident during oral surgery. Patients do occasionally die in the dental chair."

Something I'd suspected since I started going to the dentist. "But I'm just here to get a crown."

He smirked as he removed the syringe from the plastic. "I'll say that I convinced you to let me remove your wisdom teeth too."

There was no point in protesting—Dr. Lessler was diabolical. My fingers felt for the phone I'd left by my leg, and I tried to buy some time. "Why'd you do it?"

He shrugged. "Simple. Amber had become an expensive nuisance, and I wanted out of the spit business."

The word expensive reminded me of the vassal's conversation with Sugar Cherie about Amber meeting a man she'd already known at the sugaring party. "You were her sugar daddy."

His full lips thinned. "Among other things."

I located the home button on my cell. "The two of you were emotionally involved?"

"Let's just say that I'd availed myself of her professional services and leave it at that," he replied drily.

"Okay." I needed to distract him, because I couldn't

make a call without looking at my screen. "But why become her sugar daddy if all you wanted to do was steal the necklace?"

"She tried to sell it to me to cover the cost of school, and I told her I wasn't interested in buying stolen property, especially amber that belongs to Russia. Next thing you know, she came up with the idea of sugaring to pay her bills while she looked for a black market buyer." He grimaced and shook his head. "Amber was such a disappointment. She'd said she was going clean, but she was never going to be anything but a whore and a thief."

I didn't dare point out his hypocrisy. It would have been lost on him, and it might have accelerated his plan to kill me.

"I figured that if I set her up in an apartment for a month or two, I could find out where she was hiding the necklace." He picked up a small vial marked Ketamine HCl. "So I signed up with the Sugar Shack under an assumed name and went to a so-called sugar bowl party. The rest is history."

As he inserted the needle into the vial, I pressed the *Home* button.

"I don't understand," I said as I glanced at my cell screen to orient my fingers. "Why didn't you just steal the amber from the apartment, then?"

He thumped the side of the syringe and continued to extract the clear liquid. "Because I realized I could get the necklace and get rid of her when she told me about the witchcraft spell."

"How did that come about, exactly?" I tapped the Emergency icon.

"Curaçao told Amber that she'd put a hex on her back when they were working at Madame Moiselle's." He lowered his eyes from the syringe to me. "And Amber was stupid enough to believe in that witchcraft crap."

In light of that comment, I felt like a fool for thinking that I was cursed myself—although my present situation sure seemed to support the idea.

"Amber was convinced that the hex was the reason she hadn't been able to get her life together since she'd quit the club." He removed the needle and scrutinized the liquid in the barrel. "And she was afraid she never would—that is, until Eve recommended that she do an anti-hex spell on the spot where the hex had been placed."

My fingers froze when my eyes set sight on that syringe. "So, you snuck into the club while she was doing the spell and strangled her, but Curaçao came in before you could take the necklace."

"Right." The corners of his mouth turned down. "Somehow she found out when Amber was going to do the spell."

Based on what Carnie had told me, I guessed that Curaçao had been eavesdropping on Amber or Eve. "But why would Curaçao try to sell you the necklace after seeing you kill Amber?"

"She didn't see me," he replied like he was talking about spotting a friend at the cinema. "While I was choking Amber, I heard a sound and hid in the prop room. I watched through a crack in the door as she ripped the pendant from Amber's neck."

The casualness of his tone as he talked about killing gave me the mental kick in the rear I needed. As he returned the vial to the tray, I glanced at the numbers on my phone.

"And you didn't kill her and take the necklace?" I asked as I tapped 9-1-1.

"That was the plan." With the syringe in his hand, he smoothed his bangs. "But someone started unlocking the front door, so she ran to the back exit. Before I could do the same, the stripper mom came in."

My surprise at learning that Eve was at the crime scene made it easier to do what I had to do next. I sat up and started to cough to cover the sound of the 9-1-1 operator's voice.

He slammed me back into the chair with his left arm, and my cell hit the floor with a clatter. "Well, look at that—your phone." He stood up and pressed his left hand to my neck, and he kept it there as he walked around the back of the dental chair and smashed my phone with the heel of his shoe. "Try that again," he growled as he made his way back around, "and I'll make this as painful as possible."

I swallowed hard and wondered whether the call had made it through, although I wasn't holding out hope. I hadn't heard the 9-1-1 operator answer, and I wasn't even sure that I'd dialed the number correctly. "I-I wasn't trying anything," I lied.

"I just didn't expect you to tell me that Eve was there."

The tension on his face relaxed as he released my neck and sat down. "That caught me off guard too. Until I saw her at Madame Moiselle's, I only knew her as the Texan lady that owned the sugaring company."

Now I understood why he'd said that a woman with a Texas accent had called his office about Amber, but I wanted to clarify that he was talking about Eve, and not Nadezhda. "You mean, Georgia."

He rolled his eyes. "Same thing."

Yeah, like honey and molasses. "After you saw Eve there, you decided to frame her for Amber's murder."

A conceited smile spread across his lips. "Actually, you gave me that idea when you asked about her mother. If I would've mentioned Eve before, it would've been too obvious that I knew more about Amber's life than I wanted to let on."

"Why didn't Eve report you to the police?" I asked, keeping an eye on the syringe still in his right hand. "Even if she didn't know your real name, she must've recognized you from the sugar bowl party."

He leaned back on his stool and crossed his arms. "She never saw me. When she noticed Amber onstage, she dropped the grocery bags she was holding and started screaming, 'Curaçao, what have you done?'"

So Eve had covered for Curaçao even though she thought that she'd killed Amber. Protecting her girls no matter what.

His lips curled with contempt. "While she was in hysterics, I slipped out the back entrance too."

I realized that the morning Veronica drove me home from the police station, I'd probably missed seeing Dr. Lessler leave by mere seconds. "How did Curaçao come to contact you, of all people, about buying the necklace?"

"She was one of my patients," he said with a flick of his hand. "After she stole it, I had my secretary call and schedule a cleaning appointment. When she came in, I casually mentioned that I was looking for an exotic gift for my wife for her birthday, and she fell right into the trap."

My blood began to boil at the mention of his wife

because it reminded me that he had a young daughter too. But I had to keep a lid on my anger. Otherwise, my goose was cooked.

"We met at her place when her roommate was out." He laughed and shook his head. "She tried to play me by telling me that she had other buyers—a couple of Russians who supposedly knew the value of the amber and were willing to pay big bucks."

Eugene and Nadezhda.

"I pretended to go along with it, agreeing to beat the Russians' offer." He stopped and scowled. "But then she showed me a pendant that was obviously a fake, so I got pissed and offed her."

I squirmed in the chair. He was so cavalier about killing. "And you took her body to the club to make it look like Eve had killed her too."

He cocked a brow to match the cocky twist to his lips. "Pretty clever, huh?"

I didn't reply. We'd reached the end of his story, which meant that my story was about to end too.

He glanced at the clock, and the self-satisfied look left his face. "I've got to get a move on before that temp gets here and my next patient shows up."

"Wait," I breathed, winded from fear. "You don't know where the amber pendant is, and I do."

He slapped his knee. "As luck would have it," he said in a mocking tone, "Curaçao told me that she'd hidden it in that pigsty she called a house right before I wrung her naïve little neck."

For a moment, I thought that the dental chair had dropped a foot, but it was my stomach falling.

"I went there to get it, but her roommate was home, and then the cops started watching the place." He gave an apologetic smile. "Now that the killer has been arrested, though, you're the only thing standing in the way of me and that pendant."

Desperate for more time, I half-shouted, "Hold on. I still don't understand the Amaretto di Amore. Did you love Amber?"

He ran his hand over his lower face and jaw as though wiping a bad taste from his mouth. "I thought I did once. But after she left the club she cheated on me with one of her ex-johns."

Amber's death had been related to infidelity, after all.

"There's no such thing as love, anyway." He snorted. "It's like that bottle of amaretto."

"What do you mean?" I pressed, trying to keep him talking in case the police had gotten my call.

The corner of his mouth turned up, and he almost seemed sad. "You can give it a romantic name, but it's just plain old booze."

"Then why did you leave it at the crime scene?" I scanned the vicinity, looking for something I could use as a weapon.

"Lots of reasons." He sighed and rubbed his thighs. "For one thing, to remind Amber of what she'd thrown away."

I thought about the bottle Eve had seen Amber launch across the kitchen, and I knew it was from him too.

"And, you don't know this," he said, tilting his head toward me, "but my *grann* was Creole. She taught me to pay my respects to the voodoo *loa*, so I know better than to risk the wrath of Erzulie Yeux Rouges."

I marveled at the discovery that Dr. Lessler practiced voodoo, even though he'd said that witchcraft was "crap." *When was I going to learn that anything was possible in New Orleans?* "Were those your only reasons?"

"Not quite." He scooted his stool closer to my chair. "I knew that Amber's pimp had taught her voodoo, so I was trying to raise your suspicions about him too. The more suspects, the merrier, right?"

Slowly, I began to slide away from him. "That explains why you alluded to Amber's past as a prostitute and told me that she'd been wearing a mermaid *veve*."

"And it's the reason I left the rum and cigarettes for Baron Samedi, besides paying my respects, of course." He put his thumb on the end of the syringe. "But I'm going to have to skip the offerings this time since I have to kill you here in the office. I hope the loa don't mind."

I recoiled into the armrest. "If I were you, I wouldn't gamble on the gods."

His mouth turned down, as though annoyed by my impertinence. "You'd say anything to get out of a shot, wouldn't you?"

Especially one that was fatal.

He reached for my forearm. "As much as I hate to kill a fellow LSU fan—"

"A *what*?" Even on the brink of death, the Texas Longhorn in me was outraged.

"I was there when you stripped in those LSU tiger shoes, trying to lure the killer to the club." He sneered. "And now that I think about it, after that performance you deserve to die."

Since the day of my birthday, I'd endured countless injustices and humiliations—starting with turning thirty. But I was damned if I was going to continue to deal with the fallout from Glenda's stripping scheme.

Gripping the armrests, I kicked the dental tray as hard as I could, and it went flying into Dr. Lessler, instruments and all.

He shielded himself, giving me time to shove him away and leap from the chair. On the off chance that a patient had entered the lobby, I screamed, "Help!"

"Francesca?" My mother's voice was as shrill as a dental drill.

My head jerked toward the door from the shock of hearing my mom.

Dr. Lessler gripped my forearm with Superman-like strength and inserted the needle into my vein.

Stunned, I shot him a questioning look.

"Rock climber." He grinned.

The horror of what had happened hit me so hard that I fell backwards into the chair. Figuring that I had seconds to live, I knew what I had to do. "Mom, run! Dr. Lessler's the real killer!"

But even as I said those things, I knew that she wouldn't listen. When you threatened my mother's kids, she was half mamma bear and half mafia boss.

She rushed into the room and rose to her full five feet four inches with her claws and fangs bared. "What's happening?" she rasped like Vito Corleone. "What have you done to my daughter?"

Dr. Lessler turned to face her, and I cold-cocked him with the hanging light.

We sunk to the floor.

Nonna stormed the examining room holding her handbag like a club. "I can-a take-a him, Brenda!"

From a supine position, I watched as she pounded Dr. Lessler with her purse while my mom punched a number into her cell. Despite the chaos, I looked up at the dolphin poster and felt at peace.

The ketamine was taking effect.

My mother leaned over me and pressed the phone to her ear. "I told you that you should be more careful when choosing a doctor, Francesca!"

Then my appointment abruptly ended.

CHAPTER TWENTY-FOUR

"Get the hell up," a male voice demanded.

In my semi-conscious state, I realized I wasn't dead, but I knew Dr. Lessler wasn't done with me yet.

The peaceful feeling was replaced with primal fear as I remembered my mom and nonna coming to my rescue. *What had he done to them?*

I tried to open my eyes, but I couldn't. *Did he inject me with a paralytic drug?*

Two powerful hands gripped me by the biceps and shook me.

Summoning my strength, I forced my eyes open. Then I let out a hair-raising scream.

Carnie was standing over me in the Private Chicks lobby, her face practically purple with rage. And in her black strapless dress and spiky white wig, she was the spitting image of Ursula, the half-human, half-octopus villainess from *The Little Mermaid*.

"The police just held another press conference," she huffed with her hands on her hips. "It seems that my amber pendant has been found."

High heels came clattering down the hallway from Veronica's office.

"Are you okay, Franki?" Veronica asked as she and Glenda rushed to my side on the lobby couch.

"Divine." I pushed myself into a sitting position. "But get Ursula off my back, will you?"

Carnie's blue lids lowered and her red mouth frowned. "You'd best be talking about Ursula Andress, or you'll wish you were back in that dentist's chair."

Glenda swallowed a sip of the celebratory *sleuthing* champagne she'd been drinking since Dr. Lessler's arrest the day before. "What's the matter, Miss Carnie?"

She pointed a red-lacquered fingernail at me. "Your partner in cracking crime here gave my family heirloom to Detective Sullivan."

"I didn't *give* it to him," I protested. "He figured out that I knew where the pendant was at Amber's funeral."

Carnie raised a McDonald's Golden Arch-shaped brow. "Then how the hell did he end up with it?"

I massaged my temples in preparation for the headache she was about to give me. "When he came to interview me in the ER yesterday, I cut a deal to let him find it in exchange for dropping the battery charges against Bradley."

Carnie gasped. "I paid you to find the amber for *me*!"

"And I did!" I threw up my arms in an I-give gesture. "It's not my fault that it's evidence in the case against Dr. Lessler."

Veronica smoothed her skirt and took a seat beside me. "Franki was legally bound to inform the police about the pendant, Carnie. So it's nice that something good came of it, don't you think?"

In reply, she looked at Veronica like she was considering biting her with her venomous beak.

"There, there," Glenda said, patting one of Carnie's massive shoulders, "you'll get it back after the trial."

"But that could take years!" Carnie cried as she collapsed onto the opposing couch.

I wanted to tell her not to get her padded panties in a knot, but I held my tongue. After narrowly escaping the clutches of one madman, I wasn't willing to get caught in the tentacles of another.

Glenda sat next to Carnie and kicked up her heels. "Where was the pendant, Miss Franki?"

As I got ready to relive the events of the past twenty-four hours, I pulled a cushion into my lap for comfort. "In a matryoshka doll on a shelf in Maybe's living room."

Carnie, who'd turned her head away to sulk, stole a glance in my direction. "How did you know it was in a nesting doll? Did it have something to do with that nasty Nadezhda?"

I smirked as I shook my head. "It was partly because of Glenda and partly because of the nonne. When we were at the St. Joseph's Day altar, the nonne covered her up like the Virgin Mary. Then when my nonna was shooting the lemons at me, a statuette of the Virgin Mary broke in half, and it reminded me of the nesting doll because it was hollow inside and because the doll depicted a stripper. Since Curaçao was a stripper and the amber was Russian, I just knew that was where she'd hidden it."

Glenda winked. "Glad to know my body could be of service, sugar."

I took a deep breath as I prepared to say something that I never dreamed would pass my lips. "Your near nudity was a huge help. Thank you."

She raised her flute in a salute. "Speaking of naughty matryoshkas, what's going to happen to Nadezhda?"

"At the initial press conference yesterday, the police said others would be indicted." Carnie fluffed her odd updo. "You know that Russki's one of them."

Veronica cleared her throat. "I'm sure they'll charge Nadezhda and Eugene both if they can prove they conspired to steal the necklace."

The creases in Glenda's brow deepened. "And Miss Eve?"

"She confessed to withholding evidence, so she'll face prosecution." Veronica looked down at her lap and shook her head. "If she'd told the police that she'd seen Curaçao at the crime scene, they would've taken Curaçao into custody—and she might still be alive today."

Regardless of what she'd done, I felt bad for Eve. In trying to protect Curaçao, she'd more than likely contributed to her demise. And I knew that was the last thing she would have ever wanted to do.

Carnie shifted and crossed her ankle over her knee, despite her dress. "What I don't understand is why that dentist knocked you out instead of killing you."

I shot her a long look—making sure to avoid the area below her torso. "According to Detective Sullivan's theory about what happened, Dr. Lessler needed to make it look like I'd died under anesthesia."

My story stopped as I made the sign of the *scongiuri*. Given everything I'd been through, I wasn't completely cured of my curse conviction yet.

"So he gave me ketamine, which is what dentists usually use for oral surgery, but just enough to knock me out for fifteen minutes or so. In that time he could've hooked me up to an IV to make it look like the drug had been administered normally and then cut off my air supply." I shuddered at the thought—and at the fact that I still had to get my permanent crown done.

"What a sick, twisted man," Glenda said, staring at her glass.

"I'll say," I muttered. "But then, he's a dentist."

The office phone began to ring.

"That's probably my mom calling to tell me they're leaving." I rose to my feet, and the room began to spin. "Whoa!"

Veronica stood up and placed her hand on my back. "I wish you would've taken the day off."

"You know I couldn't do that." I sunk back into the couch. "My mom and nonna said they were going to stay until they were sure I was all right. And after *getting* to share my bed with my nonna last night," I grumbled, "I'm more then ready for them to go."

"You owe your life to your nonna, Franki," Veronica chided as she walked to the reception desk. "If she hadn't insisted that your mother bring her to that office…"

I grimaced. The fact that my nonna's meddling had not only helped me find the amber but had also saved my life was a particularly bitter pill to swallow—and one that would keep coming up over and over again, both literally and figuratively.

When Veronica reached for the phone, it stopped ringing. She brought the receiver to the couch and placed it on the coffee table.

Glenda drained her glass. "Why *did* your nonna want to stop by Dr. Lessler's, sugar?"

"She never told me." I chewed the inside of my cheek. "But if I had to guess, it was to try to marry me off to the man."

The phone started ringing again.

"I'll get it." I grabbed the receiver. "Private Chi—"

"Why haven't you been answering your phone?" Ruth growled.

I squeezed the couch cushion. "Well, apart from the fact that it was crushed by a homicidal dentist, I've been kind of busy fighting for my life. Maybe you saw something about it on TV last night?"

"If it's not on *Nancy Grace*, I don't know about it."

That was worrisome news.

"Now, as much as I'd love to sit here and chit chat about the ups and downs of your day," Ruth snarked, "I have work to do. This is a courtesy call to let you know that Jeff Payne just resigned from Ponchartrain Bank thanks to your sweet grandmother."

As shocked as I was to hear that Jeff had resigned, I was even more astonished that my nonna had anything to do with it—and that she was "sweet." "Are you sure it was *my* grandmother?"

"Yes, ma'am," she crowed as she popped what sounded like a cork from a bottle. "About fifteen minutes ago, she burst into the board meeting with your mother. I didn't catch everything she said because she speaks like a female Father Guido Sarducci."

That was Nonna, *all right.*

"But I did hear her likening Jeff to a *mafioso*." She took a slurp of something. "Then she started passing out the compromising pictures."

"Hang on." I shot forward in my seat. "My nonna had compromising pictures? Of Jeff?"

Veronica and I exchanged a freaked out look.

"Did. She. Ever," Ruth syllabified. "She said she'd gotten them from 'the Madonna,' but I'll tell you what—the Virgin Mary don't know nothin' about the kinds of things going on in these pictures, even if she is looking down from heaven."

"What are you talking about?" I wheezed as the air left my lungs. "What was in the pictures?"

Veronica put her ear to the receiver, and I bowed my head to listen.

"Well, he was drunker than Cooter Brown on the 4th of July, but that ain't no big whoopty doo to a bunch of boozehound bankers," she said in a teetotaler tone. "What got them was that he was all tarted up in a stripper costume, performing for a gaggle of drag queens."

My head shot up, and I glanced from Glenda to Carnie—both of whom averted their eyes.

"And he was at a real swingin' cathouse, too," she said with relish, "because some of the pictures were taken in an all-pink room with a loveseat, others were in an all-red room with a small stage, and there was even one in an all-white room with a giant champagne glass."

My eyes zeroed in on Glenda.

Her lips spread into a slow smile. "Men find it hard to resist a free coupon for the VIP room, sugar."

"Actually, Ruth…" I paused and broke into a grin. "I'm friends with a Virgin Mary who knows all about those sorts of things—because she's anything but a saint."

*   *   *

As I slowed the Mustang to a stop in front of my apartment, I eyed my Mom's Ford Taurus. For the first time in days, the *Psycho* soundtrack was gone. It had been replaced with "When the Saint's Go Marching In"—the Louis Armstrong version. And when I got out of the car and headed up the driveway, I was mentally high-stepping and twirling a baton as I led the brass band playing in my head.

Although I had a newfound appreciation and respect for my mother and nonna after they'd defended me from the deranged dentist, and I loved them more than words could express—English, Italian, or Sicilian—I was oh-so ready to see them go. Now that the case was over, I needed some rest and relaxation before getting back to the grind. And I wasn't going to get any of that by sleeping in my bedtub.

I also needed some space to work out what had happened between Bradley and me. I'd planned to call him if he hadn't contacted me by Tuesday. But now that the day had arrived, I wasn't sure whether I wanted to talk to him. I understood that he'd been under attack at work, not to mention under orders to lay low, but I was hurt that he hadn't contacted me after I'd nearly been killed. Surely he'd seen the news, unlike Ruth?

When I reached my front stoop, and the door opened.

"What are you doing home, Francesca?" my mother asked, swinging her purse onto her shoulder as she exited. "Aren't you feeling well?"

"I'm fine, Mom." I wrapped my arms around her and considered asking her about what had happened at the bank, but I decided to leave it alone. After all, everything had ended as it should. "I just wanted to come and say good-bye."

Her face was flushed as she reached up and brushed a strand of hair from my face. "Well, aren't you sweet."

My nonna appeared in the threshold with her big, black weapon on her arm. "*Bella mia!*"

"*Ciao,* Nonna." I hugged her hard, breathing in her garlicky aroma and wondering for the nth time what made her purse so heavy. I could've asked, but I decided to let that go too. Some things were better left a mystery.

"I'm-a glad you're here," Nonna said while we walked arm-in-arm to the car. "There's-a something I forgot-a to tell you. *Un piccolo dettaglio.*"

I opened her passenger door while my mother climbed into the driver's seat. "Is this 'small detail' what you came to Dr. Lessler's office yesterday to talk to me about?"

"Don't even speak-a his name, *quel criminale.*" She waved her hand as though brushing away the doctor's memory and got into the car. "It's about-a the lemon." Her eyes darted to my front door. "And you need-a to know it-a now."

My brow furrowed. *Was it bad news about the bum lemon? And why did she look at my apartment? Was Bruno lying inside in wait?*

Nonna fastened her seat belt and then stared straight ahead through the windshield. "When-a you steal a lemon from-a the altar of *San Giuseppe,* there is another thing-a that can happen."

I didn't have to know what this "thing-a" was to know that it wasn't good, especially because she wasn't looking at me. "O-kay…"

She gripped the handle of her purse. "Instead of a

husband, from-a time-a to time, you get a *bambino*."

The *Pyscho* music screeched in my head.

"But-a either way, it's-a win-a win-a, eh Franki?" She turned and winked at me, and for a split second, I could've sworn that she had cat pupils.

My mother started the engine, shaking me from my shock.

"I hope we see you before Christmas, dear," she said, getting in one last guilt trip before their car trip back to Houston. "I assume you still know our address."

I rolled my eyes. "I'll be home this summer, Mom," I replied, resuming my usual defensive tone. "You guys drive safe."

As she backed the Taurus out of the driveway, I thought back to my conversation with Theodora about Old New Orleans Traditional Witchcraft being a kind of everyday magic that great-great grandmothers used to do. And it occurred to me that the lemon tradition and all the other bizarre customs I'd grown up with could be considered a type of witchcraft that nonne do.

But whatever. Since I was planning to break up with Bradley, the odds of my having a bambino out of wedlock were zilch.

I turned toward the house and stumbled over something, hitting the ground with a thud. I looked back and saw Glenda's stripper garden gnome.

The Virgin Mary.

Jumping to my feet, I rushed inside to call Theodora about an anti-hex spell—just in case. But I was distracted by the aroma of Italian food. My apartment smelled like my mom and nonna had made some meals for me before they'd left. I walked into the kitchen to see what they'd prepared.

There stood Bradley, holding a dozen yellow roses and a glass of Prosecco.

Our eyes met as he handed me the glass, and I drank it all in—not the Prosecco, the romantic atmosphere. The curtains were drawn, and there were lit candles on the kitchen table, which had been set with fine china and crystal that definitely didn't belong to me. Napoleon was even wearing a bowtie. And although I was furious with Bradley, I had to admit that he looked handsome in his dark blue suit—so much so that I understood why my nonna had told me about the other lemon legend.

He cleared his throat. "Can we talk?"

"It depends on what you have to say." My tone was frosty, like my heart.

He pulled out a chair. "Would you like to have a seat?"

I swallowed a sip of Prosecco. "I'll stand."

"Fair enough." A muscle worked in his jaw. "I'd like to start with how sorry I am that I let the pressure at work come between us."

"That's a good place to start." I crossed my arms. "But skip ahead to why you didn't call me after you punched Detective Sullivan."

"I wanted to, Franki. I really did." He tossed the flowers on the kitchen counter and ran a hand through his hair. "But Veronica insisted that I not contact you until I knew where I stood with the bank. My gut told me not to listen, but as my attorney and your best friend, I figured she knew what was right for both of us."

Although I wouldn't have admitted it to Bradley, I had to agree that Veronica was usually the wiser one in a crisis. But still. "So, like Jeff, you thought I'd be a professional problem for you. Because I am, you know."

He winced. "That's not true, Franki. My job is dependent on me, and me alone. And it wasn't Jeff or my job that I was worried about. It was you."

My cold heart began to thaw, but just a little. "How so?"

He turned as though he wanted to pace in the tiny kitchen. "I can go home to Boston and get a job any time I want, but I didn't think you'd want to go with me."

"What?" I practically gasped the word. "This isn't about Detective Sullivan, is it?"

"No, but that son—" He bowed his head for a moment and put his hand on his hip. "That *detective* got what he had coming to him after dangling your bra in front of me and putting a dollar bill in your G-string."

"It was a five, but go on," I said, deadpan.

"Look." He sighed. "Boston is a long way from New

Orleans, and from Houston, for that matter. I didn't want to have to ask you to leave your family and friends or your work for me."

My heart continued to defrost. It was considerate of him to take my needs into account, but something didn't add up. "If you were so worried about me and my wellbeing, why wouldn't you call me after I was almost killed?"

His eyes looked anguished as he took a step forward. "I did call—over and over again."

I bit my lower lip. My cell phone *had* been destroyed.

He looked at me from under his lashes. "So, I came over to make sure you were okay."

"You did?" I asked, taking a step forward myself.

"I stayed here all night," he replied, his voice soft.

My heart warmed but promptly sank. *My nonna's enema bag.* "You didn't sleep in the bathtub, did you?"

He tilted his head. "No, I sat at the kitchen table, drinking coffee and talking to your nonna first, and then when she went to bed, to your mom."

Now *that* was devotion.

"I kissed you on the cheek before I left for the board meeting, but you didn't wake up." He shoved his hands in his pockets. "I wanted to skip the meeting, but your mom said that it was important that I go."

My heart had not only risen back into my chest, it was practically bursting. I put my glass on the counter. "I swear to you, Bradley, I had no idea that they planned to crash the meeting, and I had nothing to do with those pictures."

The corner of his mouth lifted. "I know. Your mom and nonna explained everything. They're quite a pair, those two."

I snorted. "You can say that again."

"Just like someone else I know." The smile faded from his face, and his gaze bore into mine. "Can you forgive me?"

I nodded, and he crossed the distance between us. As he cupped my face in his hands and his lips pressed against my forehead, my eyelids, the tip of my nose, and finally, my mouth I knew that there was nothing in the world that could make me break up with him.

My knees weakened, and I wrapped my arms around his neck.

And I thought of that damn lemon.

I stiffened and pulled away.

Bradley gave me a searching look. "What is it?"

Of course, I could hardly tell him about the lemon I'd lifted and the "small detail" my nonna had laid on me before she left. But I wasn't ready for this magical moment to end.

My mind raced as I tried to conjure up a way to ward off the lemon's adverse effect. Obviously, I wasn't a great-grandma or grandma, but I *was* thirty, so I figured I had some witchcraft in me too. Making the sign of the *scongiuri* behind my back, I whispered, "Nothing. Everything is perfect."

He flashed a dazzling, eye-twinkling smile. "Good, because I've been thinking about that tiger costume you wore at the club." His lips nuzzled my ear. "And I was hoping you'd show me some of your animal moves."

Grazie for reading Amaretto Amber!

Carissimo lettore (Dear reader),

I hope you had fun reading _Amaretto Amber._ Like _Limoncello Yellow_ and _Prosecco Pink_, this book reflects my longtime fascination with the New Orleans scene and my lifelong obsession with the Italian and Italian-American cultures. But _Amaretto Amber_ was actually inspired by the performances of Bianca Del Rio and Ivy Winters at my first ever drag show, i.e., "RuPaul's Drag Race: Battle of the Seasons," at Austin's historic Paramount Theatre.

When I started planning _Amaretto Amber_, I decided that it would be fun to incorporate some reader suggestions into the plot; specifically, requests to have Franki's nonna show up in New Orleans and to make Bradley pay for what he'd put Franki through with Pauline in _Prosecco Pink_. So, I would love to hear your feedback (good or bad) about my books, because it often inspires me and helps me to improve. You can write to me at traci@traciandrighetti.com.

If you would rather not write to me directly, please consider writing a favorable review of _Amaretto Amber_. Authors are dependent on the kindness of readers like you to stay in business, so thank you in advance for taking the time to write a review.

Tante grazie!

Traci Andrighetti

P.S. If you're a Franki or a Cassidi (Danger Cove Hair Salon mysteries) fan, I'd love to have you on my street team, The _Giallo_ Squad. You can find information about how to join on my website: www.traciandrighetti.com

BOOK CLUB QUESTIONS
for Amaretto Amber

Turning thirty sends Franki into a tailspin. How do you feel about the milestone birthdays?

The St. Joseph's Day lemon tradition freaks Franki out. Do you have any unusual family or cultural traditions that you observe?

In *Amaretto Amber*, Glenda takes up sleuthing, which is quite a change from stripping. If you could try another profession on for size, what would it be?

Speaking of stripping, have you ever tried it, like Franki? If not, would you?

New Orleans is known for voodoo, but it also has a well-established tradition of witchcraft. What brushes have you had with either of these two forms of magic?

The victim of the story, Amber Brown, turns to sugaring to pay her bills. What do you think of this phenomenon?

Franki's client, the drag queen Carnie Vaul, is constantly changing her look. Which was your favorite of her outfits, and how would you describe your own look?

Many works of fiction have been written about the missing Amber Room. What historical mystery or era do you find intriguing?

Bradley is Franki's favorite leading man. Who is yours—in fiction or in real life?

Nonna just won't stop interfering in Franki's life. What experiences have you had with a meddler?

ABOUT THE AUTHOR

Traci Andrighetti is the national bestselling author of the Franki Amato mysteries and the Danger Cove Hair Salon mysteries. In her previous life, she was an award-winning literary translator and a Lecturer of Italian at the University of Texas at Austin, where she earned a PhD in Applied Linguistics. But then she got wise and ditched that academic stuff for a life of crime—writing, that is.

If she's not hard at work on her next Danger Cove novel, *A Poison Manicure and Peach Liqueur*, Traci is probably watching her favorite Italian soap opera, eating Tex Mex, or sampling fruity cocktails, and maybe all at the same time. She lives in Austin with her husband, young son (who still wants to be in one of her books), and three treat-addicted dogs.

To learn more about Traci, visit her online at
www.traciandrighetti.com

Enjoyed this book? Check out these other novels
available in print now from Gemma Halliday Publishing:

www.GemmaHallidayPublishing.com